MUCKLUCKED

James Brock

ISBN: 9781092632478

Cover by Joleene Naylor

LaVation Publishing
Seattle, Washington
2019

For my brothers, Richard Eaton and Joe Brock
And all of the bush/homestead kids who experienced
the same life we did.

There are strange thing's done in the land of the midnight sun...
The Ballad of Sam McGee
Robert Service

One

The huge salmon snapped up out of the churning waves, sparkling beads of water flying from it's thick silver skin, the movement of the muscular fish sent the droplets flying through the crisp afternoon air like diamonds. Twisting wildly the glistening fish just as quickly slammed back down into the frothy chop, heavy gauge line holding the deeply imbedded lure in place despite the effort to pull free.

Kodiak DePaul, the experienced fisherman holding the pole attached to the great fish, took another cautious step forward into the rushing water. He was already knee deep in the swiftly moving colder than ice river and did not want to lose his balance on a slick rock. Small accidents led to true disaster in the far Alaskan north.

"C'mon, c'mon," Kodi hissed to himself. This one would make his limit for the day, with the season closing soon the homesteader needed every ounce of food he could get stockpiled for the quickly approaching winter. The line played out a bit more as the fish struggled, Kodiak holding statue still until he felt a moment of slack. As soon as that tiny hitch happened he began to gently crank the reel handle forward, pulling the line taunt again making him a fraction closer to winning this battle.

The struggle had been going on between he and the

fish for nearly twenty minutes, Kodiak liked the challenge; the sun was high and warm on the mid-September day and the riot of fall colors in the forest around him were a painter's dream. A rainbow of shades from fiery red to brilliant yellow, gold and tan filled the forest around him. The green leaves left on the birch trees rustled as a light wind teased through the branches, the dark green scrub spruce lining the river bank as far as his eye could see rocked gently in the same breeze.

There was no place Kodiak would rather be.

Salmon from the Copper river far to the south of the homestead land he lived on were flown directly to Seattle and California where eager crowds waited on the planes for what were supposed to be the best fish of the season but Kodi knew better. The oil rich flesh of the river wild King and Silver salmon he was bringing in were the best by far.

Four huge King Salmon and two Silver were gutted and hooked to a line cooling in the shallows ready to be put into the smoker. Back at his camp Kodiak also had a line of laundry which needed to be folded, an axe to be sharpened and the perpetual chore of wood to be cut, split and stacked for the long dark winter season. The work on a one-person homestead was never ending, it took hard work and effort to live in the remote place year around the way he did.

Planning and supplies even for one were a daunting task. The plane bringing in the last of the cold season supplies would also be arriving soon, which added a whole new list of things to be accomplished.

Back breaking work aside, having no contact with the outside world for months on end had no drawbacks for Kodiak, he kept too busy to be lonely. Everything needed to be done to prepare for the long mostly dark days lay squarely on his shoulders. Supplies arrived when there was a break in the weather rather than on a set schedule so anyone in the bush had to be prepared to do without sugar, flour or other staples. Considering needs for every situation was key to a remote life, as a lifelong Alaskan used to living in the bush, planning might as well have been in his DNA so it was rare Kodiak went without.

The plane the young homesteader was expecting was the last large supply delivery before the harsh winter set in, Kodiak had to make certain everything was set for the arrival. Once the first snowfalls hit even the most veteran bush pilots were hesitant to come this far north and east.

Fort Yukon, over three hundred miles away by air, was the nearest mechanic, doc, and hot burger to Kodiak\s homestead cabin. As well as Kodi was liked by the flyers none of the pilots wanted to be stranded with him with a busted strut or choked out carb deep in his area of the bush.

Choosing to live on a homestead in the middle of nowhere was not easy work but no one went into the Alaskan wilderness without knowing that. The acreage of homestead property Kodiak was on had been his family way of life for three generations, no one knew the dedication bush life took or loved it more.

The wilderness Kodiak had moved to had been the family homestead since his great grandfather had proved up and lived on the land in nine-teen fifty-seven. The rest of the family were now in the central part of the state in Willow, a former gold mining village where the annual Winter Carnival in early February was the main attraction. Kodi had grown up there but loved the time he had spent here in the truly wild part of the state north of the Brooks Range and many miles to the west was the Canadian border,

The fish currently on his line, which might have weighed nearly fifty pounds un dressed, leapt again, trying to free himself. The massive fish were swimming the natural migration route back to the place of their birth to die, completing their cycle of life and feeding those along the river as they had since the beginning of time.

The tip of the heavy weight fiberglass rod nosed back down toward the water as another length of line went zinging out over the frothy waves. Tightening the muscles in his shoulders

Kodi leaned back, balancing his weight against the pull of the water, not giving any more line as the fish struggled. Another few feet of reeling and the fisherman would be able to unclip the net from his belt and scoop the fish out of the water.

This time old struggle of man against nature was being played out against a back ground of jaw dropping beauty; a jagged crested line of snow-capped mountains loomed on the far side of the wide Kuskuquim river Kodiak was fishing. The wild river stretched broad and smooth at nearly a quarter of a mile wide at that point then meandered on across the upper most part of the vast state. The rugged country was filled with massive mountain ranges and crisscrossed with roaring glacial fed rivers.

The river was about three miles from the homestead property through a trail lined with tall, slender spruce, soft pale green cottonwood and pristine white birch trees which faded away near the shore line, giving way to a gently sloping gravel sand bar offering a high spot for the small tent Kodiak had pitched and gave easy access to the fishing the spot which had become a favorite place for the young homesteader to bring in his supply for the winter.

Always careful to take only his limit Kodi had arrived early and set up the light camp before casting a line. At midday he'd stopped and grilled two-foot-long Grayling trout who had been among the salmon for his lunch and left the fire to burn out in the carefully constructed sand and rock pit he'd dug when setting up his rough camp on the beach. Although there had been a decent amount of summer rain, fire was a respected commodity in the bush. Kodiak had seen acre after acre scarred by blazing wildfire flames and left barren.

Kodiak was laser focused on bringing the fish in then moving on to his next series of tasks, he was about to slowly smooth his long fingers down along the seam of his jeans to unclip the large net attached to his belt when he froze.

The air was suddenly permeated with a zombie like stench, a horrible, rotten stink which could only mean one thing.

Bear.

Hopefully only one, but there could be more. Spring time cubs were mostly grown by that time but might still be with a sow teaching a cub to fish and fatten up for hibernation.

Shuddering Kodi slowed his breath as the light wind brought the horrific stench in even more powerfully. Bear were feeding on the massive fish runs all over the region getting ready to head over to the caves in the mountain range in the distance to hibernate. They had an abundance of food in the fish and the ground was all but carpeted with wild blue berries, raspberries and cranberries ripe for the picking. However some bears were mean no matter how full they were. Mama's with cubs, even this late in the season, were especially protective.

The smell meant the bear had been gorging and rolling on rotting fish, typical bear behavior.

Normally when he was out Kodi would sing or yell now and then, making just enough noise to let any wildlife around know a human was out and about but he had been so caught up with this fish that he had let his lifetime of bush training and experience lapse.

With a sinking heart Kodi realized his second mistake was not cleaning up the temporary campsite after lunch. He had properly gutted the grayling in the river before grilling them on a rack of willow limbs he had skillfully woven together and had eaten the fish in chunks off a smooth, flat sun warmed rock. Flavored with some wild onion shoots the fresh fish been a perfect lunch. Kodi would have preferred grilling a slab of the salmon he'd been catching but every bit of that was going to be needed for his winter food supply.

His mistake had been leaving the remains of the meal on the rock. The willow branches had burned out in the fire but he had made a literal signal calling the bear in with the smell of the left overs. Kodi could not have brought more attention to himself in the bush had he rushed the bear and poked it with a stick. The young homesteader did not turn around but could hear the animal clattering among the rocks behind him.

The rifle and .45 he carried in the bush at all times were also with his gear over by the small camp. He didn't like taking the guns near the water and now regretted not having a weapon strapped to his side.

Slow and easy...he thought to himself while changing the direction of his fingers, instead of hooking them into the carabiner holding the net he fished a Swiss Army knife from the pocket of his pants and into his fingers.

Quietly snapping a razor-sharp blade out Kodiak carefully used his thumb to put the brake on the reel then sliced the heavy pound test fish line cleanly. A small *ping* rang through the air as the line went slack. He knew the noise could attract the bear, but fighting with the fish on the line was a more certain way to attract the animal. He hated losing a lure but knew with the powerful scent surrounding him that a hook was a small loss compared to what he was going to have to deal with.

The salmon would have a natural end to its journey.

Common bear training is to drop and play dead. Don't run. If you are in a dire situation you can also try and make yourself look big to intimidate the bear. All good advice which has worked from time to time but there was no advice Kodiak could think of which applied in his current situation; knee deep in a glacial cold river with a slack fish line and a bear finishing the remnants of his lunch only yards behind him. Falling down was out of the question as Kodi was right in the middle of the bear's natural feeding ground.

Kodiak knew he had to do something. His feet were well guarded against the freezing water as he was wearing a pair of treasured Mukluk boots inside over size hip waders. The soft, hand tanned handmade Caribou hide lined with glossy seal skin trimmed in Russian Wolf pelt would keep his feet comfortable in most any condition, however he could not stay in the water all day.

Mind racing Kodi heard the bear snuffling behind him, great heaving gasps of air snorting in and out as the animal began thrashing around the tent and fire pit. The overpowering scent again made the hair on Kodiak's arms and the back of his neck stand on end and skin pebble.

Staring straight ahead, fishing pole still firmly in hand, Kodi realized that he might very well make it across the rapids if he had to, but if he made it into the deeper water that hypothermia would set in before he reached the other side if the bear did not follow him into the water. Bear could swim almost as fast as they could run.

But the homesteader could not stay rooted in the river forever, he needed to make a move so he began to turn his torso, inch by painful inch, until out of the corner of his left eye Kodi finally caught a glimpse of the bear foraging through his belongings.

Kodiak had lived in the bush most of his life and seen every type of wildlife Alaska had to offer. Moose who ran up to two thousand pounds and looked as formidable as an Alaska Rail Road engine when encountered on a narrow animal trail, bear with heads wide as a Volkswagen. Beaver the size of a wheelbarrow and porcupines so thick with quill they could cover a husky from snout to tail in moments. Like the famous giant vegetables which were farmed down in the Matanuska valley, Alaskan animals tended to be oversize.

And dangerous.

Still moving in the slowest possible motion Kodi could now see the bear full on, and what he saw was not good. Big, brown, a Grizzly for certain. Black bear were generally not found that far to the north.

Kodi's plain white t shirt stuck to his muscled body as he began to sweat, something he had hoped not to do. The day was not that hot but having a bear with jaws that could crush his bones like toothpicks mere yards away was anxiety producing. While bear may not have the best sight their sense of smell was as dead on as radar, the odor Kodiak had begun to give off might as well have been neon letters sent out over the airwaves spelling out fear.

The bear suddenly rose onto its hind legs, massive forepaws swinging in front of its torso as the huge animal slowly swiveled its head back and forth, snout raised it snuffed at the air. Dead center on the bear's chest was the rough outline of a white cross, a mark running roughly four feet down the center of its body with a slash about two feet long between the front paws. Kodi had seen many bear rear up like that over the years but always from a distance. He had never seen anything like this huge marked bear, especially up close. The distinct marking not only made it rare, the bear was also trophy size for certain, over twelve feet tall standing on hind legs the massive animal. While terrifyingly close, the bear was also as awe inspiring as the mountains in the distance and the powerful glacial fed river rushing around Kodi's legs.

The animal certainly had by then seen the man in the river but its hunger had been sated, the massive bear was more curious about the flapping tarp on the tent and the different scent left by the cooked fish to be wildly attacking as it usually would have been.

Dropping back onto all four paws the giant beast moved across the smooth gravel of the riverbank to the water in a few fast, easy strides which brought the animal closer to Kodiak than ever.

Movement in the water caught the bear's attention, scooping a paw into the river the bear lifted the line of fish Kodi had just caught. The bear brought the stringer up to its flaring nostrils and gave an appraising sniff, the huge fish looking like minnows compared to the animal.

Opening it's jaws the bear ripped one of the fish open while dropping the rest of the line back into the water.

The great animal swallowed most of the fish in one gulp then suddenly seemed to see Kodiak for the first time, making the homesteader cringe as the animal gave a huge roar.

A shudder wracked Kodi's body, he knew he had only moments before the animal charged.

The bear would take him down in the shallows in seconds, he would drown before the bear skinned him alive.

Neither option appealed to him.

What happened next could be called fate, a miracle or just one of those chance happenings of a lifetime.

A flat bottom skiff suddenly roared around the wide bend in the river, the boat headed right toward Kodi and the bear, it would have been hard to imagine which of the two. Man, or animal. were more startled at that development of the afternoon.

The boat seemed to anger the bear, shaking its head the huge animal gave another roar then charged into the water, galloping at startling speed past Kodiak into the river, giving Kodi the chance to move-and move fast.

Not even ten feet were between he and the bear, who was now thankfully ignoring him as it plunged into the roiling water, standing on hind legs, head thrown back and giving another primal roar as the stranger drove the boat closer then slowed.

Kodiak managed to scramble back up onto the river bank, getting to his shredded tent where he fumbled to wrap his hands around the rifle. Throwing himself down on the smooth river rock he pulled the strap around his fist and sighted the back of the bear's head. Taking a breath, he lined up the shot and exhaled just as he heard whoever was in the boat start to yell.

"HI BEAR HI! GET OUTA HERE, HI BEAR HI!"

The yelling caused the bear to stop, and Kodiak to back off on the trigger as the shot was now lined up directly at the person in the boat. It would be just plain bad form to shoot the person who had just saved him.

"HI, HI BEAR!" the boat drifted slowly toward the massive beast as the boat pilot kept a steady hand on the tiller.

Taking another long slow breath Kodi again lined the shot up on the bear, holding the sight tight. The homesteader doubted the bullet would even penetrate the massive skull of the animal, it appeared to be pre-historic. The huge hooked claws extending from the bear's massive paws looked to be about ten inches long and capable of opening an SUV roof as if it were a tuna can.

The small skiff continued drifting toward the enraged animal, Kodi figured the guy in the boat was giving him time to get away but he was taking no chance on trying to out run the bear. They were at a stale mate.

Smacking helplessly down at the water, massive paws sending spray arching high into the air, the bear lowered onto all fours, back and head still high above churning waves, which would have been chest deep on Kodi.

If the boat would move away Kodi would have a clean shot at the bear, but the driver of the skiff was now drifting even closer to the bear. While Kodi appreciated the boat driver making a distraction at this point the boat was not helping the situation.

Thinking back to the trail leading from his camp to the river Kodi knew there were a few tall birch trees he could scramble up, but the dash would leave him winded and there was the danger

that the bear would just stay at the base of the tree until Kodi fell asleep and tumbled out. Or that with the size of this animal that it could easily start ripping limbs off then break the tree off at the base.

The bear was now fully focused on the boat, which was dangerously close to the animal by then. The driver had eased the throttle off and was playing some sort of horrible cat and mouse game with the bear. Kodi did not recognize the skiff as belonging to any of the villagers along the river, it was too new and well maintained. The village boats belonged to a very poor population; besides, any natives in this area would have already taken care of the bear and Kodi would be taking them back to his camp for a potlatch feast to celebrate.

No, the driver of the skiff was likely some rich guy up from the states who had the means to come barging into the wilderness looking for a trophy like this who could afford all the toys, bells and whistles to pack the skin and head out while leaving the carcass here to rot. Kodi hated hunters like that as, like the natives he had grown up with, sustenance hunting was what got the family through the season.

The only thing confusing him was, if this were a hunter why had he not shot the bear yet?

Perhaps the hunter was concerned if he shot the bear in the water that he would lose his trophy and was waiting for the animal to head back to the shore. This thought infuriated Kodi, making

his trigger finger itchy enough to want to fire a round off even if it drew the attention of the bear back to the shore.

And him.

Frustrated and growing angrier by the moment Kodi silently cursed the man in the boat, which had not moved closer to the bear, but now the bear appeared to be moving closer to the boat-the huge hump on the back had slowly sunk farther into the water. Kodi wished the boat would restart the engine at least to be at the ready to move out of the bear's reach.

The homesteader had just about decided the bear was far enough away that he could rise from the beach would be safe in walking backward toward the trail head when the bear rose from the water again.

Animals, even this far north in such a wild area where they may never see a human in their lifetime, are smart. The old bear in the water had outlived many enemies, you don't grow old in the wild without learning a thing or two and this bear was indeed smarter than the average.

Standing suddenly the bear revealed that it had not been going deeper into the water, just lowering its massive body deeper down *into* the water.

Through the scope of the rifle Kodi could see that the boater, fooled by the illusion that the bear would not be able to move as quickly in the deeper water, was startled by how close he had drifted to the animal.

Lifting it's great paws, the bear threw it's head back again, giving a mighty roar it swept both paws down against the wide, flat bow of the skiff. The aluminum crumpled like cellophane as the bear gave a hard push, forcing the boat on down into the water.

The startled boater had seconds to push himself away from the sinking craft and begin lashing out for the shore in the icy cold water.

The bear, occupied by the debris floating around the sinking craft, did not turn as the swimmer managed to stumble to the shore. Kodi was dumbfounded, not so much by the action of the bear but that the boater had allowed himself to get so close to the animal. And that the man had now managed to pull himself up onto the shore and was stumbling toward where Kodiak lay.

Standing Kodi motioned the soaked man to follow him, leading him back toward the tree line where the well beaten trail was.

"Holy Fuck! That thing must be fourteen feet tall!" the wet man panted.

"Probably only twelve and *shut up*!" Kodi hissed back, "don't give it any reason to pay any attention to us." With that he stepped onto the trail leading into the woods then looked back at the wide river only to see that the huge bear had lost interest in the flotsam in the water and was now striding with purpose toward them, stepping back up onto the scree on the river bank yards from where the two men now stood, again frozen.

"Drop and play dead." was all Kodiak managed to say before shouldering the rifle and managing to get a shot off just as the bear dropped back down onto all fours and began galloping ward them.

Two

Of the strange situations Kodiak DePaul had found himself in during his nearly twenty-three years of life the one he was in at the moment was among the strangest.

After firing off one round from the rifle Kodi had dropped down on top of the wet stranger, letting the weapon clatter onto the rocks next to them and started breathing shallowly in the hope that the big bear would think him dead. It might not be a good ploy, if attacked by a black bear yelling and fighting was what you were supposed to do. You were not supposed to yell at a brown unless he was on you the way this one was. Even then you were in danger in case the bear just wanted to "play" with your body using knife like claws. However the acting dead tactic was the only option open at the moment.

Of course this was not just any bear, black or brown. This animal was bear like a Maybach is to a Toyota. The homesteader hoped if the bear was intent on death that those claws and jaws would act fast and the end would be quick with mercy.

Kodi was not happy to be dying with a stranger, especially one who could have avoided the whole situation by not acting like a total moron, but that ship had sailed.

Well, sunk if one wanted to be technical.

The (wet) stranger was bony; a hip, knee or elbow of his was sticking into Kodiak in a very sharp and uncomfortable way. Still it was nice to have something to focus on other than the rampaging grizzly bringing probable death.

The ground rumbled as the massive bear approached, it felt like an earthquake, a train loaded with coal, an eighteen-wheeler running wild down a highway with the pedal stuck to the floorboard heading toward them.

Kodiak could feel his heart beat and became strangely calm, he had always loved nature, was at home in the wild and certainly did expect to die there someday. The day of death had just come sooner than he expected. He tried to relax, waiting for the cold feel of the nose of the bear against his neck, to have his nostrils assaulted by the horrible stench of the bear up close as the animal whuffed hot breath onto his sweat damp skin.

But none of those things happened, in fact as he lay there trembling slightly on top of the stranger the thrumming of the ground as the bear's massive paws slammed into it was growing faint. There was no snuffling, no bone crushing teeth tearing into the tendons of his neck.

Kodiak was grateful to be alive, for the moment at least, even if he was on top of a wet guy and quite uncomfortable. It had been a long time since he had been this close to another man but this was not the time for *that*.

After what he had been through Kodiak DePaul was done with men, sex and love.

Mentally kicking himself back to reality Kodi tried to listen for sounds beyond that of his heart pounding in his ears. He focused on the steady flat *whump* of the giant bear pads as they slammed into the ground but growing faint. The fact that the bear was still moving meant one of two things; the bear was running *to* something or *away* from something.

The first meant a food source more appealing than the pile of human pate likely followed by a salmon course. The latter meant something more terrifying than a giant bear. Kodi could not think of anything which would run off a bear of that magnitude short of a Tyrannosaurus.

Wolverines were one of the fiercest predators in the far north but even the largest, most vicious of those would not have gone after this bear. Unless it were a mutant giant wolverine, an idea Kodiak did not even want to consider.

The positive was that while he was still wet, the warm body below him at least made the dampness tolerable. Still, like being trapped in the river while the bear was on the bank, something had to be done. The ground was no longer throbbing and there was no stench in the air. Although there were no signs the bear was totally gone Kodi had to check, and the animal could still be close enough to charge again.

Slowly lifting his head Kodi flicked his eyes upward, seeing nothing but a wide stretch of wild grasses. Holding that position for a moment, happy a giant bear paw did not smack his head off his shoulders like a golf ball off a tee, Kodiak took another deeper breath and gently pushed himself up off the man he was on top of. His field of vision was higher now, he could see into the clearing stretching along this side of the river. The canvas shelter he had set up using silvery gray branches of drift wood were shredded, nothing was left of the tent but streamers of material flapping in the wind. Slowly lifting his body up Kodi saw the massive bear charging on through the grasses and caught just a glimpse of the hindquarters of a moose or caribou disappearing into the tree line. Probably a young bull born early last spring who had just separated from it's mother. A fast and better meal for the bear than both men put together. Today was not the day Kodiak would die. Someday yes, but not that day.

Reaching down Kodiak laced his fingers around the arm of the soaking wet man on the ground and found it to be thick with muscle. In another place and time the homesteader would very much have liked to have explored the arm farther but if the bear lost interest in the moose, or just plain lost him in the trees, it could just as easily and quickly come back toward them.

The man pushed up off the ground with his other arm, rising he stood nearly nose to nose with Kodi, who liked what he saw but again quickly put *that* thought out of his head.

The stranger looked to be in his mid-twenties, a sweep of thick brown hair plastered to his head. The cap Kodi had seen on him through the rifle site had been swept off in the river when the bear sank the skiff, the strangers exposed face presented deep brown eyes fringed in coal black lashes, the men briefly stood together nearly nose to nose, the beautiful eyes locked into Kodiak's bright blue eyes. The men stared at each other for a long moment, Kodi felt his body reacting to the man so close to him so he took a step back and sternly reminded himself again that he was through with men in that way. His heart would never heal after the last time and there would be no next time.

"Thanks," the stranger said. "I," he began, only to be

cut off by Kodiak.

"Quiet! We've got to move in case that bear comes back." The homesteader hissed.

With no further directive Kodi quickly salvaged his weapons from the small camp and scraped sand over the fire pit. He hated leaving the stringer of salmon but had to. Unbuckling the heavy rubber waders, he peeled them down over his body, reaching out to grab the strangers shoulder involuntarily to steady himself as he kicked out of the heavy boots. He hoped to get back soon and retrieve all the gear but at that moment getting space between them and the bear was the most important issue on Kodiak's mind.

That and feeling the corded muscles in the shoulder he was holding onto.

The gear might detour the bear for a moment, the scent the pair would leave behind as they moved over the trail to the cabin was a bigger concern. The bear might be distracted right then but Kodi did not want to chance attracting it or another bear with an easy snack for the taking.

They would need to hustle over the trail leading back to his camp and the heavy load of fish would weigh them down. The salmon would be running for another week or so, which meant he'd have to work harder to catch up but being interrupted by bear in the middle of a project was part of life on a homestead.

Slinging the rifle over his shoulder Kodi wordlessly turned, moving toward a trail leading into the woods, the other man following close behind.

The well-worn path had been beaten by animals going to the water for a very long time, Kodi had been using the route for a much shorter time but had memorized every tree, rock and square inch of mossy ground cover between his camp and the river. He usually made the distance at a leisurely pace in just about forty-five minutes but was now moving at just under a run and stepping as carefully as possible to avoid snapping any branches underfoot. If he kept the pace he was at he would cut the time back to camp in half.

"Hey, hey! Slow down!" the man behind him panted just as the pair reached the halfway mark back to camp. "C'mon man, I'm *wet,* that water was freezing."

Ignoring the plea Kodiak kept up the pace as he tried to remain deaf to the pleas, cajoling and threats which started coming from the man who by then was lagging farther and farther behind him.

Stopping short Kodi finally caught his own breath and let the young man in the soaking wet clothing catch up to him.

"An Olympic sprinter can be clocked at 27 miles an hour. If you were dry and in prime condition you could probably run for a few minutes at ten miles an hour," he said while trying not to gasp himself, "that bear can hold a pace of thirty miles an hour. Some of these trees are big enough to slow it down but they won't stop him if he wants to eat us or just rip us to pieces."

Chest heaving the attractive man behind him said nothing.

"Besides, we aren't running, just moving fast. Moving will help you warm up. At the cabin I have a Thirty Ought Six, a Luger and half a case of flash bang grenades. And even with all that if the bear wants us the bear will get us but at least we have a fighting chance once we are there."

"I know what a bear can do. I'm a game warden," the

handsome, wet young man said flatly, plucking at the dark green jacket he wore while turning so the insignia patch on his shoulder was visible. Kodi's stomach knotted. If this guy was here it meant that Tom Ridgley, who had been the assigned warden for this region foe decades had kept his word and retired. Kodi had hoped Tom would have held off a few years. Tom knew the people and animals of the region. He also knew when to turn a blind eye to an extra salmon or a moose taken out of season when the natives were starving.

But he'd deal with all of that later.

"Well, *officer,* unless the state has started issuing magic brooms for you to fly on I suggest we get moving because we still have well over a mile to my camp." With that Kodiak turned and began striding down the narrow dirt trail, the man falling in behind him.

"How long have you been with the department of Game anyway?" Kodi asked, not bothering to look back over his shoulder.

"Nearly two months, and flash bangs are illegal. Regulation AR 7-4229 states," the young warden began with authority. Well as much authority as a man whose uniform was soaked to the skin could manage that is, "that no shell artillery,"

Stopping short again Kodiak turned and stared the wet young man down. "Really? Now?" was all he said before turning and speeding down the well-worn trail again.

"I have the authority of the state of Alaska behind me as well as two degrees and a Masters in conservation education so I *do* know that I am talking about."

"Show your degrees to that mad griz and see how he feels about 'em." Kodi muttered over his shoulder. The

Game department were scraping the bottom of the barrel. The cute dope's actions could have gotten them all killed but Kodiak saw no reason to bring up the obvious right then.

The pair were still far from the safety of camp and had just been spared being gutted yet the wet guy behind him suddenly felt the need to Alpha challenge Kodi. A surge of rage rose in the homesteader but he pushed it back down, along with the urge to take off running and leave the young man to the fate of the wilderness. This one was going to be difficult. Seasoned, understanding wardens like Tom were as valuable as contained fire in the bush, rookies made mistakes and this one behind him had already made a doozie by getting close enough to an angry bear to get dumped in the river. He was lucky to only be wet.

Taking a deep breath Kodiak reminded himself that nothing lasts forever and this little saga would be over soon. He was far enough north to only merit a ranger visit once or twice a year.

Tom had been a valued friend, so those times had been looked forward to. Alaska is a huge state and sadly, had more than its share of guys who had to feel important. Kodi had been around men of self-stated importance like this all his life and had long ago learned that it was better to be patient than prove you were right to them. If the time came the guy would see that Kodi could handle any of his weapons like an expert, he had been taught well as a child and continued to practice even when he was not hunting.

"You can quote regs all day," the homesteader said while picking up his previous pace, "I'm heading home. You are welcome to come along with me or stay right here. If you stay it will be helpful if you write up a little good-bye note and pin it to a tree. I'll make certain it gets to your next of kin. And before you say it, I know pinning something to a tree is destruction of state property so just add that to my growing list of infractions." Kodi was far enough ahead of the young warden that he doubted the snarl and snark was heard but he didn't care if it were.

"Without regulation and proper management of natural resources," the young warden began, his voice again close in behind Kodi. The homesteader smiled to himself. The guy may have been sexy and was green as spring grass but somewhere a survival instinct had kicked in and he was now following obediently.

"Save the speech for your next Department of the Interior conference, man." Kodi snapped. He didn't know if it was his tone or his pace that quieted the game warden following behind.

Both now panting the pair soon arrived at the first building in the compound Kodi called his camp, a long low log structure with a wide plank door. Turning a hand lathed wooden latch Kodi stepped inside, finally feeling safe back inside the thick log walls for the first time since seeing the bear.

Round sky lights flooded the large, warm room strung with lines of drying laundry with natural light.

"Wow!" the warden gasped as he glanced around the cabin. "Is this where you live?"

"Nope. This is the wash cabin, I just work on projects here." Kodi said with pride. One of the first rules of living in the bush was that clothing had to be clean to stay warm. Choosing this parcel of land to live on had been based on being truly independent, he felt lucky that a natural hot spring had been harnessed as part of his life. Kodi hung the pack he had grabbed from his day camp spot on a wooden peg on the wall. The rifle and gun still in its holster were hung on another peg.

"You mean you are taking state resources for your own use!" the game warden sputtered while looking at the steam rising from water coming out of a free-flowing tap.

Kodi sighed to himself, he liked showing what had been harnessed but this guy clearly was not going to appreciate the work he had put in.

"If you need to put it that way, yes. I am stealing from the state," crossing the room Kodi opened a large armoire made of rough-hewn wood planks and brought out a pair of denim pants, a red and black plaid shirt made of thick wool, underwear, socks and another pair of hand tooled mukluks, beautiful tanned leather boots lined in waterproof seal skin which laced up to the knee.

"Here. Go dry off and put these on. We seem to be about the same size, you can change in there. You'll find towels." With a nod of his head he directed the warden toward a small closed door. "Bring your wet clothes back out and I'll hang them up to dry." Kodiak mentally kicked himself for offering to hang the clothes up but he like organization and structure. Those things were key to survival in the bush. He just plain did not trust that the warden who had almost gotten them killed know how to operate a clothes line.

When the man representing himself as a game warden disappeared into the next room, Kodi wasted no time in getting back to his work and began un clipping the clothing from the lines. He neatly folded the clothes and sheets, rolled pairs of socks and put them away into the hand crafted armoires in the room.

The freestanding closets were packed with extra winter gear; wolverine and seal skin parkas with lynx ruff which could withstand the coldest temperatures like no commercial jacket and more handsewn mukluks made of the softest hand tanned caribou skin lined with seal skin and totally waterproof. The shelves also held thick mittens made of marten and fox most caught by Kodiak's childhood friend Sam Chigliac who made his living running a trap line when he was not carving the figures he sold through shops in Anchorage and Juneau. Sam was an artist, his beautiful craft work coveted by galleries from the panhandle to Fairbanks but he still gathered the furs, tanning the hides and picked the ivory he used himself. He had learned the carving and fur work from his grandmother, who had been a friend, mentor and teacher to Kodiak's mother, who had hand crafted much of the clothing in the wash house including thick, warm socks and carefully knit caps woven from the thick fur combed from Musk Oxen. The clothing in the wash house had been neatly and, efficiently kept in place for winter and or emergency use. Which alone in the far north could be at any time day or night.

Kodi had split the logs into planks to build the rough but serviceable clothing and bedding storage cabinets. On the back wall stood an antique wooden cradle washer, the machine had been shipped to the state by ferry by Kodiak's great grandfather years earlier and had served his family on the homestead since. Lengths of hollow bamboo brought up from the states not nearly that long ago had been carefully run from one of the many un charted hot springs in the state and served as the pipeline to bring the 108-degree water into the wash house.

Another series of bamboo lines brought water from one of the many spring fed small rivers in as well. Hot and cold running water with no metal leeching in from pipes.

The walls of the cabin made of thick logs were lined with heavy hand-hewn shelving holding rows of gleaming jars of homemade and canned jam made of local wild berries; black, blue, raspberry along with both high and low bush cranberry. Small jars of honey glowing like amber, some with comb in them, made from bee drawn nectar from the delicate pink flowers of the fireweed plant and tundra clover sat alongside the other jars. Small jars of syrup carefully distilled from Birch and Spruce trees were on a shelf above the honey. It took a lot of time and effort to craft the syrup but was often just the touch of sweetness needed on the darkest of winter mornings here in the middle of the silence deep in the bush. Another shelf held several rows of sealed jars containing sliced wild mushrooms packed in a heavy layer of virgin olive oil. Only an expert woodsman would chance getting the right mushrooms; one bad one could poison a diner, causing severe sickness. And that far from medical help, possible death. The taste of summer and good things to come were sometimes all it took to keep motivated.

Newly canned salmon and gleaming jars of crisp red stalks of rhubarb which would later be mixed with his hoard of now frozen tiny, sweet wild strawberries to make delicious cobblers weighed the shelves as well. Thick freshly smoked salmon fillet hung from racks on the walls, large wooden bins on the floor were lined with straw were over flowing with huge potatoes, cabbage, carrots, turnips, beets, and yams. Fifty-pound bags of flour, cornmeal and beans and oats sat on hand cut wooden pallets.   Fresh vegetables like snap beans, peas and tender wild asparagus had been put in cold storage for winter use in a glacial cave several miles away.   One shelf held carefully lined up rows of home canned bright green pickles.

Kodiak was rightfully proud of the supplies he had worked so hard to lay in for the long winter to come. Tending the garden, harvesting, canning; the fishing and curing took all of his energy and every waking hour of the days of extended arctic sun but also kept his mind off the past.   From time to time he craved companionship in both the physical and mental sense but usually the homesteader was too worn out to think of anything but his list of daily accomplishments and what he still had to face in the coming days to prepare for winter.

Another hand-hewn table for folding clothes, worn smooth by years of use, was against one wall.   The room the warden was changing in was the bathroom proper for the homestead.   The large room held a huge stone with a naturally smoothed out hollow large enough for Kodi to stretch out in fully for hot bathing.   He had rigged a shower in the room as well, another sectioned off room held a fully compostable toilet.   Kodi's homestead accommodations were better than most of the rooms at the developed hot springs hotels in the central part of the state.

Technically the facility was an outhouse, but a deluxe outhouse compared to the now dilapidated single hole log outhouse once used by Kodiak's great grandfather.

"You have a full bathroom in there!" the warden exclaimed as he came out of the room toweling his head. He was shirtless, his smooth chest tight with muscle and arms that looked as if bocce balls had been inserted at the bicep. The scruffy game warden who had just about gotten them killed a short time ago was hot, Kodiak suppressed a gasp as he continued creasing the sheet he was folding. It had been a long time since he had been this close to another man even partially naked and he was human, he had to hold back the yearning flooding through his body. Feelings in check Kodiak turned away from the sexy form Hunter presented.

"Thanks Sherlock." he flatly as he turned to tuck the sheet back into one of the cabinets, wanting nothing more than to shut the young man up by pressing their lips together in a long passionate kiss.

He took a quick, deep breath before turning back around. Those days were behind him, those days when kisses were plentiful and easy. No one wanted to kiss a freak. He had learned to live without them but still had to convince himself that he did not need them. Need and want were two different things. There were more than enough things which needed to be done to survive on the homestead and kisses from hot strangers were not needs.

Or so he worked to convince himself.

"What happens with the waste water. You can't just randomly let water, detergents, soap, shampoo, all of that, go without proper disposal," the young man dropped the ends of the towel, letting it drape around his neck as he sat down on one of the hand-built chairs next to the folding table. Leaning forward he began to snug his sock covered feet into the soft, hand tooled boots Kodi had handed him.

Kodiak stepped into the bathing room to scoop up the game warden's wet clothes then came back into the washroom and set about hanging them to dry before responding.

The only mirror on the homestead hung in the small room, glancing up at it Kodiak stared at his reflection for a split second then grabbed the small brush he kept on a shelf next to the mirror and gave a few fast strokes to his nearly shoulder length blonde hair then snagged a length of leather he'd hung on a peg under the shelf and pulled his hair back then tied it off at the nape of his neck before going back into the main room.

Not that many people had ever been to the homestead, the ones who had were usually amazed at what Kodi had accomplished. This guy, though, was like a different breed and a small part of Kodi regretted that the bear had chosen moose for lunch rather than have a game warden burger.

"You said you were with Fish and Game, not the EPA but nothing I use is not biodegradable and I have a proper waste water field. You are welcome to go outside and inspect it if you like. I doubt the bear with the giant razor-sharp teeth and claws followed us this far."

"You may live in the wilderness, but you are still part of civilization, part of a society," the game warden said while tightening the laces on the boots. "With governing laws,"

Kodiak cut him off again.

"I'm sure the Supreme Court will be very interested in the case you seem to be trying to build against me but we are temporarily stuck together here so could you just chill for a few? Be happy we are alive for a minute?"

There was a pause before the game warden stood and crossed the room, extending his hand, the sexy grin crossing his face causing a knot to form in Kodiak's stomach.

"Hunter Davis."

Drying his hand on his jeans Kodi introduced himself then finished clipping the last of the warden's wet clothing to the line. Since Hunter had made the gesture of finally introducing himself (although in fairness there had been a great deal of more important things going on that afternoon, like running from a giant angry bear, for them to have wasted time giving proper introductions) Kodiak decided to prove he could be social so returned the handshake with his name as he hooked a rifle off the peg then suggested the men move on to the camp cabin.

Cocking his head Hunter reached up to the shelf holding the pickles and plucked one off, turning it slowly around in his hands.

"Don't tell me these are part of your bounty as well?" he asked, sweeping the jar around toward the cabin packed with supplies. "I know you can grow a lot of stuff up here, but this is pushing it."

Kodi was secretly pleased Hunter had noticed the pickles. He was not crazy about telling Hunter anything but it was rare to have any outsiders on the property and he was proud that he had kept the place running and productive.

Talking about his accomplishments also helped him focus his eyes on something other than the muscled outline of his imposed guest's still bare chest. "I have a greenhouse built out of old windows, manage to get some more delicate crop like small cucumbers out of that." he kept his voice as flat as possible, trying not to show any excitement over his hard work. He could have enjoyed the encounter with the hot game warden had the hot game warden a short time early almost gotten them killed.

Hunter replaced the jar on the shelf then without

asking reached for a side arm in a leather holster hanging on a peg on the wall.

"Hey!" Kodi said with a glare. "Don't you ask to touch anything? Especially another man's piece without permission."

"You have the rifle, I should be armed too."

"Uh uh. I've seen you in action quickdraw. No dice. I've got us covered."

Thankfully the game warden wordlessly let his hand move away from the sidearm and followed his reluctant host back outside while shrugging his shoulders into the thick, flannel shirt and beginning to button it.

As they moved down the well-worn trail Kodiak pointed out his raised cache, a small cabin with a moss-covered pitched roof made of logs set on thick poles made from birch trees. About ten feet off the ground a sturdy, well-built ladder reached up the small doorway. A few yards away from the food cache the homesteader pointed out the long, low smoke house made of the same materials and now filled with freshly caught salmon in various stages of preservation. Next to it stood the small green house made of salvaged glass windows.

"Buncha bees over there," the game warden commented, pointing at a small cloud buzzing around behind the smoke house.

"Coupla hives give me all the honey I need." Kodi said without turning around.

"This far north? Have you talked with the University at Fairbanks? They probably need to be studying this."

"Look Ranger Rick, what I do up here is *my* business, ok?" Kodi stopped to turn and glare at the ranger.

"It's Hunter, not Rick, and alright, alright."

Kodi turned away, still leading on the path.

"And I'm certain you have all the permits for keeping bees in place."

The homesteader kept moving, glad the ranger could not see how red his face became at the jab. He imported a few Queens each season from a breeder in the states (*Lower Forty-Eight* or more commonly *Outside*. Alaska had been purchased for two cents an acre from Russia in 1867. While Alaska has been an American State since then Alaskans often act as if the state is still its own territory), the bees came on their own from the surrounding fields where they collected nectar from the wild purple and white clover and the beautiful magenta fireweed blossoms which grew wild all over the state. The fact that the swarm stayed in the hives conveniently provided by the DePaul homestead where Kodi collected the resulting honey was incidental.

"Outhouse? With that indoor privy back there?" Hunter asked, pointing to a small windowless log cabin not far off the path.

"Sauna." Kodiak said with justifiable pride. He had properly lined and vented the small building and could quickly get the sweat lodge as hot as he wanted.

"Pretty sophisticated living way out here beyond no-where. I don't hear any dogs, don't you run a team?" the game warden following Kodi asked as they made their way along the path through the woods.

"Takes a lot of food to feed a team through the winter and hauling in commercial food is still too expensive. Got a buddy who runs his team along his trapline about ten miles out," Kodi growled, "he lets me use his team when I need to." Kodiak had no reason to explain anything to this stranger and was glad they were so close to the cabin to end the grilling.

"No snow machine either?' Hunter asked as they moved along the well-worn trail through the woods.

"Little transportation obsessed, aren't you?"

"Just curious how people get by up here this far north." Hunter said with a shrug, tying to blend in as the new guy learning the territory.

"Same as with running a team," Kodik finally responded, "no-where to get fuel and too much cost to get and keep a supply on hand."

While all of the reasons given by Kodiak for not having a dog team or motorized snow vehicle, the truth of the matter was that he liked being as cut off and remote as possible. Someday he would have dogs and or a snow machine but for now he was content with walking and flying out when needed. He wasn't ready to have easier access to the world just yet.

And Kodiak DePaul was certainly not ready for the world to have any kind of access to him.

Rounding a sharp corner on the hard-packed path the men were suddenly in front of a snug, classic log cabin, the peeled wood gleaming blond in the afternoon sun. The place looked like it had been copied from a tourism poster, complete with moss-covered roof and a wrap-around porch stretching across the front of the building. The solid door was centered, small, thick windows were to the left and right of the doorway. Set on the top of a small ridge the cabin overlooked a narrow, fast moving mountain stream.

Mounting the stairs of the porch Kodi unfastened the hand carved device created to keep the thick door latched. A bear might eventually force the door open with power and weight but the handle with its puzzle like twists and turns was not easily opened.

"Someone put some work into that," Hunter said from behind Kodi.

"My great grandfather was sleeping inside when he just had the walls up. No windows were in and he just had burlap hanging over the door opening," Kodi said while pushing the cabin door open then stepping back to allow his enforced guest to step inside first, "he had his rifle and ammo in the mummy bag with him zipped up to my chin and woke up one morning to pressure on his chest. He opened his eyes and found a big black bear standing above him with one paw resting in the middle of his chest."

"Whad' he do?"

Kodi shrugged, following Hunter into the small, neat cabin.

"He yelled and started to cry. The bear must have gotten bored because he took off and my granddad never saw him again. He built this version of a bank vault door that day and it has held firm since. I oil it up once a year."

"I'm glad he didn't have to take an animal out of season. Nice in here, too." Hunter said as he glanced around the interior of the cabin.

Kodi felt his stomach clutch again, this time for the people of the region this guy might be covering as this greenhorn would be lucky to last one season.

The well-made cabin was made of stripped, uniform logs hand polished to the color of deep caramel and fit so tightly together you could not have gotten a piece of paper to slide between them. A massive fire place made of river rock was at the west side of the cabin, taking up most of that wall with a huge wood box which fed from the outside. A thick sofa was in front of the fireplace, a set of gleaming moose antlers with a 72-inch span hung above the heavy beam mantel of the smoothed stone fireplace.

A kitchen area with a small, old but still gleaming wood cook stove trimmed in silver was on the east wall along with a sink set into the counter with working taps. Built in cupboards lined the rest of that wall. A small round dining table with a set of four rustic hand-made chairs completed the kitchen area. Books were stacked everywhere there was a flat surface, the rest of the walls of the small cabin were lined with bookshelves packed with colorful dust jacketed hard cover books and paperback volumes. The living room looked more like a small library that a wilderness camp cabin.

Two doors leading to bedrooms dominated the south wall of the cabin. From the living room Hunter could see a double bed in each of the two bedrooms.

"I'll start some food, you are going to be in there," Kodi said while pointing to the doorway to the left.

"Do you have a radio? I need to get back to my camp and without that boat I'm going to need a fly in."

"No radio, no contact. You'll stay here tonight. Lucky for you the supply plane is coming in soon. He won't mind dropping you off. I'll pay him to take you if I need to."

Hunter let the dig slide.

"That little creek is too busy and small for it to land on." the game warden challenged, using his chin to point at the small river tumbling outside the kitchen window.

The snark was more exhausting to Kodi than being chased by the bear.

"There's a lake farther behind the cabin. Plenty of room there."

"Ok," Hunter said, pausing before heading in to see what the bedroom held. "That'll give us time tonight for you to tell me the truth about your face."

Three

The bear was not the biggest surprise of the day.

The comment by Hunter Davis was a verbal rock thrown from his mouth.

An actual karate chop to his shoulder would have surprised Kodiak less than the comment about how he looked.

Kodiak for the most part did not think about his face, the deeply trenched scars running down over his left cheek from his forehead along down to his chin were usually covered with a beard and mostly out of sight. A few pulled, shiny raised lines of skin twisted up over his left cheek moving back toward his left ear were the most visible of the damage. He wasn't pretending the scars were not there, he simply saw no reason to look at them as the past could not be changed and the doctors had done all they could.

"I'm from just outside Palmer, all my life." Hunter had gone on, naming another of the larger cities in the state. "You are about as famous in Alaska as they come and everyone is curious about what really went down " Hunter continued, voicing what Kodiak was hit with any time he was around other people.

Which is why he had chosen to be away from society as much as he could be.

For a short time Kodiak DePaul had been as famous

in Alaska as Captain James Cook, William Seward or Sarah Palin.

And for a short time, he had been more infamous than the three of them put together.

He was famous not because he had run a race, rescued anyone, sung, danced or acted his way into the spotlight.

An international spotlight.

Kodiak DePaul had been a constant on a nationally televised modeling program, which had brought him to the surface of the little pond of the big state he lived in. News can be slow in Alaska, the same politicians round the same corners; the same bears attack the same tourists, the same moose chase after the same local's year after year. The cruise ships come and go spring to fall and snow closes roads October to May.

But every now and then something extraordinary happens.

Jewel is heard on the radio.

Tom Bodett writes best-selling books.

Kodiak DePaul is chosen for Top Model Search.

Second of three sons in the family Kodi, named Kodiak for the bear famous Alaskan island, had always hated being singled out for the way he looked. But there was nothing he could do about that. He had always been made over, told how handsome he was, and the proof of that pudding had come his senior year in high school when a photographer caught an image of him at work at the Winter Carnival. Kodi had both a look and a hook; smokking guy from not just small-town USA but from the frozen north, which was hot that year because of its politics.

A stud in hand-made mukluks.

A week after high school graduation Kodi was taken to Anchorage and put an airplane bound for New York city to begin the competition.

Pretty heady stuff for a young guy who had never even seen the television show he had agreed to be a part of, let alone never having left the state of Alaska.

Briefed on how the contest would work before leaving Alaska, the reality of what he was undertaking hit the moment Kodiak found himself at the airport in New York when the he picked up his bag and was met by the show handler assigned him.

Used to mountains and space the Alaskan found himself in canyons of steel. The noise, smell and movement of the city were overwhelming, Kodi was thankful when he finally found himself in a hotel room alone. Undressing he fell onto the single bed, trembling while wondering what he had gotten himself into.

It seemed like his eyes had just closed when the door to the room flew open and the out, proud, loud (and stunningly handsome) guy who was to be his roommate for the competition swept into the room in a whirl of glitter, rainbows and old school disco.

Until that moment, when Charles Porter entered his life, Kodi had never been around anyone who was openly, happily gay. Kodi understood his own sexuality but had no idea how to express it.

Charles changed that.

"Sweet Jesus in the stable look at that ass! And in *Tar-Ghee* tighty-whities no less! Did they scoop you up over at the Port Authority? Mmm, mmm, that butt! Looks like you got a coupla honeydew melon stuffed in there! Now roll over and let me see your face baby!"

Kodiak dutifully rolled over, when Charles spoke

people listened. The garishly bright overhead light caused the Alaskan to grab at the coverlet and try to pull it over his muscular body.

"Don't be coverin' that up child! You got it, why you are here! Mercy!" Charles, tall, beautiful with a smile full of mischief, drew in a deep breath and sighed at the work muscled body Kodiak presented him with.

"You are fine!" And with that Charles, jaded at nineteen himself and firmly of the belief that closets were for clothes and kinky sex, took young Kodiak under his wing firmly and hostage like.

"Get up, get up-hate to cover that body but put on some party clothes! We are in New Fucking York city and I have a handful of fake ID's. Let's go get some hot guys to buy us some cold drinks."

While Kodiak had never questioned his sexuality, his attraction to guys was as natural as breathing; he had also never had a chance to act on it, either. Mostly home schooled he had spent most of his life deep in the bush with only his brothers as playmates. This adventure into a big city offered an opportunity to explore in a way he never expected. With a guide like Charles offering the keys to the city and life this was a chance not to be missed despite Kodiak's natural quiet reserve.

It was also like giving a kitten a vial of nitroglycerine.

They were handsome young men with the means to get into clubs; that night they used their looks like a super power.

Despite the warnings from the program that the contestants were not to leave their rooms without permission Kodiak let the charming, charismatic man soon to become his best friend lead him out onto the mean streets of the city, the two of them quickly giggling like school boys playing with matches.

Moving deftly though the throngs in Times Square Charles led Kodiak through the flashing valley of neon while explaining that the contest was secondary to his rise to stardom. The *exposure* was what this experience was all about, and as he was a triple threat (model, dancer, actor-with a giggle the handsome man admitted that he could not carry a note in a bucket and that God needed to give every piece of perfection a *flaw*) so it was his destiny to be a star but he would graciously let Kodiak hang onto him for the meteoric rise.

Their looks, and Charles fierce, fearless attitude, got the underage pair into club after club, where paid for drinks were offered and the virgin Kodiak, who had only had a few sips of beer in his life up until then, was quickly stumbling drunk, making out with strangers and soon nearly drugged.

The more experienced Charles, who had not believed Kodiak's protests of virginity and not having tasted hard liquor, had been watching his new roomie like a hawk, swept in just as Kodiak had been handed a drink which had been doctored with a notorious drug. Charles managed to snag the drink out of Kodiak's hand just before the young man collapsed onto the dance floor. Charles had simply let the container slip from his hand and shatter all over the shoes of the guy who had slid the beverage to Kodi.

"Oopsie," the imposing model said, his beaming smile firmly fixed in place, "now why don't you move along before someone drops a house on you." He said, using the term in a far more menacing way than could ever have been conceived by Billie Burke.

Taking Kodi by the shoulders Charles led him to a

small banquet, shooing the group huddled over drinks at the table away with the hushed whisper that Gaga had just secretly entered the club and was getting ready to go on stage.

"Who'z at? Should we go see her?" Kodi had slurred, trying to push himself up off the red leather seat. He had no idea of what was going on, the pulsing music shaking his bones, his senses were overloaded but he was having the time of his life.

One drink had left the young man from the north wobbly and disoriented. The six more he had downed since that one had him flying.

"Sit back down hot stuff," Charles had ordered another drink for himself and two bottles of water for Kodi. Hot as he was it was the young man's naivety that attracted Charles to Kodiak.

Aside from that rocking ass.

Over the course of the competition the pair had eventually traded life stories, but even on that first night as he led Kodi back to the hotel that night Charles had become fiercely protective of Kodi. Smiling to himself Charles unwound his new roomie from around his body early the next morning pleased he had kept the young Alaskan's virginity still intact.

For that night at least.

As quickly as the competition had begun the models become household names in some circles, developing fiercely loyal fan clubs on line.

Kodiak might have made it farther into the competition if he'd had the ability to pretend to understand the challenges or be enthused by them. He did have a natural smoldering look which the camera picked up, but his lack of modeling experience showed;

while grinning did not come naturally to the young Alaskan, he was chided and lost valuable points round after round when he smiled, unable to suppress how he felt about some of the clothes he was assigned to wear or runway moves the contestants were asked to perform. Stern faced models were successful models and Kodiak could not suppress himself with unwanted smiles in shoot after shoot.

Brash, hot, funny Charles who had the advantage of several years of experience in industry made it to the final round. By the time the last tapings were happening Kodiak was knocked out in the sixth slot but had been spotted by a manager and agency ready to sign him at the end of the competition.

By the end of the filming Charles had introduced Kodi to a world the young Alaskan never dreamed existed. A place where you could openly love anyone you wanted. While Alaskans leaned toward the independent and liberal, Kodi never imagined growing up that there were places where he could publicly have a boyfriend. While he missed the wilderness and hated the noise and people packed streets of the city Kodi did enjoy the freedom of being himself, having the option to walk down the street hand in hand with another guy and feel safe was a treasure which could not be bought.

Novice Kodiak soon fell into a natural rhythm of the work once the pressure of the show tapings were over and quickly became one of the sought-after new *IT* models in the industry, a fleeting title at best.

He also learned that models were treated as meat to be used, from the stylist who randomly let their hands wander down much farther than needed when tucking in a shirt to agents who offered work only after favors had been traded to photographers, who felt as artists they could simply take what they wanted.

Kodiak, naive but not stupid, quickly caught on, learning to pull away when needed, to say *No* in a friendly and firm enough way and smile his way out of any situation. He did not want to offend anyone and this was an opportunity to earn enough security to go back to the bush for good.

At least he thought he had mastered easing out of uncomfortable situations.

A photographer with a brilliant career tapped Kodiak to come have shots done in his studio late one afternoon. Obliging Kodiak moved naturally, gracefully in front of the lens and flash, allowing the man to ease him out of more and more clothing and move in closer and closer, until the final shot was nothing more than a lip lock, the man lunging forward to press Kodiak onto a lounge.

Fighting back even as the photographer hissed *relax, I'm going to make you a superstar* over and over. Raising his voice Kodiak fought back, calling out for the stronger man to stop as he rolled him over and took advantage.

At the end of the event as Kodiak slowly re dressed, dazed at what had just happened, the photographer said casually, *you shouldn't be so hard to work with man, might hurt your career.*

Kodiak kept the rape to himself, never even telling Charles.

Four

Tall and lean with his head of long, glossy blond hair streaked naturally by the sun Kodiak had the angular features and lithe body of a clothing designers dream. With his perfect skin and big, blue eyes he had a magnetism which easily translated from Boy next Door to Cycle Slut, putting no effort at all into switching gears depending on who he was walking for. While the attack scarred him deeply Kodiak resolved to keep that out of his mind and move forward. Not an easy task for the quiet young homesteader but it was the only way for him.

With Charles at his side at nearly every gig Kodi had met a who's who of the city, usually not knowing anything about the people whose names were in the paper but unknown to the young Alaskan.

The world, New York in particular, was, however, full of beautiful people who flocked there to break into modeling. Or acting or singing, all of which in addition to talent (or looks) took work. Hard work, self-promotion, agents, managers, a never-ending list of connectors to help make that big break happen.

Big paying modeling gigs were still few and far between despite the exposure from the show.Kodiak did get a nice share of work due to his Alaskan story but still never enough to cover all his expenses. Clothes were at least at the bottom of his concerns list as he was still most at home (and looked his sexiest) in his worn jeans and faded flannel shirts.

While his looks did pay the bills and the exposure from the television show put him ahead of guys with more experience Kodiak needed to work for his daily expenses so he signed up with an elite event company, while they were handed trays of food to pass the models were not much more than eye candy, back ground entertainment for people who were at these events all the time and used to pleasant looking things. And people. A steady diet of the same canape, same fundraising speeches and never-strong-enough drinks were all made easier to deal with when you had young, hot models holding the trays.

There were many opportunities to work in the sex industry, but the agency made it clear that if even *one* picture of Kodiak naked showed up that he would be finished in high-end modeling.

So, the mindless work for a decent wage was easy enough for Kodiak, who had ripped his muscles chopping wood, hauling water and shoveling snow and now kept up a grueling routine at an old school gym filled with grunting body builders heaving weights over their heads.

Kodiak never bothered paying attention to who might or might not be looking at him, the usual fuss that went on behind his back about his attractiveness went un noticed by the sexy homesteader.

The show and living in the city did not change how he felt about himself, but it did afford him the chance to explore in ways he would never have had the chance had he not left the wilderness.

He had been kissed by a beautiful young model while huddled under the Eiffel Tower during a sudden spring rain storm. Shared pasta with another handsome man at a bistro across from the Coliseum in Rome. He learned to enjoy sex and had a number of short relationships, but was never in love until meeting Jimmy Dugan.

The night he met Jimmy might have been just another serving gig had the staff not been asked to wear something "native", beads, a feather; just a touch of something to lighten up the usual uniform of black on black. It was a sweltering New York afternoon, but Kodiak was accommodating and wore his mukluks. Beautiful reindeer hide lovingly hand tanned and beaded by his mother, a ruff of white Russian wolf ringed the top of the one of a kind mid-calf boot. The boots were works of art Kodiak and his family all wore without thought.

The newly minted model was standing behind the MET amid the catering trucks and tents taking a short break near the end of the night when someone behind him spoke.

"Now those are some fancy shoes!"

Turning Kodiak, for the first time in his own life, felt his heart beat just a little faster when he found himself face to face with a small group which included Jimmy Dugan, his boyfriend and some pals who were attending the event and found this a convenient place to smoke.

Jimmy's wide smile and flashing blue eyes locked with Kodiak as his boyfriend called out to the model,

"Kenneth Cole? Ferragamo? Jimmy Choo? C'mon Chief, where 'dja get 'em?"

Kodiak had no idea who the designers listed were. It did not matter anyway as his hearing had stopped at slur "chief". He did not need to be in the city know this type, they were of the wealthy group who could do what they wanted when they wanted. Arrogant bullies. He had been around their kind all his life, he'd heard his lifelong friend Sam Chigliac called "Chief" and far, far worse and had always come to his fast defense, using his fists when needed.

"My mother made these," Kodi said, the words coming out slowly and tinged with anger.

The slur had come so natural and easy, the young man had not even noticed that he had used it. Kodiak doubted he ever did. Just like the summer fishermen and hunters from outside Alaska who easily insulted Sam and the other natives with thoughtless slurs. A hot blush of shame flashed over his cheeks, he felt as if he had been punched in the stomach.

"No shit! Lemme see! C'mon, c'mon." The drunken man with Jimmy Dugan yelped as he lightly pushed Kodiak down onto a stone bench and plopping down next to the young model. Reaching down he grabbed Kodiak's left foot, lifting it he began examining the Mukluk in detail.

"Your old lady knows her way around a needle, then," Jimmy said with a nod toward the building behind them, "do you have any idea how much artifacts like this are worth?"

"They aren't artifacts. They are my boots." Kodi said as he pulled his foot away and stood. moving so quickly the young man who had pulled him down onto the bench lost his balance and tumbled to the ground. Kodi could tell by the smell that the guy had imbibed enough of the event's open bar cocktails to cushion the short fall. He was mocking Kodi and the young model was having none of that.

"Hey, HEY! Do you *know who I am?*" was yelled from behind him as Kodiak kept walking, the other young men helping their friend up off the ground. "I can keep you from working any event in the city! HEY, I'm talking to you, Chief!" Kodiak heard behind him as a hand reached out and gripped his elbow.

Fast as a flash of lightning the homestead kid turned, sweeping his left leg behind the young man grabbing at his arm, sending him back to the ground with a solid "whoomph", for the second time in less than five minutes the expensive tuxedo had been smoothing the grass of Central park.

"Leave him alone man, let's go," one of the pack said from behind as Kodiak kept moving.

"No, he's pissed me off. I want an apology. And those boots!" were the last words Kodiak heard before he was tackled from behind.

The friends for the most part scattered as the young man who had taken Kodiak down tightened his arms around the model and began to pummel his fists against Kodiak.

"Yale boxing, rube. Fucked with the wrong guy," he boasted while pounding on Kodiak, wildly swinging lunging blows which connected mostly with air. A few shots got Kodiak before he managed to squirm away.

Kodiak pushed himself up off the ground at the same time as the young man, whose thick hair now swagged thuggishly down over his eyes, the guy was adapting his stance as Kodiak lunged forward and stuck a stunning blow to his shoulder. The young man went to his knees as Kodiak turned around to leave.

"You will never work in this town again asshole!" was shouted at Kodi's back as he moved into the building and moved on past the server's station, continuing forward out one of the front doors, making his way defiantly out as disheveled as he was and ignoring the rule of the help entering and exiting through the back.

As he reached the bottom of the broad steps of the iconic building a figure suddenly appeared next to him. In defense mode again, Kodiak found himself face to face with the sexy guy he had seen with the group in back, who's bright eyes and smile had made his stomach clutch.

"Sorry, he's not usually a jerk like that. He's drunk. I'm Jimmy, Jimmy Dugan."

He offered his hand, which Kodiak wordlessly let hang un shaken.

"The boots really are beautiful, and they really should be on display in there." He said with a nod back toward the museum behind them.

Kodi just stared at the handsome stranger blocking his way.

"Some of the guys'll take him home and he'll be sorry when he sobers up. I'll make certain he doesn't try to get you blackballed."

"Let him do whatever he likes." Kodiak shrugged as he turned and stated to move away.

"Tell me about her, your mother." Jimmy called after Kodi. The sliver of emotion which snaked through him could not have been identified by Kodiak but it was the beginning note of love.

Love can come fast or slow, it can be a slow realization or a punch in the soul.

Kodiak, who was used to the ways of the bush but not of the heart, did not understand the

rattle snake swift way he had been taken with Jimmy. Especially after dusting Jimmy's rude friend.

You see someone and your heart races, mouth

becomes dry, palms damp and you just know.

Even though he had just been assaulted and decided to leave New York on his brief stomp from the west to the east side of the museum, at the base of the steps, looking into Jimmy's eyes,

Kodiak DePaul fell in love with Jimmy Dugan when he asked about his mother. Jimmy had the charm of Jay Gatsby, other than Charles he was the first person in the city who made Kodiak feel totally at ease, as simple and easy as that. He let Jimmy apologize for his boorish friend, buy him a drink and from there the two fell into a natural rhythm of each other's lives. Jimmy's touch was slow and gentle, easing Kodiak into a comfort he did not think possible after the brutality he had been met with at the hands of the photographer.

The photographer who had suffered no repercussion for his actions against Kodiak.

The worlds of the two young men could not have been more different. Jimmy's east coast elite world was about as opposite as Kodak's working-class rural world as you could get but there was a natural symmetry to their love despite the difference in backgrounds.

The relationship would likely have remained sunshine and roses had it not been for the asshole who assaulted Kodiak, the young man Jimmy had most recently been dating.

The spoiled, pampered son of a prominent politician Finn Carson was used to getting his way. A trust fund baby who got what he wanted, when he wanted, Finn was furious when Jimmy left him for Kodiak, beginning an immediate campaign of hate directed at the handsome couple as soon as he sobered up from the attack on the model.

Finn, Kodiak's attacker, had finished the relationship with Jimmy two weeks earlier but just had not gotten around to telling him, being the kind of guy who wanted something (or one) he really did not want just because he did not want anyone else to have anything he fancied. Finn made the character played by Ryan Phillipe in the movie *Cruel Intentions* seem like nothing more than a fun stand up kind of guy. Hannibal Lector and the Wicked Witch of the West might have suggested that Finn re consider his actions and attitude toward others in general. In the right mood, which was not often, Finn charmed the birds from the trees. His laser focus of attention could captivate. But he was a young man with a short attention span and interest. He needed the constant next thing to be happy and had the means to get what he wanted. When he lost interest it was on his terms or he turned ugly.

The luxuries of time and money gave Finn the ability to do what wanted, when he wanted. Being young, handsome certainly did not hurt, either. He had been thrown out of some of the finest learning institutions on the east coast and a paternal trust fund gave him all he needed to drink, swagger and, when the time came, focus all his energy and attention on torturing Jimmy and Kodiak.

Neither heart, Jimmy or Finn, was broken when Jimmy eased Finn off his arm and onto Kodiak's as both Jimmy and Finn were used to dating in their circle of friends and social set.

Finn was only angry Jimmy had booted him first, and that Jimmy was dating below what he considered their standard. As Finn's former plaything he was outraged that Jimmy moved along to Kodiak without a second thought, which was when the campaign against the model began.

At first the taunts took the form of simple slam jokes and put down (*Kodiak! Be a pal and fetch us a round of drinks! What did the model put behind his ears to make himself more attractive? His ankles! What are the only similarities between Kodiak DePaul and the Victoria Secret Models? They are all hungry!*), when comments embarrassing enough to stop conversations stopped shocking Finn escalated his attacks to making certain they knew he was following them if they were going out for the night or just for coffee. Had a work-a-day Joe spent the time and money on the campaign Finn launched he would have been labeled crazy and arrested. Money and the freedom it brings allowed him to be labeled "eccentric".

Finn escalated his harassment by hiring people to harass Kodiak when he was alone, paying off models to put itching powder in the young model's underwear and saran wrap over toilet seats Kodiak might use. These things were considered harmless pranks for profit in a career where work can be plentiful for the few at the top, making the plentiful extra offered by Finn for the pranks easy to take from already starving models who lived in sardine tight packed quarters all that much more appreciated.

Finn, frustrated by Kodiak's lack of outrage at his treatment, finally took a more exacting revenge on a fateful night in Chelsea.

Jimmy, Kodi, Charles and some other friends had been out to a club. The small group leaving had blended in with a larger group walking in the same direction, a group of young men flirting, laughing and having fun as they made their way home after a long evening of dancing on a hot summer night.

A car, dark was all the few survivors could agree on, bore down on them from behind. Traffic had been light on the street so another pair of headlights bearing down on the men from behind was no surprise. As the car came up even with the small group it slowed, then stopped.

Doors flew open. Overhead and interior lights had been darkened, the car had stopped just as the group reached that slightly faded intersection where the light of the overhead street lamps over-lap, the only other illumination on the street came from a few closed store fronts and the ambient light of the city.

The group was slow to react to the figures in dark clothing swarming out of the car toward them. The surprise, the unexpected happened like lightning.

None of them yelled, at first. By the time the realization that something out of the ordinary was going on Kodi had been singled out and pushed up against the building next to the street. A scuffle began, Kodi lurched forward but was held back by at least two of the attackers. The young model screamed out, as he did a white-hot sting of pain seared his face. The last thing he remembered as his arms were dropped and he sank to the dirty concrete was the sound of small caliber gun fire going off in flat, hollow bangs as he hit the sidewalk.

As quickly as they had begun the attackers finished, turning back to the idling car, doors slamming as they efficiently scrambled inside. The dark rig darted down the street, the hit happening in no more time as if the car had just slowed to avoid a pothole.

Days later Kodi woke to a face which had been

disfigured by a vial of acid, swathed in gauze and throbbing to the very bone and the news that Charles, who had fought the attackers, was dead.

Others in the group had been wounded and Jimmy's family had sent him into hiding. It took weeks for Kodi to even begin processing the tragedy. The loss of his new friend Charles was devastating, the disappearance of his first love, Jimmy, overwhelming. He did understand for the first time what money, *real* money, meant. As Fitzgerald said, *the rich are not like you and me.*

Jimmy was an asset to be protected. He had loved Jimmy and was certain Jimmy had loved him back despite their different stations. Kodiak learned then that fairy tales are just that, real life brings harsh realities.

He never saw or heard from Jimmy again, heart crushed he vowed to never be vulnerable again.

Kodiak had felt alive with Jimmy for the first time since leaving the bush, the handsome young man made the homesteader smile and laugh, they could get caught in their own world in a crowd, the giggled like conspirators and for the first time since the death of his mother the shy, sheltered Kodiak had begun to feel at ease with himself. Finn, at the same time, had suddenly left the country for extended stay in Europe.

Once the initial twin horror of grief and loss washed through and the wounds began to heal an anger like Kodi he had never felt build. Rage worked through the grief. His anger turned to revenge for Charles.

Kodiak also made a vow to never let his heart be taken again. He had quickly come to see what a come and go commodity feelings were, and that they could lead to the kind of deadly game Finn had played. So, no more love.

In the long months of account draining time Kodiak spent in the hospital, the few friends he had slipping off more and more from visiting due to their own hectic lives and work schedules, Kodiak had time to think.

And plan.

It had not been difficult to track down the attacker, after years in the bush hunting Kodi had the time and patience to stalk and wait out his prey. The strong-arm thugs hired by Finn to do the deed had been methodically tracked and punished. and only Kodi would ever know if the knife which had been thrown and killed the suspected murderer of Charles was actually thrown by the Alaskan bent on Bush justice.

Kodiak had been arrested on suspicion of committing the knifing but there was not enough evidence for a jury to convict him.

The case, however, had been huge, social media exploding over the trial of the disfigured homestead model tied up in murder. The headlines remained constant even in the fast-paced world of ever-changing electronic news flashes there was a morbid fascination with Kodiak and the crime. Accusations as to who had really done what to whom were thrown thick and fast, the media hounding Kodi day and night until he could only escape by returning home.

There was a time when people could go north to Alaska and disappear, but technology had followed the gold and oil booms, even back in Anchorage he was followed day and night, camera's snapping to get the best picture of his scarred face. The story was sexy; gay content, the modeling world, Alaska, murder and a high-profile court case. Which meant the media was willing to follow it, even back to Alaska.

Anchorage is a small town to start with, the tiny former gold mining village of Willow where Kodiaks family lived and ran a small service station nothing more than a dot on the Parks highway which cut through the middle of the state between the cities of Anchorage and Fairbanks.

When a pack of reporters swarmed that quaint village and began rooting around at the school house, tiny library and general store looking for information about Kodiak his family suggested he go north to his great grandfather's homestead land, a place the family used as a hunting and summer camp. Kodiak had now been living there full time for two years, turning the property into the nearly self-sustaining show place the homestead had become. He luxuriated in the privacy of the woods and could never imagine that he had left Alaska for the contest in the first place.

The statement about his scarred face had caused Kodiak to nearly drop the pan holding huge fillets of freshly caught salmon to the floor of the cabin kitchen.

"Follow me," Kodiak snarled at Hunter. The homesteader felt the steady throb of pain begin to pulse along the line of his longest scar, the one now hidden in the line of his thick hair which ran on down the side of his face nearly to his chin. The scruff of beard he now wore kept most of the wounds hidden. The modeling world would have been happy to have had Kodiak back but he refused to limit his exposure to just being classified as a disfigured freak to be used as shock value.

Kodiak loved the solitary life he had carved alone here in the bush. He'd known love, he'd known true friendship in Charles. Both were gone now, and he now was fine on his own.

Or so he convinced himself.

"Hey, no offense man! Everyone knows about the famous Kodiak DePaul, if you go getting pissed at everyone who is going to ask about what happened then you aren't ever going to have any friends." Hunter had kept pace behind Kodi as they went back out of cabin doorway.

"Where are we going anyway?"

Kodi's stomach knotted, would this buffoon never shut up!

"We are going back to the wash house so I can see your ID. If you are a fucking reporter you are back out in the wilderness on your own, asshole."

Hunter stopped, laughing for the first time. "Wait a minute, you are going to force march me back to my wet clothes to see identification? You *saw* the patch on my sleeve."

Kodi shrugged.

"You can get those at any surplus store."

"I *earned* the honor of wearing that patch and will not have you disrespect the authority it represents."

"Fine," Kodi said, stopping short, "I don't have to see your credentials. Just go. I'll walk you back to the wash house. You can wait there, spend the night if you want, and leave from there in the morning. No one comes this far north unless they are looking for something. Or someone," Kodiak continued darkly. "And since I don't think you are really a game warden or a hunter I think you are snooping on me or a reporter. So, unless you can prove yourself, I don't trust you."

"Are you kidding me with this?" the ranger asked, eyes flashing.

"Up to you. All you have to do is prove you truly *belong* here. And frankly you storming off into the bush with no gun while that big crazy grizzly is out there will go a long way toward proving you are who you claim to be."

The game warden smiled again, Kodiaks stomach knotting as the young man's scowling features changed. The smile made him handsome, sexy, and that was the last thing Kodiak wanted on this homestead. Turning on the trail he started walking again, Hunter falling in behind him.

"I get it, I get it. You are known and want privacy. Well you found it, and you must think a lot of yourself if you think anyone is going to come all the way up here just to try and get information about you."

Kodi did not respond. The guy had no idea how many people had already tried to get information about his ordeal. Even in this isolated place Kodi knew of at least two book deals being shopped about his story and one treatment for a cable movie.

"But telling me to prove myself by going unarmed back to my camp is crazy, man." Hunter weakly protested as they stepped up to the wash house and Kodi pushed the door open, holding it wide to allow the game warden to go inside ahead of him.

Stepping over to a taunt span of cotton rope serving as the clothes line the young man began rummaging in the pocket of his pants hanging on the line, then in the pockets of the brown jacket with the ranger patch on the shoulder, Kodi watching carefully.

Two, three times Hunter dug his fingers into the wet material, bringing them out empty. He finally pulled the lining of the pants pockets out, letting them drape down over the outside of the pants.

"Guess I lost my cap *and* wallet," Hunter muttered, still digging into the wet material. "I had it when I left camp," he went on, voice trailing off. "Sorry man, I just remembered. I took my wallet out of my pants when I got on the seat of that skiff. It was holding me up on one side so I put it in a bag I had. All of that went down with the boat and is lost in the river."

A plausible story and still just that. A story. Kodiak knew he was taking a chance but also knew the days were getting shorter and that if the guy was on the level as a game warden that he would never forgive himself if he sent him away to his camp and he was taken by the marauding bear, which was certainly still in range of the camp. Bear are territorial, to send this guy out with no protection was the same as signing his death warrant.

Of course, if the guy turned out to be a reporter Kodi would feel equally bad. But only for the bear who would miss a meal as Kodiak knew places to put the body where it would never be found.

Keeping himself to the homestead, living on the modest interest earned by money made from his short modeling career Kodiak knew little of what was going on in the rest of the world, nor did he care. His work now was survival in the cold, harsh beautiful land. He had installed solar panels, a wind small generator and was working on a simply hydro converter to run in a nearby river in the next year to harness that energy. The power provided lights, charged an iPod which fitted onto a BOSE speaker and gave him the ability to play a library of old movies on DVD. He could likely have rigged up a broad band radio or connected with a satellite but even on the rare occasion when he had to go to Fairbanks,

Anchorage or home to Willow, Kodi turned a blind eye to the news. Having lived in the eye of a hurricane he simply had no interest in events happening in the rest of the world.

Or, more ominously, that the news might again contain a story about him.

William Powell and Myrna Loy in *The Thin Man* series was about as current as Kodiak wanted to get. Once a week he did allow himself the luxury of listening to messages sent out by powerful radio station in Fairbanks. Anyone needing to connect with someone in the bush could call in a message to the station and they would announce the information over the air. It was limited and one way but a connection to the world those in the far north would not have otherwise. Radio programs like *North Wind* and *Muckluck Telegraph* were important to life in the bush if someone could not fly or walk in and a bush rat needed to be reached.

Suppressing the urge to tell Hunter he was going to leave him to sleep in the wash cabin, Kodi turned and stepped back out onto the trail leading back to the cabin, Hunter following close behind him quietly.

"Look, I know you have been through a lot," Hunter began from behind Kodi. The homesteader turned sharply, so quickly the game warden almost ran directly into him. "You. Do. Not. Know. Anything." Kodi growled, eyes flashing.

Hunter had the good sense to just lift his hands in surrender and was smart enough to take a quick step back.

Turning sharply back around on the well-worn trail the homesteader strode forward.

Back in the cabin Kodiak began slamming pans

around in the kitchen while Hunter quietly went into the room Kodi had pointed out that he was to sleep in, staying there until Kodiak emitted a grunt of *Dinner* from the tiny kitchen.

The meal of fresh salmon, huge garden grown potatoes which had been baked in the wood stove oven along with the fish, and sweet carrots fresh from the homestead garden would have cost fifty bucks a plate in Seattle was eaten in near silence. When the men were finished Kodiak set about cleaning the kitchen while Hunter wandered to the other side of the room and casually began looking at the objects lining the thick beam from a long abandon gold mine which served as the mantel over the fieldstone fireplace.

"Wow," Hunter finally said, breaking the by then hours long silence. "These are pretty amazing, your work? If I'm not being too nosey." The warden added quickly. The intricate carvings would be worth a small fortune in Anchorage or any of the pan handle cruise ship ports.

Coming back into the small book filled living room Kodi turned on a floor lamp, a soft yellow light was cast around the room, making it look very cozy despite the glacier wide quiet which had formed between the men over the course of the afternoon.

"No," Kodi finally responded, suppressing an urge to reach over and snatch the tiny carved dogsled Hunter had picked up out of his hands.

A smile of nostalgia crossed Kodiak's face.

"A kid I grew up with carves them, Sam Chigliack. Nice guy. His grandmother taught my mother to sew," Kodiak said while lifting the delicate figure of a seal pup from the mantel and stroking the glossy smooth ivory.

"Runs a trap line so I see him a few times a year. I won't take any money when he stays here so he carves something for my collection. I feed him and bring up some candy but nothing I do would be able to pay him for this kind of work."

"No liquor, though." Hunter stated with authority as he put the miniature ivory carving down then picked up one of the tiny huskies lined up in front of the sled. It was illegal to bring liquor into any of the native villages. Like their other native north American counterparts Alaskan natives had been stripped of their land and alcoholism ran rampant among the quiet, gentle people.

This time Kodi did act, carefully placing the seal figure back onto the mantle he snagged the tiny dog carving from Hunter and carefully replaced it in line with the others.

"You know enough about me to know I am from here. These people are my people too. You don't need to say crap like that."

"Some people don't know," Hunter said with a shrug, moving on down the mantel where he picked up a tiny carving on a native dancing. "The darkness in this piece looks like it might be old, mammoth?" Tusks from the ancient beasts still popped up out of the deep permafrost and were dislodged by changing river channels and were openly hunted. Sold by the pound they were made into carvings and beads to be sold at extremely high prices. If the tusks were not preserved once they came out of the ground they began to rot. The two scrimshaw carved pieces carefully carved and polished by Sam Chigliac were now hanging next to the fireplace could easily fetch five thousand dollars or more at an Anchorage or Juneau gallery.

"This collection is probably worth a lot." Hunter said with a nod toward the pieces on the mantel. "You aren't just really handy with a knife and snagging walrus ivory and carving it up yourself, are you? 'Cause that is illegal and immoral. Natives only can do that."

"Listen, I'm really starting to regret not letting that bear have you for lunch." Kodiak said with a glare. "These were gifts, if any of these are walrus they were carved by Sam Chigliac. You are in my home and unless you knock off your accusations and insinuations right now I'm change my mind about bunking you in the wash house." Kodiak then lowered his voice a notch before continuing ominously with, "Or walk you off my property and let you hike back to your own camp alone."

"Sorry, sorry," Hunter said, turning away from Kodiak. Stepping back toward the kitchen the thick cuff of the heavy shirt Kodiak had loaned him caught on a small handle sticking out from one of the smoothly polished logs, pulling open a section of the wall.

A small bar set into the dark niche appeared.

"Well, well, well. What have we here!" Hunter said with glee. "Vodka, Rum…I suppose this is for medicinal purpose only."

"As a matter of fact," Kodiak said flatly, "it is. "And the wash house is right the hell down that path unless you close that and get to bed."

Before bringing his hand out of the carefully carved in niche Hunter paused to let his fingers curl around something else pushed back into the dark inset, bringing out a small yellow and black plastic box, a SPOT emergency satellite signal phone used by most people who were spending time in the bush.

"Another nice touch of civilization," Hunter said with

a grin.

"Can't you keep your paws off anything?" Kodiak snarled while taking a menacing step toward his guest.

Pushing the phone back into the chamber and closing the door Hunter lifted his hands again in a signal of defeat then turned and went into the bedroom.

Closing the door, he moved to the small desk built in under the window. Sitting down on the rough-hewn log bench and turned on a small desk lamp. A note pad was open to a blank page.

Hunter pulled it toward himself then lifted a pen left next to the pad. With a smile crossing his face he carefully wrote the word Jackpot! across the top line, followed by a series of numbers, 27.7079 N., 80.0642 W.. The co-ordinates of where he had launched the boat for the homestead land he was on. Hunter had committed the degrees to memory before shoving off into the river and had been fighting to keep them correct in his head all afternoon.

Making notes on the afternoon he was quickly satisfied that he had gotten a good start. He gave the words he had written a fast review before undressing for bed.

Bunching the plaid shirt Hunter could not help but bury his face into it and inhale; the last skin other than his own touching the material had been Kodiak's. There had been a washing between wears so all the smell Hunter got was the clean, fresh scent of air-dried flannel- but in his mind he was smelling the hard-muscled body of Kodiak in his hands. He wanted the young homesteader desperately but even if Kodiak had given him a signal that it was alright to make a move Hunter would not have. There would be plenty of time and money for guys later.

For now, he had to move with caution. He did not want to mess up this opportunity.

Turning out the light he smiled, sliding down into the sheets of the very comfortable bed he had been offered for the night, grateful he was not curled up on the wash house floor or swatting plumb size mosquitos while making his way through the woods along the river looking for his own camp while on the look-out for the huge angry bear which had sunk his skiff earlier in the day.

Five

Kodiak woke the morning after bringing Hunter back to the cabin fully aroused and furious to find himself in that state. An erotic dream involving the game warden in the next room had caused his morning excitement, he was livid his body had betrayed him. The game warden would soon be gone and the young homesteader hoped it would be a long while before he would ever have to deal with the green horn again.

Calming himself Kodiak had let his thoughts drift to Jimmy since he was in the sexual neighborhood. Their affair had been hot and intense, while Kodiak was a true loner he found waking in Jimmy's arms had been one of the most wonderful and unexpected things he had ever experienced. He missed that more than all the other thoughts and memories he had of Jimmy however there would be no love's lost kiss for Kodiak. He was finished with love and romance.

The solitude of his world in the bush would be his passion, his life. He would not lose his heart again.

Refusing to visualize the game warden, Kodiak took a few minutes to go ahead and indulge in some fond memories, then hurried out of bed. Shuddering he dressed quickly, the temperature had plummeted overnight and a chill had settled into the cabin. The day before had likely been the last true day of the summer season.

Kodiak hurried into the kitchen and built a fire in the vintage cook stove then scooped a portion of sourdough starter from a mason jar on the counter. The starter had been growing continuously since the time of his great-grandfather and had likely been around much longer than that. If you kept the starter in a cool, dark place and fed with fresh flour the starter would live indefinitely. Hot cakes, rolls, pie crust and breads could all be made with the organism. Not only was the starter vital in the diet of a generational homesteader like Kodi, but it added to the thread of continuity on the family property.

"Something smells good," Hunter said from the doorway of the bedroom, he was fully dressed save for the beautiful hand sewn boots Kodi had loaned him the day before. Kodiak shuddered on seeing Hunter, his body reacting to the wide grin and tousled hair of the game warden as he crossed to a chair in the living room and sat down to slip on and lace up the soft mukluks.

"Hot cakes," Kodi said while sliding a spatula under two of the rounds of batter. With an expert twist of his wrist he flipped the dough just as both had turned golden brown."Coffee's hot, mugs over there," giving a nod to the coffee pot simmering on the back plate of the wood stove top Kodiak slid the spatula under two of the hot cakes ready to come off the surface of the stove. Sliding the finished hot cakes onto a platter Kodi lifted the door of the warming oven above the stove then slid the platter in while gritting his teeth, trying not to imagine Hunter naked.

"There is no danger of you starving up here, you know your way around a stove," Hunter said with a beaming smile as breakfast was finished. The table had been dressed with the platter of fluffy golden sourdough hotcakes, which now sat empty alongside their plates, margarine and a now nearly empty pitcher of fireweed honey Kodiak had put on the table. He had some freshly churned butter he had bartered for stored down at the wash house but he was not about to share that special treat with Hunter. The game warden had almost gotten them both killed the day before. While Kodiak would not let anyone starve he also saw no reason to cast pearls before swine or offer the efforts of his hard work to a jerk.

Even if he was a cute jerk.

"What time is that supply plane due?" Hunter asked as Kodi began clearing away the plates.

"Dunno," the homesteader shrugged. "hopefully today, if weather hit's it might be a week,"

Kodiak shrugged, "it'll be soon enough."

"Well then let's fire off a call from that SPOT locator and get someone's attention!" Hunter replied as he made a step toward the small bar door set into the cabin log.

"That is not a device to use like you are calling for a cab! The SPOT is for *emergency* use only. You'll be patient and wait until the plane arrives or you are welcome to head on down to the river and hope the bear doesn't pick up your scent."

Hunter started to reply then thought better of it. The more time he was with Kodiak the more information he could gather.

"You are playing that bear card like we are in a casino." Hunter smiled while reaching for the fork next to his plate.

"You are gonna have to keep yourself occupied until the plane does get here and I have chores to do, so stay out of trouble." Kodiak said, lifting his own fork as the men turned to the food, eating in a comfortable silence.

When they finished Hunter stepped to the front door and had one foot on the porch when an eerie animal call suddenly echoed through the silence.

"What the fuck was that!" Hunter said, the words coming out of his mouth before he could stop them.

A small grin crossed Kodiak's face, causing Hunter's crotch to twitch. He would have done most anything to have seen more of that smile on Kodiak's handsome face. The homestead/model had left his hair hanging, the soft unbound lengths of hair framed his handsome face making him almost unbearable for Hunter to keep from lunging into his arms.

"A guy who claims to be an Alaskan, and an Alaskan game warden at that, who's never heard a Loon." his tone assured Hunter that the sound was game warden 101 and that he had failed a basic test. "The majestic water bird with a white band around their neck, they mate for life and the same pair come back to the same lake every year to raise their chicks." With a smirk Kodiak turned, his heart always lurched at the sight or sound of the Loon as he felt he would now never be mated as they got to be.

"So, you've never heard the legend either, huh? the homesteader said, sexy grin still in place.

Hunter had to shake his head no again.

"There are several versions, but the basic story is that a prolific hunter and provider went blind. He had always given his family and the village the best game and in return was given gifts of blankets, beads and necklaces, some very elaborate. His wife was a vain woman who became angry when the hunter could no longer provide her with many beautiful things when he went blind so she threw him out of their cabin. He left to go die in the woods and ended up at the edge of a lake where a Loon found him sobbing. The Loon offered to help and told the man to hold onto him and bury his face into his dark feathers. The man did and after several dives under the water the man opened his eyes and could see. He was so grateful he removed the exquisite shell necklace he was wearing and graced it onto the Loon's neck. And since that time the Loon has had a white band on its neck."

Smirking that someone claiming to be an Alaskan did not know such a basic piece of folk lore. With that Kodiak turned again, heading out toward his woodlot, leaving Hunter behind.

"Now you know the story," he said loud enough for Hunter to hear but not turning around. "I know a lot of other legends. Tell you another after dinner tonight. By the time you leave here you will at least have an education for your game warden *character*."

After watching Kodiak disappear down the trail into the woods Hunter went back to the bedroom, where he reminded himself he had to be more careful. Stupid little mistakes like not knowing the call of the loon could easily blow his cover. He quickly made up the bed and picked up the notebook again. He was sorry to have lost the cameras in the bear attack so would sketch what he could to work with for now, he'd have to come back for pictures. In this case they would be worth quite a lot more than that proverbial thousand dollars per shot.

Interest in the Kodiak DePaul case had not waned in the years he had been out of the spotlight. The few times he was spotted in Anchorage he was immediately swarmed as soon as he was recognized, the national networks and tabloid programs always placing the sightings at the top of their programs. There was money to be made in images of Kodiak, Hunter did not like what he was doing but it was a dog eat dog world.

Going outside Hunter began working on a series of sketched views of the exterior of the homestead cabin. He was hardly an artist but was pleased with his work and the rough sketches.

Kodiak seemed like a good enough guy and Hunter felt bad that he was doing this, and he had to keep steering his thoughts from the young homesteaders ripped biceps. The scarring across his face only made the former model sexier. There were few clear photographs of Kodiak's face in existence after the incident despite the intense competition of the paparazzi to capture his image.

Hunter had hoped to sail in and secretly get some good shots and be gone before Kodiak suspected a thing but the appearance of the bear had changed the way he planned to meet the infamous backwoods man. He would be penalized for not having photo's but this, being here with *the* Kodiak DePaul and having actual quotes from him (even if several them were curses at Hunter), would have to be enough.

For now.

When Hunter finished drawing, he would list as many of the book titles in the small cabin as he could before Kodi returned. If things worked as Hunter hoped it would never be known that he was the one who supplied the detailed information of how Kodiak lived. Of course, Kodi would figure it out, but as far as he was from civilization he might never know.

Hours flew by, giving Hunter time to finish off more sketches and lists in detail. When he finished with the book titles Hunter carefully tore the pages from the note pad then folded them and slipped them deep down into his shirt then smoothed his hands over the material to make certain the paper did not crackle before he put the pad back in place next to the pen.

Hurrying back into the living room Hunter scanned the collection of carvings on the mantel. Luckily there was a wide array of tiny items, most of them in the deeply yellowed ivory he suspected as being walrus.

Selecting an intricately carved moose complete with a wide set of antlers along with several other small pieces he figured to be made from ancient tusk Hunter slipped the carvings into his pants pocket then carefully re arranged the others to fill in the gaps, hoping it would be a while before Kodiak missed the pieces. The pieces he selected were signed with the initials *S.C.* carved into the bottom. While he would not have paperwork on the art he knew those initial's would be recognized and help get a little more for the pieces. He hadn't intended to become a petty thief in this venture but was too far in to stop now. *If you are going to steal a loaf of bread you might as well steal a million dollars h*is mother had often said. The words haunted him now, if he was stealing the details of Kodiak's life and planned to come back to steal images of him then in for a penny and in for a pound. What was wrong with taking a few of the many carvings Kodiak had on the mantel as well.

Tucking his conscience aside Hunter left the cabin, reflecting on the beauty of the place the moment he stepped back onto the small, neat front porch.

The snug log structure had been set deep in the heart of a thick grove of trees, giving it a natural wind break. A wise move in this usually cold place. Hunter swatted at the large mosquitos buzzing around, the natives had lore of the huge pests driving white men crazy but Hunter had spent enough time in the bush to learn the trick of ignoring them while staying on guard not to let them start feeding on any exposed skin.

Wandering along the well-worn trail leading to the wash house Hunter slowed his pace, a smile spreading on seeing an adorable animal moving toward him.

The porcupine, whose summer diet of berries and tender shoots had fattened the animal, who had likely never encountered a human had no fear. Hunter's smile extended as he lowered himself to his haunches. The animals were generally not aggressive.

"Hey little guy. Hey there," Hunter said softly, extending the back of his hand toward the snout of the animal which was making a deep, low chuffing noise. "I'm nice, it's ok to say hello," he assured the animal in an even voice.

Giving a few strong sniffs at Hunter's offered hand the animal must have decided Hunter was not to the trusted, faster than the young man ever could have expected the porcupine gave a short hiss and tried to scramble around him on the narrow path.

"Hey!" yelped the startled Hunter, who did not have time to pull his hand back as he fell over as the porcupine unloaded a thick bundle of quills, one of them catching Hunter deep in the flesh of his thumb.

"Ow, FUCK, OH FUCK!" Hunter stammered, jumping up and down while squeezing his hand at the wrist to try and cut off the blood flow to stem the pain. His stomping scattered the other released quills to the sides of the path.

Contrary to myth porcupine cannot shoot their quills,

they do release them in defense, the ivory colored black tipped quills had been known to make the largest of bear turn and run from the much smaller animals.

"Fuck!" Hunter shouted again, fully forgetting Kodiak's directive about the use of that word as the porcupine picked up speed, it's waddle turning into a run as it hobbled down the path in the direction opposite the game warden.

As Hunter leapt away from the porcupine he suddenly caught a glimpse of what appeared to be a wolf staring at him from a stand of trees not far away.

Money or not he was ready to get out of this Wild Kingdom. Hunter half expected to see a young woman in a red hood and cape standing next to the wolf when he looked again. While Red Riding hood did not appear, another turn of events startled Hunter as if she had.

"Yukon! Stay!" A deep voice said sternly from behind the beautiful but deadly looking animal, which had now stepped down onto the beaten path and was delicately sniffing the packed ground where the porcupine had just been. Moments later a tall handsome young man with blue black hair gleaming in the morning sun, a back pack strapped around his body, had stepped onto the trail just as a startled Kodiak raced up behind Hunter.

"What the hell is going on!" Kodiak exclaimed while bounding around to stand in front of

Hunter. "Sam!" he yelped with equal delight on seeing the man behind Hunter. "Yukon!" he said with equal joy, squatting to throw his arms around the magnificent husky Hunter had thought to be a wolf. "Pretty girl, that's what you are!" Kodiak beamed at the magnificently beautiful lead dog from Sam's team.

"Careful," Sam cautioned, "quills on the ground. Don't want her to get one in a paw."

"Dammit, I told you not to get into trouble," the homesteader sighed, standing as Hunter grimaced, his stomach was knotting from the pain, but he still felt a thrill of excitement with Kodiak standing so close.

"Pull it out!" Hunter growled through grit teeth while blinking back tears and feeling his heart beat through his aching thumb.

Grabbing Hunter's wrist Kodiak turned and began leading him toward the wash house, Sam and Yukon following close behind.

"Be careful where you step," Kodiak warned, nodding down at the spill of quills on the ground. "Bad enough you have one of those in you. Get one in your foot and you are screwed. What the heck were you trying to do, pet a damn porcupine?" Kodiak growled, the idea of a real game warden getting tangled with a porky quill made it even more clear that his "guest" was not who he was representing himself to be.

"I wasn't trying to pet it," Hunter snarled back through grit teeth, knowing that he had indeed tried to do just that. Palmer was cosmopolitan enough that his encounters with the cute but dangerous animals had been very limited. How was he to know how quickly those quills could be released.

"Learning a hard lesson, man," Kodiak said with a shake of his head as he led Hunter into the wash house where he sat him in small frame chair and sat him down then crossed the room, returning with a first aid kit. Sliding the plastic case onto the table next to Hunter he opened it,bringing out a paper wrapped sterile pad he opened it and again grabbed Hunter's hand.

Kodiak's work rough fingers tightened around his made a pit at the bottom of Hunter's stomach despite the physical pain he was in.

"This is going to hurt, can't lie."

"Fuck!" Hunter yelped. "Gimme a slug of that *illegal* booze to get me through this?"

Kodiak smiled, despite the horrible situation he had seen worse. He had seen dogs hit with a muzzle full of quills that took hours to extract. This guy was a phony and a liar, but he also was a liar on Kodiak's land and was in pain. He didn't even bother honoring the intruders' question.

He had re locked the tiny liquor cabinet and hidden the key. Hunter also did not know that to extract a quill in that location that Kodiak was going to have to push it forward, not pull it back.

"These quills are filled with air," Kodiak began while bringing a multi tool out of the First Aid kit. Placing the tool on the edge of the sterile pad he brought out a bottle of rubbing alcohol out and poured it over the tool. Following that he pulled a sealed sterile pad out, ripped it open then swabbed both sides of Hunter's thumb.

"Much repair needed out on the line, Sam?"

His native friend nodded *No* in silence while stroking the soft fur on the dog's head. He had extracted many quills on his own and knew what was coming. Sam knew the question had been asked as much out of idle curiosity as to distract Hunter from the lightning bolt of pain to come.

"Mostly just re setting traps. Some wolverine damage, one set was destroyed by bear." the handsome native said as Kodiak continued arranging the equipment needed for quill removal.

"There's a big rouge griz out there," Kodiak continued, swinging around he grabbed a thick strip of leather hanging on a peg on the wall next to himself and handed it over to Hunter.

'Here, bite down on this. *Hard,* and try not to pull away."

"Saw some scat and pretty big paws down along the river," Sam replied, stroking the dog's silver fur.

"We both saw the bear. Biggest I've ever seen, ten, twelve feet tall. Sank the skiff this dope roared up on."

"Hey! I told you," Hunter started, then wisely closed his mouth at the look Kodiak gave him.

Clamping his teeth down onto the leather Hunter did not avert his eyes as Kodiak quickly picked up the tool and used it to snip off the end of the quill. The hot homesteader then squeezed the ivory colored quill flat and looked Hunter dead in the eye. Despite the pain Hunter felt his stomach knot again as Kodiak's brilliant blue eyes bored directly into his. If Kodiak had leaned in and kissed him Hunter doubted he would have felt anything going on around his thumb.

Since the kiss was not going to happen Hunter bit into the strap, hoping the model could not see the unadulterated lust emanating from his crotch.

"On three."

Hunter nodded, despite the calm he was trying to exude beads of sweat formed along his hairline.

"One," Kodiak began while tightening his grip on Hunters wrist. Kodiak felt sorry for this city dope pretending to be a game warden. This was not the young homesteaders first time dealing with quills, he'd removed them from dogs, his brothers and himself.

"Two,"

Kodiak had not lied to Hunter about the pain, he also had not told him the entire truth of what he was about to do. Porcupine quills are barbed on the end, piercing flesh like tiny razor sharp fish hooks they cannot be pulled out. To be properly removed they must be pushed on through when possible, a process which takes a little longer but does less damage to the intended target.

Kodi knew telling the tenderfoot stranger any of this would only add to his anxiety.

He didn't like the thrill holding Hunter's hand was giving him either.

On a whispered *three* Kodiak pushed as hard as he could, driving the quill through the thickest part of Hunter's thumb, the bloodied end of the quill punching through the skin and on out the other side as Hunter's eyes grew wide, his breath coming in deep jagged spurts.

With practiced skill Kodi grabbed the multi tool, cracking the jaws apart while still holding tight to Hunter's wrist as tears brightened Hunter's eyes then spilled down over his cheeks.

Turning the tool around Kodi clamped it down over the barbed end of the quill and pulled it on through Hunter's thumb.

Laying the tool aside, the quill still gripped in it, Kodiak grabbed the base of Hunter's thumb, forcing a large bubble of blood out of the hole he had just created and grabbed the bottle of rubbing alcohol, he liberally poured the clear liquid over the wound as Hunter dropped the leather strap from between his teeth.

"OW, OW, OW-THAT FUCKIN' STINGS!" Hunter yelped while trying to yank his hand away, but Kodi held it tight.

"YOU DIDN'T FUCKIN' TELL ME YOU WERE

GOING TO *PUSH* IT THROUGH!" He snarled just as his eyes rolled up into the back of his head, the whites suddenly exposed and the possibly faux game warden slumping forward then sliding off the side of the chair, thumping clumsily to the floor.

Pushing away from the table Kodiak lowered himself to the silent young man and lifted the hand he had just removed the quill from. Squeezing the wound again, perhaps slightly harder than he needed to, he brought another bead of blood to the surface then reached up to grab the opened gauze pad and roll of gauze from the table and quickly wrapped it around the wound.

This part, the passing out part, of the quill removal process was not any more surprising than the screaming and cursing part of the removal process.

"Guess he will leave the porky's alone now, huh Yukon." Kodiak said to the beautiful silver dog by then up on all fours and alert to help if needed.

Looking down at Hunter as he scooped his limp form up from the wash house floor Kodiak again allowed himself to acknowledge how cute the stranger was, and how rapidly he was growing tired of him. Kodiak was no more convinced that Hunter was an actual game warden than he himself was a game show host.

Still he was not heartless enough to let the young man lay there sprawled across the floor like a bearskin rug.

With a nod toward Sam, Kodiak waited as his trapper friend unstrapped the back pack he still carried and leaned it against the log wall of the wash house. Scooping Hunter up he and Sam

then carried/drug the moaning Hunter, arms akimbo, along the path back to the cabin.

Aside from the brief time he had been on top of

Hunter the day before it had been a while since he had been this close to another man. He liked the feel of a body against his and allowed himself to smile down at the handsome face admitting to himself that even in this most passive state he missed holding and being held.

Not that he ever intended to allow that to happen in his life again.

The two men managed to get the still unconscious Hunter up the steps and into the cabin, pulling him into the bedroom where they stretched him out on the bed. Once Hunter was settled Kodiak checked the bandage then got a wash cloth from the kitchen and rinsed it under cold water then lay it over Hunters forehead before he and Sam slipped back outside.

Sometime later the throbbing white-hot pain in his thumb woke Hunter, his cheeks flushed when he slowly recalled passing out. He hated that he had done that, but had no control over how his body had reacted to the quill removal. Pulling the damp cloth from his forehead Hunter slowly sat up in the bed, thinking of Kodiak. He wanted to get this business over with before he started to have feeling for this guy, the guy who had on the one hand saved him from life with a quill projecting from his thumb and who had also inflicted searing pain on him when removing it. Smoothing a hand down over his stomach where he had hidden his notes and sketches Hunter sighed in relief that he they had not been found and confiscated. He quickly slid the information he was carefully gathering out of his shirt, sliding it under the pillow on the bed for safety.

Grimly he realized at the same time if Kodiak had found the detailed information that Hunter would certainly have woken stripped bare and staked out down by the river covered in fish guts and being used as bear bait.

He was about to swing his legs off the bed when he heard the front door open and the soft *whumphs* of Kodiak's boots moving across the cabin floor toward the bedroom. "You didn't tell me you were going to fucking push it through." Hunter snarled as Kodiak came through the bedroom doorway.

"First, that is the only easy way to get them out. Second, you are welcome. Third, please find another word than the eff bomb. Little respect, man."

Hunter said nothing, reflecting only on the fact that the sexy scruff of beard Kodi had grown since the disfigurement only served to make him even more ruggedly handsome than before. His stomach twisted as Kodiak unbuttoned his shirt and shrugged it off his broad shoulders, revealing the damp wife beater tee shirt plastered to his body. The homesteader's thick muscles were slick with sweat from swinging an axe all afternoon, causing Hunter to forget about the throbbing of his thumb. Despite the pain in his hand Hunter felt himself thicken then tried to ward off the feeling by reminding himself that he could never have Kodiak DePaul.

The homesteader, oblivious to the show he was putting on, stripped off the tee shirt to reveal a torso like it had been carved by one of the masters, a six pack of abs ending in a narrow V of a waist. Hunter did not avert his eyes as Kodiak rummaged in the freestanding dresser before pulling out another shirt which he began to slowly un button as Hunter openly scanned up and down the length of Kodiak's body, appreciating the half-naked torso.

"Don't you get lonely up here?" Hunter asked, finally swinging his legs over the side of the bed and standing.

"No, never." Kodiak answered without hesitation as his fingers worked the buttons up over his chest. "Even as a kid was more at home in the bush. I always felt sorry for the kids who lived in Anchorage and Palmer, Wasilla even. Yeah, that is Alaska, but this," he said while pointing out the small window, "is what Alaska is all about. Solitude, time to think. Self preservation."

"But don't you miss talking to anyone, let alone intimacy." Hunter pressed on, standing, feeling his own yearning for Kodiak building like fire in his crotch. "Even though I see you do have hot friends stopping in now and then," Hunter said, referring to Sam. "Do you and he, y'know…"

"Not that it is *any* of your business but Sam's only through with the team a few times a year running his trap line and we are like brothers. I give him chocolate and he gives me thousands of dollars-worth of ivory carvings. He's already back on the trail." There was a pause before Kodiak continued. "When he does stay over we both read. We don't need a lot of chatter to make our time together quality."

"Is this some kind of a round-about come on?" Kodiak finally asked, his tone even. Despite his resolve, Hunter was hot, and Kodiak was young and human. His physical desire since Jimmy had not gone away, he was just used to solving the problem alone and quietly.

But when you have been eating hamburger for a while and a steak was suddenly standing in front of you….the homesteader was torn. What was a fast-good time in the long run? Even if Hunter were not who he was presenting to be and told the outside world they had fucked what

would it matter? It would always be his word against Kodiaks, Kodi knew Hunter had no

camera or recording device, the plunge into the river would have destroyed them. Kodiak

DePaul was single, beholden to no one and although he might not *like* this guy he could serve a purpose, which would be the memory of a long, sweat slick and fun afternoon to get Kodiak through the long winter months until he got back to town and chose to have some fun, if he wanted.

It had been a long time since he had touched a man and Kodiak had no idea up until that moment if he ever would again.

Hunter said softly with a shrug, "It can be whatever you want it to be." He also knew that intimacy, fun as it would be, could either greatly help or hurt this project.

"I didn't know models got inked," he said softly while reaching out and lightly tracing the small pattern of black stars on Kodiak's chest which formed a dipper and the north star in the pattern of the Alaska state flag.

"I got that after that part of my life ended," Kodiak replied quietly, the tension between the two causing them both to begin breathing slower. Hunter's finger's lingered on Kodiak's chest as the homesteader shuddered, it felt like lightning had been etched over his skin and he hated the feelings he was having.

"The dipper stands for the bear, ironic after what we went through, huh. The North Star so we can always find our way." Hunter whispered.

Kodiak had to hardened his heart, his un invited guest had just described the meaning of the symbols on the state flag. Which certainly did not mean he was a game warden or even an Alaskan for that matter.

The men stared silently at each other for a long moment as Hunter's fingers slowly pulled away from Kodiak's skin, the sexual tension between the pair could have been sliced like cheesecake. Despite his resolve to be alone and stay alone Kodiak felt the siren call of desire racing through his body, his fingers faintly trembling as they stopped working to close another button on the shirt he had skinned over his muscular frame and he felt the urge to begin reversing the button to re-open the top of the shirt.

The encounter would not be like anything he and Jimmy had enjoyed. But nothing ever would match that. This was just getting by, survival sex; storing a memory to get him through the long cold winter.

Opposite him and still sitting on the bed Hunter swallowed hard, he had wanted Kodiak for so long and here was the opportunity presenting itself, but physical involvement would make the job more difficult, no question about that.

He was torn between choosing satisfaction for a moment or the stability this job would give him for a long time in the future.

Kodiak, shirt tail still not tucked in which conveniently covered the fact that he was beginning to be aroused by Hunter, stared to speak but went silent as the drone of a small plane engine broke the silence of the wilderness.

And the temporary spell Hunter seemed to have thrown over him.

Six

The men stood looking at each other for another moment before the homesteader-turned model-turned-bush rat finally pulled his eyes from Hunter.

The sound of the plane arriving had instantly broken the heated attraction taking place in the room. Once the intense moment had passed Kodiak's fingers firmly re seated the button he had been fiddling with firmly back into the *closed* position. Turning he quickly stepped out of the bedroom and back into the living room, grabbing a small leather satchel with straps attached to slip over your shoulders. In the bush a plane with a link to the rest of the world was more important than an encounter of any kind. The biggest part of the former model was grateful the plane had intervened, knowing in the end he would have regretted an encounter with Hunter as much as he would have enjoyed playing around.

Hunter followed Kodiak from the bedroom, also frustrated and relieved the plane had arrived at that moment. Just when it seemed as if he was on the verge of having something happen with the man who, despite the deceit of his mission, was becoming the man of *his* dreams.

"Your clothes. Your boots are still wet, but you can keep the clothes and keep wearing the mukluks." Kodiak said as he thrust the small bag at Hunter.

Hunter looked down at the exquisitely made pair of handmade mukluks he was wearing. Soft tan Caribou skin formed the outer shell, an intricate design of tiny blue, green, yellow and black beads ringed the top of the boots along with a ruff of soft, tawny lynx. Thick fur seal, acting as waterproofing, lined the inside of the worn but still beautiful boots. Reaching down Hunter drew his fingers through the thick fur, a slight smile crossing his face.

"I can't take these man! These things sell for a lot." In addition to being beautiful the boots were without question the most comfortable footwear Hunter had ever put on.

"I didn't say I was giving them to you," Kodi said sharply while crossing the room. The "jackass" as the end of the sentence was only implied. "I put a mailing address in the pack so you better fuckin' mail them back. My mother made those and I want 'em back."

"Let's get to the lake, he'll be landed by the time we get there." Kodiak said, turning to move toward the front door.

Leaving the cabin Kodi paused to pull a small flat cart with four sturdy wheels out from under the porch of the cabin then moved back down the well-worn trail with Hunter following.

A few yards down the trail the pair passed the woodlot where Kodiak had spent the morning. Several neatly stacked piles of wood were neatly squared off, a large chopping block in the middle of the cleared area was surrounded by carefully split rounds which had not been stacked yet. A razor-sharp axe leaned against the chopping block. Hunter felt a shiver of attraction run through his body again as he thought of Kodiak's muscular arms arching up over his head again and again, as he brought the axe down into the carefully cut wood, rivulets of sweat tracking down over his muscular body.

Steeling himself Hunter sternly reminded himself that the brief opportunity of sex with the hot homesteader had passed and now needed to remain a fantasy which would never be. He had no idea he would be this attracted to his quarry.

A few minutes later, the trail winding the pair through some of the most amazing wilderness Hunter had ever seen; they crested a small rise to see a pristine wilderness lake spread out in front of them. A long, narrow dock extended out into the deep, clear water. A tiny white boathouse had been built on the shore next to the dock. Lashed against the dock was a Cessna 208 on pontoons, painted in the state colors of blue and gold. The decal of the state flag was on the passenger door, eight stars of gold on a field of blue. The small plane normally held eight passengers and the pilot but four of the seats had been removed to allow for cargo.

Stacks of boxes had already been carried to the door of the boat house, the pilot of the plane turning to wave at the young men as they crested the small hill.

"Joe! Good to see you!" the happiness on seeing someone Kodiak clearly liked caused Hunter another pang of regret, knowing he would never get a greeting like that from the homesteader.

With a nod to his companion Kodiak made a mumbled, cursory introduction to Hunter then explained to the pilot the favor he needed in having Hunter extracted from the homestead.

"You know I'm always happy to help, Kodi," Joe began as the men began loading non perishable supplies into the boat house then loaded the cart with boxes of eggs, more fresh butter, sugar and candies. Niceties which would be greatly appreciated in December and January when the snow was piled deep and the nights long and very dark. In addition to the dry goods and perishable food stuff there was a box of mail for Kodiak. responses to which might have to wait until spring. "Dropping him would normally not be a problem. But as soon as we secure this stuff," the pilot swept a hand over the inventory of the wagon, "I have to take you back in

with me, too."

"I can't leave now!" Kodiak cried, while sweeping his own arm over the supplies. "I'm not finished with my wood or fish, not to mention getting these eggs into cold storage for the winter. And there is a big brown on the prowl. Sam was just here checking his trap line and saw more fresh tracks. We had a bad time with him down by the river yesterday and I've gotta get this stuff secured in case the bear comes this direction."

"You have to come back with me Kodi. Your Dad had a heart attack two days ago. He's still not conscious."

"Damn," Kodi hissed under his breath, the color draining from his face as he grabbed the handle of the loaded wagon and started back over the trail toward the cabin. Closing his eyes, the young homesteader took a deep, calming breath then started to move forward. Not only did he have to go back to Anchorage to see his father and family but while there he would likely have to face a gauntlet of press at some point but he had no choice. The press were going their job, no matter how vicious or callus they could be, and he had become part of that process.

"Then let's get this stuff stowed and get outa here."

"Sorry son," the older man said to Hunter as they began moving briskly down the trail. "I can't afford a detour right now. Time wise it is touch and go. We need to get back to Anchorage. You are welcome to ride along or try and make it back to your camp if Kodi will loan you a rifle. With a big griz out there you shouldn't try to hike it unarmed."

"Guess I'm going back with you then." Hunter said, a new plan formulating in his head.

Arriving in Anchorage hours later was not as startling as the day Kodiak arrived in New York from Alaska but it was still a jolt to have flown over the most-vast wilderness left in America to suddenly find yourself back in a bustling, lively, dirty city.

Joe drove Kodi to the hospital, dropping Hunter and his small pack off at a city bus stop.

The exhausted young homesteader was in a certain level of shock by then and all but ignored the possibly faux game warden as he got out of the small utility vehicle. Suddenly the mystery of who Hunter Davis really was or was not was a very small matter in Kodiak's world, he hoped to never see the attractive young man again.

At the hospital front desk Kodiak, numb, raw with exhaustion and concern, was given directions to his father, making his way through the maze of corridors until he found the waiting room outside of the intensive care unit. There he found his brothers and sister in law, as he topped in the doorway everyone in the room froze for a split second.

With no mirrors to remind himself of his face Kodiak

was for a moment puzzled as to the reaction those closest to him even had to his disfigured face. The looks of shock twisted with sympathy made him cringe. At the same time, he was thankful he now lived a sheltered life free of the looks and stares, whispers behind his back. On television photos of the model were always shown as a before and after split screen as if the then and now difference in how he looked needed to be accentuated.

Kodiak was thankfully no different on the inside than he had ever been.

Those looks coming from the ones he loved were bad enough; the looks from stranger were even harder to stomach. It was as if he were a vandalized work of art which could never be repaired and was now useless.

The former model looked each person in the room directly and gave them a moment to collect themselves before stepping in.

Named after Alaskan places, his older brother Denali after the great mountain, Kodi after Kodiak Island and Cord, the youngest short for Cordova, this generation of DePaul brothers could nearly have passed for triplets, save for his height and the nose ring and purple streaked hair of the youngest, Cord, which gave him a distinct separation. Denali was a near mirror of middle child Kodiak, the acid scar now giving them a permanent distinction.

The gap in their ages was just enough that each brother had for the most part felt pretty much like an only child. With their father working long hours at the garage after losing the boys mother in a small plane crash they had become a disjointed family. She had been the glue holding them together in times like this. On their own it was difficult for boys to find their way back together in this time of crisis. After the initial hesitation the three young men came together in a crush of hugs then slowly eased back apart to separate corners before Denali filled Kodiak in with a report on their father.

The heart attack had been mild, but even a mild heart attack is a heart attack.

Two mesh stents had been inserted into the veins around their father's heart, recovery was expected to be complete but he would need to rest to regain his strength.

After the young men were allowed a brief visit with their father the family went to the home they had maintained in Anchorage for over thirty years, when their great grand-parents had sold some of the original homestead property just north of Willow they had invested in property in Anchorage and Seattle. Wise investments which had turned out well for the family. The Anchorage house was always at the ready for any of them to use. Denali and his wife lived in and maintained the Seattle property.

After a fast dinner the group settled into the living room to decide what the next move should be.

"He's coming back to Seattle with us until he is cleared to go home alone, that's it. Even after that we will hire someone to help him with meals and groceries." Denali pronounced, as oldest he was used to making decisions he expected the others to follow without question.

"Good plan but he's not going to let anyone take care of him, you know that. And what about Cord? He can't stay alone even just while Dad recovers. He can't even leave the state." Kodi

said with a nod toward the sullen teenager trying not to be part of the conversation by staring at the phone cradled in his palm.

Always quiet and introverted the youngest DePaul had been acting out since the death of their mother. The eighteen-year-old may have legally been an adult but had yet to recognize that.

The family had ignored the cigarette and pot smoking; the rebellion and not coming home for days on end until Cord had finally begun ping ponging back and forth from the Anchorage teen detention center to a privately-run Christian run camp, where he had spent the last six months.

His use of drugs had been escalating; from now on the courts were not going to be so lax. Intervention by the state through the court system had been the best decision for the young man. The last months of the rehab program he had been in included not only staying clean but staying home, his case having been fit with a provision that he not leave the state. Cord had been home just about three weeks and re enrolled in high school but had not yet been started again when the heart attack had happened.

Denali exchanged glances with his wife then spoke again. "Then you'll have to stay here. Enroll him in school and take care of him until Dad is healthy again." he said to Kodiak.

"I can't do that, and you know why." Kodiak said flatly.

"Then take him north. He can do a home school course, we know plenty of bush kids who do that and have had fine lives."

"Fuck that!" Cord shouted, his face lifted from the device he held for the first time.

"Hey! Language!" the older brothers shouted almost in unison.

"You will do exactly what we tell you to do," Den's voice steel. Cord had sullenly turned his eyes back down to the device he held.

"Cord you don't have any option," Kodiak had always been close enough to the kid, while he did not want to be responsible for Cord he felt sorry for him and knew he had to pitch in on this family situation. "It probably won't even be for the whole year."

Lifting his eyes to meet Kodis, Cord said evenly, "Fuck. You."

Before the others could object the teenager went on.

"You two get off on that bush shit, not me. I want to be here in civilization where there are movies and pizza and *life*. Where you can get Starbucks when you want. As soon as I can I'm getting the fuck out of this whole stinking state and never coming back."

There was a moment of silence, outside of court hearings this was about the longest speech the young man had made that any of them count remember in years.

"It's not all it's cracked up to be, out there." Kodi said in a low voice.

"Just because *you* lost and got fucked up doesn't mean I shouldn't have a shot." Cord cried out.

"You'll get your chance Cord. If you'd straighten up and fly right the University of Washington is less than a mile from our place in Seattle. But have to get out of high school first. You have a whole life time to explore the world but right now you are going to go stay with Kodiak while we take care of Dad whether you like it or not." Denali remained a total optimist that Cord would clean up his act over-night.

"Why can't he just come here then?"

"You know why, Cord." Kodi said quietly. "Pictures

of me sell for a lot. I'd be hounded, you'd be hounded. Eventually even someone we know, one of your friends perhaps, would be tempted by that bounty if the paparazzi couldn't get a shot on their own. I wish it was different but it's not." Kodiak also wished he could tell his brother how much he regretted leaving the state in the first place, the guilt he felt because Charles was dead because of him. The love of his life ripped away. Things which could never be fixed, returned or replaced. Even if he could tell Cord he knew the kid would still need to learn hard lessons on his own to truly believe how hard life could be. The Dorothy-Gale-click-you-heels-three-times-because-you-have-had-the-power-to-go-home-on-your-own-all-along syndrome.

Words were there and stuck in Kodiak's throat. He had put his family through enough, Cordova was never going to understand until he had the chance to make his own life, and now was not the time for that.

The next few hours were one long shouting match between the brothers, Cord threatening to run away, offering to live with friends, demanding emancipation, all his ideas, wants and suggestions shot down until an un happy truce was met, with the four finally separating to their own rooms to get some much-needed rest.

When the brothers went back to the hospital the next day their father gave the final decree, no argument or discussion. Cord was going back into the bush with Kodi.

Using the truck kept in Anchorage Kodiak, a hat pulled as low down over his face as he could manage, made a quick round of supply houses for extra provisions as he was outfit for one for

the season. He then arranged for Joe to fly the

brother's back north the next day. Cord still refused to acknowledge that he was going to the homestead property, so it was just easier for Kodiak to make the arrangements rather than try to force the teenager to help with the chores even if they would directly benefit him.

The city was stressful for the former model under the best of circumstances, given that he had almost lost his father and now was saddled with his angst-ridden younger brother did not make time in the congested place any easier. Especially when coupled with the fact that he was concerned about being recognized at every turn. His story was still too fresh and close at hand to have been forgotten.

Then the inevitable happened.

Kodiak had come out of a giant warehouse store and was loading goods into the secure box in the back of the truck when he had one of those feelings, not a psychic connection, just that feeling of being watched, that someone was *paying attention.*

Working as quickly as he could without rushing Kodiak was strapping the last parcel in place when a flash strobe suddenly exploded through the windshield of the pick-up. Trying not to react Kodi pulled the strap tight as he fished the key ring out of pocket and slipped in behind the wheel, his name by then being called by at least two people, more lights from flash guns temporarily blinding him.

He hated these situations, it had been months since he had last been here and had this kind of assault happen. He had not looked at the morning newspaper or the television news so Kodiak could only imagine that information about his father's condition had been broadcast so the press were expecting him.

"Kodi! Kodiak! Over here, man!" the voices were muffled by the tinted glass of the truck windows but in his head as loud as they were each time he had gone in and out of a courtroom in New York. While the man calling to him was standing alone a cluster of other photographers were at that moment charging toward the truck.

"Damn," he murmured to himself, stomach clutching as tightly as the night the acid had been thrown in his face. Panicking was not going to help he reminded himself, just go slow and steady. Evading the press was something like homesteading, hard work which required a steady hand. The last thing he needed was to have the police sweep in and stop him for speeding or some other dumb driving infraction.

"C'mon Kodi, just one-shot man, just *one!*" the vultures implored. As if that *one photograph* would sate their curiosity. Carefully shifting he eased the truck out of the parking spot, gripping the leather laced wheel so tightly his fingers turned white as he headed toward the exit of the lot.

He knew the city well but it would take maneuvering to get back to the house before the photographers. The property was well known by the press, by the afternoon, unless there was a thermonuclear war to report, every media outlet in Anchorage would be lining the usually quiet street outside of the small family home.

In a matter of hours his mental prediction of what would happen once back in the city had come true in nightmarish reality.

"We are going to have to take you guys out the back way tonight," Denali said over dinner, the family were gathered in the dining room with the drapes pulled tight against the small army of press camped in front of the house, every television station in the city had a satellite dish there as well as a truck with a CNN logo lined up as if Kodiak were going to come out and make a speech or pose for photographs. Selfishly Kodiak wished a small war *would* break out to lure the press away from him.

"It'll be the only way, they won't leave as long as I'm here. But they are here as much about Dad as me, though. You'll have to arrange getting the supplies up with Joe later." Kodiak added.

"Doesn't matter why they are here, they're here." Denali sighed, "and we have channels four, seven and thirteen checking up on our house like they are the FBI just in case you slip into Seattle. Five's there too but they will go to the opening of an envelope," Denali got a small smile out of Kodiak with that ancient joke, Cord kept his eyes on his plate, silently shoveling food into his mouth.

"Hey, lighten up kid," Denali finally said to Cord, "Dad's going to be ok, you just have to get with the program and work with us." With unusual speed Den had cleared the home school course with the judge who had last sentenced Cord and made the arrangement to transfer the minor's custody to Kodiak.

The glare in the teenager's eye said *Fuck you* even if he did not vocalize it. Kodi knew he was in for some rough time with Cord but would just have to take it step at a time.Kodiak was also glad he had not mentioned the bear attack in the time he had been in the city.

From the time he was born Cord had a natural terror of bears, a gripping fear which kept him out
of the woods even when other kids were playing with him. The story of Kodi's recent encounter with the giant

bear would never have seen Cord getting on the plane back to the homestead.

The plan to get the pair out of the house that night was worked out quickly. Since Kodiak had become the reluctant media star of the state the whole family had learned to think fast. With summer on the wane and the world famous 24-hour sun now setting closer and closer together the brother's said their good byes, Cord silently enduring hugs from his brother and sister in law before he and Kodiak crouched and dashed across the tree filled back lawn and into the neighbor's house behind them. Sliding into the back of a black SUV the brothers were driven across town to a small lake not far from Joint base Richardson/Elmendorf where a Cessna with pontoon floats soon was moving them smoothly across a small lake and quickly had them in the air.

Seven

The small plane landed in darkness on the runway in Talkeetna, the bush village where climbing expeditions for the highest mountain in North America, Denali, set out. Joe was waiting for the brothers, hustling the pair into his van and on to his cabin for the night. Even the most experienced reporter could not have found them in that remote place.

The bush pilot did not have time in his busy schedule to take the young men on that far north, transporting climbers to Denali ran from late spring to mid-summer when his work switched over to freight hauling to remote homesteaders like Kodiak and rural villages dotting the far north.

Joe was a life line to the world to places where there were no roads or rail lines, the weather was changing quickly and the farther north he flew the more likely it was that the lakes he was used to landing on with pontoons were freezing over. He was in the middle of changing over from pontoons to skis for winter landing which was time consuming. But the bush pilot had known two generation of the DePaul family and was always ready to help. So when he was called to say that Kodiak needed to get back into the bush he arranged with one of his pilots to take the brothers on up to the homestead property from Talkeetna. It was the Alaskan way, the way of life in a cold hard country where relying on one another was the only way to truly live in the harsh world of the remote bush.

The next morning the farther north they flew, the darker the teenaged Cord's mood turned. By the time they landed on the small lake near the camp, the pontoons cracking through a skim of ice which had formed over the crystal-clear water, Cord was not speaking to anyone. The pair unloaded the small amount of gear they had brought aboard onto the wooden dock and Kodiak called out his thanks to the pilot while Cord huffed and stomped his feet.

"Fuckin' cold," he muttered as Kodi reached down to pick up the duffle he had brought.

"Let's get this straight, Cord. I don't want this, you don't want this. If you hadn't worked so hard at messing up you'd be going to Seattle. But that's not what happened." Kodiak tried to keep his voice calm and even, "You're here, and as long as you are here with me you are going to do your share, help out and do what I say. And I say that your gutter language doesn't belong here." Kodi made a mental note at the end of the speech that he needed to search the duffle bag of gear his brother held. He did not want to be the enforcer but the last thing he needed here alone with just the two of them was to have Cord using. Small events turned into large ones quickly if you were not paying attention.

"You ain't Dad and I don't *fucking* belong here."

Kodi took a deep breath and turned toward the trail, deciding it was not worth the time to have a fight over language there on the dock. It *was* cold and the sooner he got Cord settled into the cabin the sooner things might calm down.

"Let's go," he said quietly, stepping off the dock and onto the trail, not looking back to see if Cord was following. Just breathing the air Kodiak began to feel himself relax. In such a short time his life had gone from homestead bush kid to cover model to being trailed by the press because of scandal. Knowing how many miles were between himself and the nearest flash gun put him at the kind of ease he had felt before he had developed an unwanted army of followers.

Despite his hate at being there young Cordova was smart enough to know that he could not stand on the dock waiting for another plane to pull up and whisk him back to the civilized world. He had no option but to follow his brother toward the family homestead cabin.

They moved quietly through the woods, Cord seething while Kodiak mentally began listing the chores he needed to accomplish in no short order while trying to put the most recent appearance of the paparazzi out of his mind.

At the wood lot Kodiak noticed the axe was missing. It had been leaning against the huge, solid round of wood he used for splitting. The axe was not only gone but the quarters of wood which had been piled around the splitting wood were scattered around the area. Kodiak hadn't stacked the wood he had been cutting and there were no beaver on the lake the plane landed on, the nearest beaver lodges were about two miles south of the homestead. Not that there were any people any closer, but if they were they would not have taken the time to scatter the wood. Some of the pieces were gone others had been slammed so hard against the surrounding trees that dents were in the trunks.

Beaver might have moved the wood cuts or drug them

back to their hut's but the scattered wood had just been randomly slung around.

Which meant only one thing.

Bear.

Slowing his pace Kodiak lifted his right arm, a bush signal to be calm and quiet, then slowed to a stop, listening carefully for any sound or noise coming from the cabin ahead. Cord had not noticed the wood pile and suddenly stopped short by slamming into Kodi.

"HEY!" he yelped while shoving his brother's shoulders.

"Quiet!" Kodi hissed back.

"What's going on." Cord's voice went low, he might have been a screw up and delinquent but like any kid born into a bush family he knew the rules of the land and played by them as well as anyone living in the woods.

"Just stay quiet," Kodi cautioned, slowly slipping the backpack off and easing it to the ground. His mind raced while thinking of the size of the bear he and the alleged game warden had seen a few days before. He'd never seen one bigger, and had certainly never seen one sink a boat. This wasn't an animal who was hungry, the loaded berry bushes all season and river full of salmon testified to that. Even a monster of that size could have eaten it's fill several times a day in anticipation of fattening up for the river.

No, a bear who showed the kind of rage Kodiak had witnessed that day at the river with Hunter, and now in his own woodlot was an angry and or sick animal, the kind who would kill for sport. The only reason he and the game warden were here today was that the moose had distracted the bear from them.

"C'mon, it's cold!" Cord whined from behind Kodi,

his voice had been lowered so he knew something was up.

"Wait here," Kodiak hissed while cautiously moving forward on the trail. Because he had left in an emergency situation Kodiak had not brought a weapon. The guns were all inside the cabin, he and Cord were exposed and vulnerable if the rouge bear were to show up.

The snug cabin was just around the corner, Kodi could hear nothing but even the largest bear could move through the woods like a shadow making no or very little sound as they stalked prey.

Taking small, careful steps Kodi rounded the bend, his stomach clenching when he finally saw the cabin.

A bear, perhaps not *THE* bear, but clearly a bear of size and might, had been trying to rip the place apart. The thick front door stood in place but the front window to the left of the door had been smashed out. Even from the distance Kodi could see thick tufts of fur sticking out from the edges of the frame, the animal had tried to get in and failed. A scatter of paper and envelopes were trampled onto the porch floor, a trail of paper had blown off into the trees surrounding the cabin. The supplies Joe had delivered had not been secured so the animal had simply fished around inside of the cabin, destroying what it could and the mail sack and egg flats had been closest to the window.

Kodiak took another step forward then felt a blast of air on his neck, causing him to jump as if he had been hit with a bucket of cold water.

"I told you to stay back there!" he challenged, realizing with relief that the air movement he felt had just been caused by Cord following him, the younger brother all but in Kodiak's back pocket.

"Holy fuck," Cord hissed, the color drained from his face, cold forgotten. "That's bear damage, Kodi."

Kodiak did not respond, it would be pointless and just further scare Cord to agree. The destruction was certainly not the work of men from Mars.

Knowing it was useless to get Cord to stay in place Kodiak moved on toward the cabin.

Normally when he left the cabin for an extended period of time Kodi carefully bear proofed the place as much as possible. Thick shutters attached next to the windows were pulled closed and latched with boards from the inside. The door was secured; there was even a plug he put inside the flu of the fireplace. But the day they left he had left in such a hurry that none of the usual pre-caution had been put in place.

Step by step, with Cord all but glued to his back, Kodi moved around the cabin, grateful when he saw the small bedroom windows intact.

Long curls of wood from the cabin logs were freshly shredded all around the back of the small cabin, as if the bear had been considering pulling onto the roof then had decided against exploring the thick moss covered top of the house.

Back at the front porch Kodi told Cord to stay at the bottom of the steps. Just to the right of the small steps leading up to the porch Kodiak saw a huge, clearly defined paw print. The pads had left dimples in the soft dirt, the claws stretching ten inches out from the paw print itself.

Kodiak's stomach clenched, he hoped Cord would not look down at that moment.

"Do you think it is inside the cabin?" his younger

brother asked, face ashen and looking and sounding like he was ten instead of just over eighteen.

Suppressing a laugh Kodiak shook his head no, but based on the paw print he had just seen he was fairly convinced that the same animal had been poking around the cabin. However, it was laughable that the animal were inside the cabin as there was no way its bulk would have gone through that opening.

"I don't think so. I'm going in. If something DOES come out, though, you shag ass to the wash house and lock yourself in and stay there." Kodi hoped the thick walls of the work house would hold against the rage of the monster bear if it had somehow gotten into the homestead cabin and came charging out. Bear were curious by nature, if the big angry bear had not taken to the foothills to find a hibernation place it could very well be back. Kodi was concerned that the bear had shown up at all, that it had tracked the human scent from the river.

And that if he were locked in the wash house that help would eventually come for his brother.

Moving to the top of the stairs Kodiak crossed the small porch and slowly worked the wooden latching device. When it clicked open he slowly swung the door open with his extended arm.

Only when the well-oiled hinges had turned allowing the door to silently swing all the way open did Kodi finally step into the doorway.

His eyes were drawn to the mess near the window, then scanned the rest of the cabin. Nothing else seemed out of the ordinary. The open living, kitchen and dining area were intact. He could see into the open doorways of the bedrooms that nothing seemed disturbed there, either.

Moving on into the cabin Kodi did a quick check and

finding the place thankfully bear free he stepped back to the porch and motioned Cord inside.

"All clear, get inside while I grab my pack."

Wordlessly Cord followed Kodi back down the trail to where his pack had been dropped.

Kodi indulged his brother by saying nothing as he followed him like a lost puppy.

In the cabin Kodi set about cleaning up the mess. Scraping the egg mess off what mail could be saved, including what he could salvage from outside of the cabin, and stacked it to dry. About half of the eggs were lost, and while un refrigerated eggs can last several weeks Kodi did not want to take any chances of losing the rest of this precious cargo. He was going to need to crack them open, bag them up and get them up to the small cavern in a glacier several miles from the cabin to freeze so he would have eggs for the winter-if he lost them in addition to the occasional treat of condensed milk he was going to be eating powdered eggs until spring.

Fresh foods were a commodity taken seriously in the bush, so you made what you had last. The eggs had to be put aside as well through. Just beyond the wash house was a small work house where the tools were kept and some materials for repair, which luckily included some panes of glass which he would need to re fit the window. The broken window had been one solid piece of glass and the only one he had which would fit had wooden framework, which was actually better for security. For both actual security and the peace of mind it would bring his brother.

Cord followed him almost silently for the whole day, setting about the assigned task of cleaning the broken parts of the window with a diligence Kodi had not expected to see from Cordova so soon on the homestead.

By the time the sun had begun to set Kodi had re fit the window and seamed it with a thick bead of caulk. By morning the window would be set, it was smaller than the original but Kodi had shimmed the sides with some thick pieces of wood which when stripped of bark would match the cabin. Improvisation was the name of the game in the bush.

Over dinner Kodi explained to Cord that he had the cabin as secure as it was going to get and that he had to head out moose hunting the next day. The short ten-day season was already three days gone and time away from the camp had eaten into the few days of salmon fishing left.

Kodiak decided it was better to take a chance and get a moose if they were going to get through the next few months the meat was necessary. Cord knew how to handle a rifle, Kodi did not like the idea of leaving Cord at the camp alone but liked the idea of taking his brother out into the wilderness even less. He also told Cord that he was not to go fishing, the one activity of wilderness life his younger brother enjoyed.

What he did not tell Cord was that in addition to hunting moose that he also planned to try and track the bear which threatened their very existence in the wilderness.

Kodiak loved the wilderness and being alone in it. He understood the economics of his time in the city and was grateful for the security it provided. Most of the money he had made modeling was gone to legal fees, so he held onto what was left tightly, the supplies and flights were expensive which was why he wanted to live off the and as much as possible. Other than being in Jimmy's arms there had been nothing about being in what was known as civilization that he appreciated.

And with his fame/infamy he could hardly waltz into any business and get a job with a pack of photographers blazing a trail behind him and he certainly was not ready to capitalize on his destroyed looks to model as a freak when he could live off the land.

Change, though, is the only constant in life. While Kodiak had looked forward to another winter of reading and enjoying the solitude of the remote homestead he was pleased to be able to do what he could toward helping the family. Even if keeping Cord, a city kid at heart, from getting the dreaded "cabin fever" was going to be a challenge taken day by day.

The next morning, food for two days packed and a weather proof sleeping bag strapped to his pack along with a heavy but powerful thirty-ought six rifle hung on his shoulder Kodi left a list of work he expected his brother to accomplish while he was away. Chores which Cord would likely slack off, he'd be bored out of his head but he had spent enough time in the bush to know how to take care of himself, including preparing his own meals.

Without being obvious Kodi carefully circled the cabin until he found another clear, huge bear track which pointed him in the direction the large animal had moved. There were not likely to be any moose anywhere near where the bear had been, and Kodi really did not want to run into the animal but wanted to make certain the huge animal was still not circling around his camp. A grimace crossed Kodiak's face as he suddenly doubted that the heavy rifle he carried would even slow the bear if it came after him.

The weather had remained crisp, although he had stripped his gear down to a bare minimum in case he did get some game to take into his version of cold storage he had quickly broken into a light sweat as he made his way through the underbrush, carefully looking for freshly broken branches with strands of fur caught on it.

Kodi managed to follow the prints of the bear for what he estimated to be two miles, the trail of the huge animal disappearing when he reached the fork of the Kashwitna and Sheep creek rivers, both churning waters thick with spawning and dying salmon. It was likely that the big bear had slogged into the water and sat gorging before wandering off, it would be impossible to tell where the bear might have gone out of the water.

Kodi was not fully comfortable with the distance from the homestead buildings he had trailed the bear, but at least the animal had kept moving forward instead of circling the camp.

After a fast lunch of cold smoked salmon Kodi pressed on, not crossing the rivers he doubled back from the direction he had come, now moving toward the low foothills in the distance and toward the glacier he used as deep cold storage for the fish and his winter supply of meat.

Moose were often in one of the two wide meadows near the mouth of the caverns, a low swampy area filled with easy to reach water grasses made a fine grazing area for the largest members of the deer family. His hope was to get a young bull and dress it out closer to the caves. If he got one he would quarter it then go back to camp and get Cord to help with the butchering project. He knew Cord would not like the job, but it was what needed to be done for their survival.

Day turned into night, Kodiak pressing on as quietly as he could but seeing nothing-no sign of bear or moose. A thick, low layer of clouds blocked out what would have been a nearly full moon light so the hunter finally stopped for the night while still inside the tree line, breaking spruce boughs to cover the ground. The boughs would keep moisture at a distance, he was close enough into the area of the meadow that the blanket of moss on the ground would make it like sleeping on a down comforter.

Buried deep down inside his comfortable arctic rated sleeping bag, the sky over head a brilliantly flashing canopy of electric looking white stars which quickly lulled the exhausted hunter into a deep and easy sleep.

Kodiak woke several times in the night, the rustle of ground squirrels moving through the dark; possibly a porcupine or two foraging through the woods all just helped to put him back to sleep. A non-bush person would likely have thought of the huge bear with its fierce teeth and claws and beat feet back to the relative safety of the cabin. The wood world experienced Kodiak let the sounds of the night filter around him then closed his eyes and went right back into a deep sleep.

The soft light of morning finally woke Kodiak, rested he stretched his way out of the sleeping bag and tightly laced the handstitched waterproof mukluks up over his calves. After another cold breakfast Kodiak was on his way, picking his steps carefully as he slowly made his way along side of the wide, rolling ground of the moss-covered meadow which smoothly led to the first of the distant foothills. Day had fully broken, the sun was up over the edge of the horizon, flooding the wide meadow between Kodi and the mountains with golden light. Stopping for a moment he took the scene in, knowing he would never lose his sense of wonder at sights like this sunrise.

This was Kodi's world, a place where he felt totally at home and at ease. Nature had a simple flow which he understood. As he walked, the springy moss under his feet muffled his foot falls,Kodi absently reached up and scratched at the longest scar on his face, the one which ran along the curve on the left side of his chin. His looks had never mattered to him, he had never even thought about his features until the one of the producers of that dumb television show he had not only never seen but had never heard of had seen him.

The man who had snapped the photo of him, a professional model scout in Alaska out for an adventure, had persuaded Kodi's father to let Kodiak be on the show. The money offered was not all that much, but the description of the work which could come as a result was more than the entire family would have made in five years' work.

Kodi had immediately hated everything about the city, the noise, smell, the crowds. Especially the crowds. But his bond with Charles and the experience with Jimmy (despite it's sour ending) made up for the other bad parts of his modeling career.

He missed Charles with all his heart. Jimmy, well a part of him would always love him as his first boyfriend but the bigger part of him would always hate him for not being there when he woke in the hospital. On a realistic note Kodi did not blame the attack on Jimmy, that was done by a psychopath with money. But Jimmy could have been here in this beautiful world with him.

Kodi's heart ached at the thought of the life they could have shared. Their worlds had just been too different and far apart.

He did not miss the city, the runways the often-stupid clothing he was paid stupidly amazing amounts of money to wear. He didn't miss the luxurious apartment Jimmy had moved him into or the weekends at the family estate in Connecticut or weekends on the family yacht in the Bahamas or Bermuda. They were all nice and he appreciated them but the thing he missed was Jimmy, and his friendship with Charles.

The guilt Kodiak felt over his friend being killed far overshadowed the scarring on his face. He could live with that, he could live with losing modeling jobs due to his looks and notoriety but the waves of guilt he felt over his funny, loving friend being killed as a byproduct of the attack was more than he could handle at times, the staggering pain of remembering at times brought Kodiak to his knees.

This was rapidly becoming one of those times, he drew in a deep breath, doing what he always did when the emotions overwhelmed him-thinking of Charles being funny and snarky and reminding him that while he was gone that Kodiak still had a life to live.

Only get the one child, make it count! he'd heard Charles say over and over.

Bringing a finger along farther down his face his vision suddenly blurred as Kodiak realized he had teared up. Quickly blinking the tears back he was about to swipe a finger over his eyes when he heard a series of twigs snapping, the sound bringing him out of his reverie.

Slipping behind one of the scrub spruce he turned his head to scan the terrain. Before he found the focus of exactly where the low sounds were coming from a young bull with a rack about twenty inches across stepped out of the woods only a few yards from where he stood downwind.

Carefully lifting the barrel of the rifle Kodi managed to seat the long tube of metal against the tree, sliding it carefully down until the barrel wedged against the trunk and a branch. Controlling his breath he closed his left eye as he rested his cheek against the rifle and found the magnificent animal it the sight of the weapon.

As his finger curled around the trigger Kodi suddenly caught a familiar scent in the air and froze. The scent of a bear is the scent of a bear; they all eat the same diet and tend to roll in the dead fish which make up a big part of their dinner, but this smell was unmistakable. It had to have been the same bear he and the (possibly pretend) game warden had encountered on the river from the gagging stench filling the air.

Just as Kodi caught the scent the moose flared its nostrils, picking up on the smell as well.

Making no sound the large animal eased back into the trees as quickly as it had appeared, the wide antler paddles managing to avoid rustling every branch as it vanished back into the safety of the tree line.

Leaving the rifle in place Kodiak turned his head toward the expanse of meadow as the huge bear rose from behind one of the low, rolling hillocks. Standing up onto hind leg the bear raised its forepaws and snout while lifting its massive head and snuffling the air.

Although many yards from Kodiak the familiar stench coming off the animal in waves made it seem as if the bear were right next to him. For the second time Kodiak saw the amazing marking on the animal. In the center of the bear's massive chest a ragged line of white fur stretched roughly between the massive front paws. Another thick line of white fur slashed down over the bears torso, forming a rough *T* outline across the bears body.

While the hunter had been calm but excited when the moose appeared, he was now grateful that he had not gotten a shot at the huge animal as the bear likely would have been attracted by the smell of blood in the air.

Kodiak only had a short window of hunting season to get a moose. His menus would include a lot more rabbit, game bird and canned chicken without the extra game meat to supplement the salmon he had frozen and cured in his cache. They would survive, but he would miss the extra protein especially with Cord eating rations as well. Either way they would make it through the winter season.

He always did.

Kodi watched as the great bear dropped back down onto all four paws, sniffing at the ground. The animal was nearly the size of a van when grazing its nose across the rolling tundra.

Sliding the gun back from the tree Kodi froze as the bear suddenly rose again, then dropped back down and began racing across the ground with a freakish speed. Darting his eyes across the tundra Kodi saw a small herd of Caribou bolting from the charging bear. Within moments the large animals had disappeared, the bear along with them.

Kodi realized his heart was slamming inside his chest like a pigeon size humming bird as he watched this *Wild Kingdom* style show play out. He had seen exotic nature shows from a front for seat his entire life but this one moved him in a way few things had. The last two times his heart had raced like were out of the state, on the night of the horrible incident and the first time Charles had taken him through Times Square.

Kodi had seen the wildest of rivers, the vastness of glaciers, huge fish and other wild game; but entering the canyon of light covered buildings in the middle of the city had made his heart race like never before.

Until now.

He felt another round of tears well up in his eyes then, sensing more than hearing anything Kodi looked up to see the young bull moose, nostrils twitching as the scent of the bear faded, had stepped back out into the clearing. Quickly re locating the rifle to its rest on the tree Kodi sighted down the barrel.

Eight

There was a chance the big bear had not gotten a caribou. That was a risk Kodi decided to take, fate turned on a dime and he might not have another chance at a shot for the moose hunting season. If the bear caught the scent of a fresh kill it could be on him in a flash.

Sometimes you had to take the gamble, and this one paid off. He and Cordova would not be without a supply of fresh meat for the season. He had pulled the trigger when there was a clear shot and had taken the animal cleanly.

Now, deep in the butchering procedure, he worked quickly and carefully while keeping a careful watch out for the bear. Well, all bears. He could not rely on smell now due to the blood now on the scene. The scent would overpower that of the bear and attract every other predator in a wide radius. Bear, wolf, wolverine, those were the animals Kodiak would have been concerned with even had he not had a second encounter with the big bear. Smaller predators like the arctic fox, ground squirrel and birds of prey would also have been drawn to the kill, but they would not have had the courage to approach the way the larger animals might.

Having killed his first big game while still a pre-teen Kodi could dress an animal with the best. With surgical precision he had unrolled the length of canvas sheathing his razor sharp knives near the kill, carefully cleaning the blades as needed and alternating the size of knife as needed.

That he had taken the animal early in the day worked in his favor. As the day warmed Kodi removed his jacket, then shirt, leaving his cammo green tee shirt on. He worked with efficient moves, economizing every movement to save energy. The job was big, and he had a lot to accomplish.

The first thing Kodi had done after checking the kill was to clear an area of debris then pulled back a layer of moss, this far north the ground was still mostly frozen with permafrost. He then gathered tinder and cut some of the scrub spruce trees filled with pitch and started a smoky fire. Bears don't like smoke; regular bears don't like smoke that is. Kodi had no idea if the smoke would detour or draw in the big angry bear who now had taken up residence in the middle of Kodiak's territory.

Cutting several green spruce Kodi stripped them, sharpened the ends and drove them into the ground. Building up the fire he attached another stripped tree branch as a crossbeam then carefully lay the ribs over the support to begin the smoking process. He would stoke the fire before taking the meat across the meadow then pick the partially cooked meat up along with the heart, liver and tongue to take back to the homestead.

Kodiak smiled to himself as he carefully sliced the lean meat, carefully wrapping the cuts in sheets of thick white butcher paper then tying each package with heavy twine. The roll of paper added to the weight of his pack but this method of wrapping while butchering made the work so much faster. He was tired but adrenaline kept him going, he thrived on this kind of work and took great pride in his self-sufficiency.

Keeping watch on the sun Kodi stopped the butchering when he felt the slightest lowering of temperature in the air. Gathering the entrails, hooves and bones he tied them into the hide, dragging the entire packet of unusable parts of the animal half a mile through the woods back to the Kashwitna river, a raging glacial run off with water the color of slate and shoved the whole package into the flow. After the leftovers had tumbled down the rushing river Kodiak stripped his shirt off again and sluiced the icy water up over his aching muscular arms then splashed the cold water up over his face and head, scouring himself as best he could while thinking longingly of the hot water running in a continual stream through the carved stone of his bath tub. Frontier moments like this, washing in the cold river, made frontier moments like soaking in the wilderness tub even more luxurious. When life was lived in the minimal joy could be found in the smallest of things. The tub would be there when he got back and he would appreciate it even more.

Or so Kodiak told himself. He'd have swapped most anything to ease into the hot water at that very moment.

Back at the kill site Kodi stoked the fire, the red-hot coals had hardly melted down into the frozen ground. He added a large pile of green spruce boughs to thicken the smoke, then hung the moose antler rack as high as he could in the branches. He would leave them there for the season and bring them back to the homestead site when nature had stripped them.

Some of the bones were left with the smoking ribs. Kodi would carry those back to the homestead to boil the marrow out to make soup stock. He had been taught well to use every part of the kill possible.

Packing the parcels of meat into the rucksack he re-dressed then hung the rife, carefully zipped into a waterproof case, on a branch against the tree and secured the weapon with a zip tie. His roll of knives, all back in place and ready to be properly cleaned and re sharpened, was hung next to the rifle. Crossing the field at night without a weapon would not have been his first choice so Kodi had to keep this load as light as possible. He was thankful to have had daylight while he dressed out the animal. The clouds had dissipated, he was grateful for that.

Adjusting the fire one last time he eased down onto the moss-covered ground and strapped the heavy pack onto his back. Kodi had kept a thick stick at hand and now used it to help leverage himself up. Catching his balance he took a few test steps then started at a steady pace toward the foothills in the distance with the thick walking stick as his only weapon now. If a large marauder tried to over-take him in the night there was a chance he was going to lose the meat by dropping it to leave as a sacrifice and hope he could make it back to the tree line and relative safety of the forest.

As the moon rose, the sky filled with shining points of white-hot starlight, the homesteader's way over the rolling tundra was lit nearly as bright as the lights in Times Square.

As he walked, his feet sinking deep into the soft, springy moss, Kodi thought of the last few days. Life in the bush was harsh, but life anywhere could be harsh. Here at least he did not have to think about revenge and knew no strangers were going to jump out of no-where and harm him.

If he died in duel with something from the wild at least there would be an honor and dignity to his death, a completion of the natural cycle of life.

Hunter Davis, the smarmy and alleged new game warden, came back through his mind, causing an eruption of feeling in his crotch, which Kodi hated. He had tried to close that section of his life after Jimmy, who had been the one and only for him. Kodi was young to have made that decision but knew his life in the bush was meant to be a chosen sentence served alone. He remembered the photographers flashing bulbs in his face, the groupies and hangers on hitting on him; he remembered the whispers and low talking which had started the few times he had gone to a restaurant after the acid scarring. He remembered the looks on his families faces when he walked into the hospital room just a few days earlier.

No, he reminded himself, despite the come on from Hunter that part of his life was over. He would keep to himself, work hard, have the occasional fantasy and that would be enough.

Shifting the pack Kodi felt a trickle of sweat start down his neck and along the raised edge of the scar. He tried not to think of the incident, but he honestly felt his life had changed as much on the day the scout had approached him as on the day the acid was thrown.

Breathing the cold air in deeply he forged on as clouds began to slowly move back over the wide expanse of land. The temperature had dropped the day before but had warmed back up, Kodi had a slick sheen of sweat on his skin, his tee shirt sticking tackily to his body as he walked, muscular thighs pumping up and down against the give of the soft moss. Two hours in he was not far from the goal of the cavern and looked forward to getting the load stored. That was what you did in the bush, you forged on and got the job done so he forged on.

When he had less than fifteen minutes of hiking to go over the deep moss to the cavern the first snow of the season began to fall, large wet flakes falling soundlessly and quickly covering the ground, causing Kodi to lift his face and smile. Another person might have cursed the

weather but Kodiak loved the snow, thrived on it, the thicker the better. By the time he arrived at the ice caverns the temperature had gone back up and the flakes had gotten smaller, flakes of that size usually meant it was going to be the first serious snow of the season.

Kodiak felt he was nearing the glacier more than seeing it, the wall of ice fronting the glacier was massive the cold wind leeching off it hitting the hiker as if he were in a sudden wind or that he was standing in front of an open ice box door even from a distance. It would be much colder if he had to go all the way up to the face of the glacier but the cavern he was headed to was off to the side, not exactly surrounded by ice it still acted as a deep freeze in the back.

The ground began to rise as he neared his destination, thousands of years earlier the entire valley had been filled with water, which had become the glacier. As the glacier had slowly receded the ice had littered the landscape with boulders nearly the size of his cabin, the rocks growing smaller as Kodi worked his way around them on his way to the entrance to the cavern he used as a camp.

Switching on the high powered flashlight he carried Kodi found the dark entrance and went in, bouncing the light around on the rocks in the wide entry.

The natural space had a framed out single bed covered in plastic which sat on a natural shelf of rock sticking out from the wall. A fire pit, kindled and ready to ignite, was off to one side where smoke would vent out naturally. Rough plank shelves made up of scrap boards he had packed into the site held a small collection of spices and a few cooking pots and pans. In the back were a pair of Bear Paw snowshoes and a pair of surplus skis. Not a lot had been overlooked in making a rough but comfortable place to camp.   Several mining oil lamps from his Grandfather's day hung from pegs Kodiak had managed to wedge into the rock crevasses.   Kodiak always expected to encounter a bear hiding in his comfortable camp in the cave one day and was again grateful to find the space empty.

Satisfied everything was in place Kodiak moved back into the ice cave proper, where he had carved out more shelving in the permanently frozen water. He quickly emptied the pack, carefully stacking the wrapped cuts of meat then returning to the cave entry where the camp he had set up there was nearly as cozy and comfortable as his cabin. Starting the fire Kodi grilled a fresh moose steak, enjoying it with a handful of wild asparagus he had put in the cold storage months ago in the spring. The frozen wild greens tasted as fresh as they day they had been picked. The meal was excellent and much needed at the end of his long day.

Exhausted but sated Kodi took off his boots then slid the plastic off the soft mattress of moss he had gathered over the summer just for an occasion like this. The moss was contained in burlap bags, he had thrown a tarp over the bags and used another burlap bag served as his pillow.

Short of sheets the bed was nearly as comfortable as the bed in the homestead cabin. Folding up the plastic he set it aside and un furled his sleeping bag then stretched out on it, he was tired but did not fall right to sleep, he lay for a while listening to the sounds around him; the crackle of the fire, the shifting of the ice, which popped and snapped like small gun fire from the huge flow of ice behind the cavern mouth. Comfortable, familiar sounds which lulled him off into a deep sleep, a content smile on his face.

The next morning, with the fire burned out, Kodiak quickly ate then re set the cave camp to be ready for his next trip there then trekked back across the tundra to the kill site, the return trip, even with the foot of first snow which had fallen, took about half the time as the trip over without the weight of the load he had been carrying.

The walk back toward the kill site and then on to his camp made Kodi happy, he loved the snow. He would have been happier to have had the little round bear paw snowshoes strapped to his feet for the hike for the trip but there would be plenty of outings over the course of the winter in which he could use the leather strapped rounds to keep himself on the surface of the snow.

That first snow hardly offered enough to use the snowshoes. At the kill site he wrapped the partially smoked ribs, heart and tongue into the ruck sack made certain the fire was totally out and began the long, slow trek back toward the homestead cabin.

It was hard to imagine as he wound his way through the thickets of birch, cottonwood and spruce trees that it had been just a few years since he had first left the state. The whirlwind which had become his life after the contest had contest had changed his life forever, and not in good ways.

Good things *had* come out of the horror of the

situation. He had seen parts of the world, good and bad, which he never would have gotten to see had he not left the state. Of course, he'd had his heart broken as well, and that was an emotion he was never going to have again. As he pushed through low branches, the pack catching occasionally enough to stop him for a moment until he had wrenched it free, Kodiak kept his mind off the city and the bad things which had happened there and instead thought of his first visit to the lower west coast and the beach.

As the current *IT* guy in the modeling world after the contest Kodiak had suddenly found himself going everywhere, even if briefly. Italy, South America, Indonesia were all photo shoot sites. The sights, smells and exotic locations were beautiful, but it was rare the young model

Kodi ever got the chance to tour around when he was at work. He was a dedicated worker and unless he was having fun with Charles, Kodiak pretty much kept to himself.

The models, for all the glamour the represented-on runways, television and the pages of glossy magazines were treated like pretty cattle. Packed into small apartments where they shared beds and often lived in filth. Mostly self-generated filth, but still filth. The top money generators naturally lived at the top of the press heap but even the up and comers like Kodi traveled coach and lived on fast food, hope and cigarettes while fending off the advances of everyone from his own agent to the other models and hangers on of every flavor-people all used to getting what they wanted. As Kodiak was not interested in participating he was eventually all but shunned, which suited him just fine.

After the television competition, before meeting Jimmy, that had been Kodiak's life. He was making money but felt dead inside from missing time in the wilderness.

The one place Kodi opened up and ventured out on his own, of all the places he had been flown to on assignments, was Los Angeles. While New York, London, Rome and Paris were all amazing cities, it was sprawling, ugly Los Angeles which caught the attention of the homestead kid. It was the first place he went out on his own in, rode the subway and bus lines end to end; attended every tourist attraction and fell in love with the beach.

His mother had grown up in Pasadena and had often talked about her happy times in the sand and waves and playing in the crashing surf. The smell, wind and sounds of the sea were everything she had described. Just being there made Kodi feel closer to her. The first afternoon he spent there he stayed until the sun had set, marveling at technicolor streaks of orange and gold streaking across the horizon.

His mother had been attached to each of her sons in a very special way, managing to make them feel like they alone were here special favorite. All their lives she had hand made their parka's, mukluk's and mittens from the furs and skins they had trapped and traded. Her craftmanship showed in that all of the pieces she'd made for them were still serviceable and in use. As Sam's grandmother had taught the items were not only perfectly constructed but useful, everything had specialized pouches to hold small, useful everyday items unlike commercially manufactured goods.

When she was gone they had each mourned in their

own way, their father working longer hours, Denali leaving the state with his new wife, Kodi spent more time working on the homestead property he now lived on full time. With all of them spending time on their own they left Cord alone too much, which led to his deep slide into drugs.

Kodiak felt deeply guilty about this and hoped the time Cord was going to be spending with him in the next few months would bring them closer.

Despite the weight again on his back Kodi made good time getting back to the homestead. A regular hiker he was used to travelling long distances, time seemed to move faster as he came

closer to camp. He'd had a good hunt, the pantry, while not as full as he would have liked it to have been for two, was better now. The moose added a great deal to supplies. By the time Joe got the goods Kodiak had recently picked up in Anchorage he and Cord would be pretty set for the winter, when the few short daytime hours would frequently be purple grey before the long hours of inky black night quickly set in again.

The temperature had dropped during the day, there had not been as much snow at this lower elevation so walking was easier and he was also now on the wider, well packed and familiar trails leading to the cabin.

The first sign something was wrong on the homestead came as Kodiak neared the washhouse. The door was open, light from the skylight filled the cabin. As he stepped though the doorway Kodi shrugged the pack from his shoulders and let his eyes adjust. Food was scattered all over the floor; dried salmon had been pulled from the drying racks onto the floor where it was surrounded by shards of glass from a broken lantern.

Vegetables from the bins were smashed and strewn about, covered in flour, cornmeal and beans. Everything was striped with long strands of honey with small pools of the syrup he had hand crafted all over the floor. The room had been trashed, but the mess had not been made by an animal. There were no padded footprints around, no claw marks or scat.

The destruction was horrible. A wolverine or wolf might have broken into the wash house or Cord had left the door open. There were footprints but no bear tracks or paw prints; this was human destruction which made it even more heart sickening. Which caused Kodi's now rapidly beating heart to sink.

Checking for bear damage had kept him from taking the time to go through Cord's bag to check for drugs or liquor, hoping the destruction was brought about from booze over drugs. Both were bad, but liquor would wear off faster.

There was no time to assess the loss now, he had to find Cord. And face the horrible truth that his brother was the guilty party who had committed the destruction all around him. Slowly backing out of the cabin Kodiak picked up the pack. He hated leaving the mess but knew he had to check the main cabin before cleaning up. He was more frustrated than angry at that point.

From down the trail Kodiak could see that the cabin door was open, the main room a dark void in the distance. Mounting the stairs two at a time Kodi dropped the pack on the porch as he raced inside.

"Cord?" he called out while stepping across the debris strewn room; books, kitchen ware and clothing was scattered all over the cabin.

"Cordova! Where are you?"

The small door to the built-in bar had been pried open, both bottles of liquor which had been locked inside were now empty on the floor.

The door to his bedroom was closed, the door to the second room slightly ajar. Pushing it open, the hinges silently swinging the door forward, Kodi's question about the cause of the destruction was sadly answered in the form of his brother lying sprawled across the bed, face down, fully dressed. His eyes were closed, skin waxy and the color of milk. He did smell of booze but the small amount of liquor in the dusty bottles were not the only thing his kid brother had stupidly ingested while Kodiak was hunting.

Muttering *crap* under his breath Kodi grabbed Cord's shoulders and rolled him over onto his back. The body was pliant, a good sign, but he did not detect any breath at that moment.

"CORD! CORD!" he shouted, grabbing the young man's shoulders and shaking him lightly to see if he could get a response. *You stupid...,* Kodi hissed while curling his fingers around his brother's wrist, grateful to find a thin, thready pulse.

He regretted leaving Cord but at the same time knew if he had not gotten the moose-well, it was complicated and not his fault he reminded himself.

Turning Cord's face to the side Kodi stuck a finger between his brother's lips to make certain his mouth and airway were clear then brought his face back forward, pinched his nose shut then began mouth to mouth, giving a few fast careful, breaths into Cord he then paused to see if that would kick start his lungs.

*C'mon, come on...*he hissed. Not feeling any air come back up from his brother's lips and not seeing his chest rise Kodi slammed his mouth back down against his brother's lips and gently exhaled again. If he started chest compressions he knew the limitations; with no one to take over if Cord did not start breathing he was just going to do more damage to his brother. If he broke his sternum or a rib there was a good chance he would be killing him right here and now since there was no way to get him medical help.

One of the many hazards of living so deep in the bush.

Kodiak pulled his lips away and waited again, this time Cord did respond. His eyelids fluttered and he coughed lightly. Falling forward Kodi slid his arms under Cord and lifted him up, the activity causing Cord to cough again, harder this time. Holding his brother upright Kodiak lightly slapped his hands against his brother's back, which caused Cord to cough again, harder this time.

*C'mon buddy, c'mon...*Kodi thought, relief flooding his body as Cord finally began taking deeper ragged breaths.

"That's it, breathe man, breathe," Kodi sighed, holding Cord and wanting to cry at the same time. His eyes did well up with tears of anger and frustration, but he quickly blinked them back, they would do no one any good and while Cord was breathing he was certainly not out of this set of woods.

Kodi understood the forest they lived in, he knew how to fell, chop and navigate the trees around the cabin but had no idea how to understand or deal with the deep, dark emotional wilderness of his brother's mind or why he turned to chemicals to try and make things better.

When Cord was finally breathing steadily, if shallow, Kodi carefully pulled him up against the headboard, stuffing pillows behind him as he then loosened Cord's shirt collar a button.

"I don't know what you did buddy, and if this is your idea of helping please stop." he whispered.

With Cord settled, and more important breathing, Kodi went back into the main room of the cabin. It was getting late and the sky had turned a thick grey. The temperature had gone back up and all signs were pointing to snow again.

The cabin was cold, Kodi had no idea how long Cord had been out, the kid was also a physical mess which would need to be dealt with. Taking a deep breath Kodi closed his eyes for a moment to center and reminded himself that he could only do one thing at a time.

Getting a fire started in the fireplace was nice busy work. Once that was going he checked on Cord again. Still breathing. After that Kodi moved back into the main room and quickly put things to rights, moving the main clutter he was happy that no lamps were broken. Actual damage there seemed minimal.

Finally stripping out of the first layers of his hunting clothes Kodi went back into the bedroom and managed to remove the soiled bedding from around his brother. He then undressed Cord and brought in a bowl of hot water and a towel giving Cord's still waxy skin the best cleaning he could under the circumstance.

With great effort Kodiak managed to get the linen and bedding changed then tucked Cord back into the bed. He was quickly coated in a fine sheen of sweat while his brother had been mostly unresponsive during the entire process. Thankfully his breathing had grown deeper, his eye lids only fluttered a few times. Once Kodi had Cord bucked back into bed he checked his pulse again, pleased to find that it was steady and even.

Although he was exhausted Kodi still had work to do.

Darkness and the pending snow had fallen at about the same time. Banking the fireplace and leaving a light on in case Cord did end up in the main room of the cabin, Kodi picked up the pack and went back to the smokehouse and started a fire there, once it was roaring and would burn down to a hot bed of coals, he arranged the racks of partially cooked ribs and moved on to the wash house.

The mess there was daunting, so much food had been destroyed. Half, perhaps more, of the supplies he had so carefully and diligently lain in for winter had been destroyed. The honey and syrup were a special loss. Not just the work which had gone into the manufacture and harvest of the goods but the thought that there was no just heading to the store to get more. The retail giant Amazon had yet to figure a way to get overnight delivery that far north.

Sick to his stomach over the loss Kodi set about salvaging what he could, returning to the main cabin hours later he arranged the clothing and bedding to be laundered, banked the fire. He then went back to the smokehouse and banked the fire slow cooking the ribs then went back to the cabin and checked on Cord, who had not moved but was breathing deeply, then returned to his work in the wash house. The snow was coming down heavily again, this one would be the first heavy fall of the season and would not be melting off.

He cleaned off the vegetables which could be salvaged then put as many of the glass shards

as he could into a small wooden box before sweeping up the floor by the light provided by another of his grandfather's oil lanterns.

He found a similar pattern of destruction at the greenhouse, which had been for the most part smashed apart. The cache had not been opened but Kodi had not moved most of the smoked fish up there yet as he planned to use that space to keep the moose he had brought back with him. He'd have to take this situation day at a time as he was too tired to try and figure it out by then.

It was nearly two am the next morning by the time he finished cleaning. Exhausted he opened the wash house door to see that the snow was still coming down, even thicker and faster than ever by then.

Winter had officially hit the homestead and his overdosed kid brother had trashed a huge amount of their supplies.

It was going to be a long season in the wilderness.

Nine

Hunter Davis was a lot of things.

Most of his trades were self-taught; he dabbled in journalism, photography, and the occasional pot sale. Since legalization of weed in Alaska that arm of his multi-faceted business had dropped off pretty much to nothing.

He played a little guitar, badly, preferred city over rural life, was a liberal Democrat in a family of staunch Republicans and tended to fall for laid back guys with crooked grins. Kodiak DePaul had been blessed with a perfectly even smile and tended to be as jumpy as that proverbial long tailed cat in a room full of rockers around other people, as Hunter had learned firsthand. In other words hardly an ideal match, but Hunter could not help his attraction to Kodiak. The heart wanted what it wanted even though Kodiak's grin was in perfect alignment.

Like many Alaskans Hunter had developed a wildly passionate interest in the life of homegrown celebrity Kodiak DePaul. The largest state had the shortest list of celebrities, infamous counted as much as famous in the land of the midnight sun.

One of the few truths Hunter had offered Kodiak was that he was also a lifelong Alaskan. However Hunter did not hold the credentials of an Alaskan game warden. His grandfather had held that position, a stern but trusted member of the wilderness community the old man had been tough but fair. Hunter had had hiked, flown and paddled the rugged Alaskan wilderness with his grandfather all his life, some of his best memories growing up had been of the times out with the old man, who had kept hunters, trappers, game fishermen and natives on the straight and narrow when it came to natural resources. His grandfather had held hope of Hunter following in his footsteps, but Hunter had been taken off that track by his own father.

Hunter Sr. had chosen a life as opposite of his gentle father as could be. As a teenager he had used his father's knowledge of the wilderness to his advantage and began running illegal big game hunts, eventually building a legitimate business which turned its biggest profit by taking game hunters into the wild then chasing trophy animals toward them with trained dogs and snowmobiles.

This was not sport, nor was it legal or moral. But people hunting big game were often impatient, hating to spend time and money waiting to find game when it could be driven to them.

By the time his grandfather had died Hunter's father had built a reputation and empire, known in trophy circles as the man to call for the biggest and best animals Alaska had to offer. The year after Hunter graduated high school the empire, as they are wont to, collapsed under the weight of a sting operation by the state. The family losing everything and his father now confined to the state penitentiary.

As the business had grown Hunter had slowly become the official photographer for the illegal shoots, doing web site work for the business but none of the actual illegal herding. With the family falling apart and losing most everything, Hunter barely escaping charges himself he fled to New York, which was the destination of the first flight out of Anchorage after the trial, to start over.

Instead of getting lost in the city fate shoved him directly into the arms of Kodiak DePaul's nemesis, Finn Carson.

Call it The Six Degrees of Separation theory, or of all the Gin Joints in All the World theory, one introduction led to another in *New York, New York* and Hunter, being a hot rugged guy new on the scene, was soon introduced to Finn at a party not long after arriving in the city. Finn, as usual getting what he wanted when he wanted it, was more than pleased when after a long drunken night of sloppy, drunken sex Finn found that, bonus! Hunter was an Alaskan. Even though Hunter only knew Kodiak through the media, Finn offered Hunter an obscene amount of money to get into Kodiak's personal space and install a wireless remote camera. Which would allow Finn to sell the live stream of video to Kodiak's legions of fans.

Would it make a profit? Never. Would it last long due to battery life? No. Was this actionable in court? Of course.

Which was Finn's only goal, to try and draw Kodiak back out into the media circus Finn knew the young Alaskan he had damaged hated. Revenge was more than a dish served cold to Finn, it was a way of life. Although Finn and Jimmy were done by the time Jimmy and Kodiak had become an item, Finn still needed a final word.

And if he couldn't get that, he would do the next best

thing.

Try to humiliate Kodiak in the most public way possible.

On line.

Hunter Davis had fallen in lust with Kodiak DePaul the first time he had seen the handsome Homesteader with no expectation of ever even meeting Kodiak. Hunters protests to Finn that the mission was impossible fell on deaf ears. The more Hunter tried to tell the stubborn, spoiled young man how huge Alaska, that even if he got to Kodiak's cabin guarantee he could get a camera installed just caused the vindictive Finn to shrug and offer even more money for the project. Hunter's explanation of how truly remote some places are were also were ignored as even more money (actual bundled bills!) were tossed onto a table in front of Hunter.

As the pile of un taxable, un traceable cash grew Hunter's resistance faded until he found Himself finally agreeing to try finding Kodiak's cabin. Not much longer after that he found himself dragging out one of his grandfather's old uniforms and on a skiff in the river heading toward Kodiak's homestead hide a way with a wireless camera tucked into his pack.

All of which, skiff, camera and photographic equipment, was now being tumbled toward the ocean by the swift currents of the wild remote river thanks to the intervention of the giant angry bear.

Visions of the money waiting with Finn once the job was complete kept dancing through his head, Hunter tried to keep lustful thoughts of Kodiak at bay as he sat hunched over a laptop at the kitchen dining bar of the tiny motel room he had taken near downtown Anchorage.

Hunter was still thrilled to have found and interacted

with Kodiak DePaul so quickly. As an Alaskan himself Hunter had a working knowledge of how to get to the reclusive scarred and scandal plagued Alaskan reality star. Which meant he could still claim the bounty even if his first attempt had failed.

The small beautifully carved figures he had slipped off the former reality show contestant's mantel had sold pennies on the dollar for what they were worth at a downtown Anchorage pawn shop. He thought it noble and cute that Kodiak would not think he would recognize the work of Sam Chigliac. Chigliac family pieces were highly sought after, Sam's work only the latest generation to be recognized. Hunter might have gotten more cash for the carvings had he poked around enough to find a black market to have sold them on, but this job required a fast in and out time line or it was lost until next spring. Hunter hated to part with the artwork but needed the money. While Finn had been more than generous in showing Hunter the bundles of money he had not been as free to hand much over until the camera was installed and running.

If Hunter did not act quickly Finn might become bored with the whole project and the bundles of cash waiting for Hunter in New York would be lost forever.

Hunter hated the idea of invading Kodiak's privacy so kept his mind on the stacks of cash waiting in New York and not the agony Kodiak was going to go through once he found out he had been sold out and put on a web site. Hunter could not bully himself into believing that he would pull the installation of a camera in a remote cabin off without Kodiak ever finding out.

With a few deft strokes on the keyboard Hunter clicked his way to an airline ticket from Anchorage to

Fairbanks. Once there in the city in the middle of the state he would arrange a flight back up to the old trappers cabin he had set up had set up miles from Kodiak's homestead but still close enough for him to reach the former model.

Use of his grandfather's maps, some horrible lies and a random bear attack had worked to get Hunter to Kodiak. Hunter knew he could not act like a random hiker who happened on Kodi's remote location because it *was* such a remote location and was pleased to have come up with the ruse of being a game warden. He knew the wardens did sometimes overlap assigned territory and knew first hand that game wardens also sometimes become ad hoc family to bush rats, getting to know them and help. Sometimes wardens were the only connection people in the bush would have with people for months on end.

Although the bear attack had been an unexpected game changer in the end it had gotten him not only onto Kodiak's property but into his cabin much sooner than Hunter had expected. He hadn't meant to be as snarky as he had been but felt the façade was necessary for Kodiak to believe the cover story of being a game warden.

Standing and stretching, quill injured thumb re bandaged and throbbing with every pulse of his heart, Hunter glanced at the clock. The flight north was in two hours, but it was only a short taxi ride to the airport so he was not pressed for time.

Hunter did not like the mission he was under taking, Kodiak had every right to his privacy. Like most other gay Alaskans, Hunter had developed a raging crush on the quiet homestead kid whose face had suddenly been plastered everywhere in the media. He longed to sit quietly with Kodiak get to know him and see if there might be a happy ending.

Sure it was a pipe dream, and a popular one, but now it was a pipe dream which certainly was never going to happen. The money offered would stake Hunter until he figured out a new gig in life even if it was at Kodiak's expense.

Not only would he hide and activate the camera for Finn, he had both still and video cameras in his pack and had already written up the first chapters of the fast paced down and dirty book on the reclusive model in place. From his Alaskan advantage Hunter had become something of an expert on the former model's life and career, including the salacious and sensational trial. The notes and cabin sketched he had just made were now on the laptop. The book deal would quietly be made without telling Finn, of course. He didn't even need to shop the book for a publisher, on line publishing and a little press work made for a nearly ready made best seller. Stories like Kodi's used to have a shelf life, with the internet even the coldest story could be revived, though. Hunter could easily have sold what he already had to a tabloid, the story of the bear attack and Kodi taking charge of the situation, even if Hunter as the writer came off as the jerk, and sketch of the remote homestead the once headline making model had resigned himself to would have been worth a lot to any tabloid.

But Hunter was after the bigger story and bigger pay day even if it ran into his own emotions. His stomach had clenched the moment Kodi had turned to confront him on the trail leading to his camp. Hunter had seen possibly every photo, both before and after the acid throwing incident, taken of Kodiak but had barely managed to suppress a gasp when the handsome homesteader faced him. Even scarred Kodi was more attractive than any man Hunter had ever known. Kodiak had even felt the chemistry between them while changing when the plane landed.

A fast fun time then might not have gotten him back into the cabin, though.

Calling for a cab Hunter gathered his compacted equipment, scanned the room for anything he might have forgotten, then left to go wait for his ride back to the airport. He knew he was not going to be the only other person out to get a photo or story from the reclusive Kodiak so he had to be the first.

Snow had continued to fall all through the next day on the homestead property, piling up to about three feet before finally tapering off. When the snow stopped the temperature fell again, although Kodi kept the cabin fires (both fireplace and cookstove) burning full time, the window panes remained mostly frosted over.

It took nearly three days before Cord slowly came around and was steadily breathing regularly again. Had the brothers been stranded on a desert island there might have been a chance of a passing ship rescue them. Had they been in space there would at least likely have been communication with a doctor on earth who might have been able to have talked him through what to do for Cord. Whatever drug or combination of drugs the young man had done had taken him down hard.

The homestead was one of the most remote places on the planet, with no communication and supplies expected but with no idea when Joe the pilot would be able to get through to the remote cabin.

It was then early October.

More snow came through the following few days with freezing temperatures in between. Normally this was Kodiak's favorite time on the remote land, there was a kind of peaceful quiet which came with the newly falling snow which he loved. He would keep the fires burning and read and re read favorite books for hours on end, feeling content he had accomplished all he needed to survive the winter in the middle of no-where.

Now he tried to read but could only get a few lines read over and over before going to check on Cord, or managing to get some broth and water into his brother. He rigged up a small private area in the corner of the bedroom to Cord him with other personal needs. Not that Cord knew much of what was going on, Kodi was all but dragging the young man back and forth across the bedroom to the jury rigged privy.

Kodiak had carefully checked the cabin, wash house and Cord's bag but found no sign of any kind of drug or liquor. If his brother had hidden any of them out of doors they would at least be covered in snow by now. Of course, his brother had some wilderness experience as well so he would know how to hide something and still find it under a layer of snow.

Kodiak tried to push aside thoughts that Cord had brought a stash and used the entire stash at once in a suicide attempt. That idea of that was more than he could handle, obsessing over things he could not handle were not going to help the situation. Wilderness life required calm in the face of any danger or storm. Kodi had not lived the fast life in those big cities for long but he had seen enough messy situations in the modeling world to last his lifetime. Anorexia, bulimia; pills, pot, clouds-not everyone had been involved to every degree, but he had seen enough to be determined that he was going to save Cord.

The upside was being on the remote homestead was that there was no way his brother could run away, he was smarter than that, and Kodi certainly was not going to help supply him with anything.

The downside, of course, was that if Cord had hidden a stash of dope or drink somewhere it was very unlikely he was going to tell Kodiak where the things were hidden.

Cord remained sullen and so far had refused Kodi's most basic request for help; to bring in wood, help with dishes. It was several days before Cord had finally gone to the wash house and bathed, although that had not been one of Kodiak's requests.

Cord kept his phone charged with a solar charger, listening to his huge library of music while Kodi continued keeping the small cabin in good repair, carefully calculating the supplies left in the wash house, smoke house and food cache before spending a few hours reading each night.

The pair fell into a quiet if not comfortable routine. Kodi had not brought up the wanton destruction of the food or the black-out binge to Cord, knowing the accusation would only lead to an argument if it was not timed right. Cord knew only vaguely what he had done. Kodi also did not want to alarm his brother that much of their cache of food for the winter had been impaired. They would be relying more on the frozen salmon and vegetables in the cavern than Kodiak had planned.

It was going to be a long winter.

Leaving the airport in Fairbanks, the second largest city in the huge state located just shy of the center of Alaska Hunter gathered his bags and hailed a cab over to a smaller airfield which serviced bush communities with smaller Cessna style aircraft.

"Son you already owe me for that first flight north," the pilot said as he hitched his cap back onto his head. "And the weather is turning fast on top of that."

"C'mon man. I'm good for it," Hunter said with a wide grin on his face. He always had the feeling the older man who had been a life-long friend of his grandfather, had a thing for him and he was willing to pay the price of passage however he needed to. "That old trapper's camp is just the place for me to get some great shots for my portfolio. I've got a buyer back in L.A. for these shots," he said with a straight face, "Why the hell do you think I'd come back up here this time of year? A studio guy saw some of my out of doors shots and wants them for advertising on line for one of their new movies." This new set of lies rolled easily off his tongue as easily as he had lied to Kodiak about being a game warden.

"Well you ain't got much here in the way of supplies son."

"Shouldn't take me long to get the shots I need."

"I dunno, if the old man was here he'd have my hide for taking you up there at all."

"Well he's not and I need to get north now. If you won't take me, I'll just find someone who will."

"No, I'll take you." The pilot said with a sigh. "You earning money is the only way I can get paid back I guess. Let's get your gear loaded. But weather is moving in, dark is coming."

Dark meant the long winter month's when there were only a few grey hours of gloomy daylight between about nine AM and three PM.

"I know, just take me. I'll be fine." Hunter wanted to believe that, too much was at stake with this. He had every intention of paying the pilot back, a debt like that would haunt him the rest of his life but ironically, he was enjoying the class and comfort of the mukluks loaned to him by Kodi that he had no intention of returning them to the model at the end of his photography session.

Smiling Hunter began tossing his meager bags into the small hold of the plane, knowing he was very close to his goal.

The experienced pilot was right, the weather had gotten worse the farther north the small plane went. Although Hunter had logged countless hours in the air in all size bush plane in all kind of weather and this was the first flight he had ever gotten sick on. In decent weather the flight into the northern wilderness would have taken just over two hours, with thick snow beginning to fall that trip took nearly three, the small plane bouncing around in the air like a beach ball on ocean waves.

"I do not like this Hunter, not one little bit I don't mind telling you," the experienced pilot said once the plane had slid to a stop near the edge of the wide, still unfrozen river, daylight rapidly draining from the sky.

"Don't worry. I'll be alright. Always have been." Hunter shot back while opening the door of the small plane. The pilot knew how close Hunter had been to spending time in prison with his father, he knew the young man had seen hard times, but he hated to see anyone going off into the wilderness at that time of year un prepared. It would have been a death warrant for most, the pilot had known Hunter's grandfather so had to trust that the young man had enough experience to get through until he could get back up to fly him out of the remote territory.

Stepping out onto the pontoon Hunter grabbed a landing line tucked up under the wing then managed to jump onto the snow-covered shore. Holding the plane he pulled the line taunt and scrambled up the embankment and secured it to a sturdy cottonwood tree. The experienced pilot hadn't liked the abandon trappers' cabin when he brought Hunter and the skiff the bear had sunk up before the snow had fallen and liked it even less now.

Glancing up at the old cabin, dark, sagging and uninviting Hunter shuddered as his stomach turned to a knot of liquid, wondering if he was making the right decision to move this plan forward. He had no lifeline set up, a limited amount of supplies and was literally putting himself on the line for a stack of money. At that moment he could still have gotten back into the plane and flown back to civilization.

Taking a deep breath Hunter turned his attention back to the task at hand, helping the pilot unload his gear he invited him to stay the night. Thanking him the pilot said no, that he would have just enough light to get back to Fairbanks.

"Give me a month." Hunter said as he again stepped from the plane then slogged through the snow, scrambling up the low embankment he watched as the small yellow craft smoothly eased back down the river then lifted off into the darkening sky.

Hunter had spent a lot of time in the bush but was never comfortable there, even with his beloved grandfather. He also still believed in the mission he was on but with the plane pulling away and snow falling even thicker he suddenly felt more alone than he ever had. The die was now cast. Moving on up the bank of the river and back to his meager gear, in the haste of moving his gear from the plane Hunter did not notice the small bag he had packed with fire starting equipment had fallen into the churning water and been carried away by the dark, frothy water.

Ten

The fight seemed like it had lasted forever.

Darkness had fallen, as it now did earlier and earlier each day, by the time the DePaul brothers had stopped trading vicious blows.

Kodi stood next to the sink, head tilted back, fingers pinching the bridge of his nose to stem the flow of blood leaking from each nostril, his head feeling like an anvil had been dropped onto it cartoon like.

In what he had thought, hoped, would be a moment of clarity Kodi had asked Cord in a calm, non-confrontational way if he had any other drugs or alcohol hidden away in the cabin.

That had been hours earlier. Cord's screaming denial turned into punches and the two of them thrashing around the cabin, which led to Kodiak trying to restrain Cord, which had led to the actual altercation.

Both healthy and strong, Kodi had the advantage of the more muscular frame and ability to keep himself calm before he managed to pin Cord several times. But the younger brother had the strength of adrenaline on his side and managed to buck his brother off each time they were down. Cord had managed to latch his fingers around a length of stove wood and got in the powerful blow on his brother's already scarred face, which had knocked him out cold. Dropping the wood while screaming in horror

Cord had bolted from the cabin, leaving the front door wide open, into another round of falling snow.

Kodi had woken just as the snowfall was ending, a skiff of white drifting over the threshold of the front door. The fire was long out, the cabin interior now felt the same feel as being out of doors. Head throbbing Kodiak had pushed himself up off the floor, a blast of pain caused the room to spin for a moment. He caught his breath and, head feeling like it was filled with splinters of glass, stumbled to close the door then checked the rooms for signs of his brother, but the small cabin was empty. Picking up the piece of wood Cord had belted him with, a slash of his own blood trailed over the bright white bark of the piece of birch, with a grimace he tossed it into the fireplace.

Kodiak knew without checking the washhouse mirror that his face was a mess and that his eyes were undoubtedly blackened. He had to try and find Cord, it was going to be a daunting task no matter how he looked. He was most likely holed up down in the wash house.

But how he felt to get the job of finding him done was another story. Stripping out of his shirt Kodiak dunked his head into the sink and wrenched the faucet on, hot and cold water mixing as it sluiced down over his head and neck. Pulling his head from under the flow of water he let the rivulets stream down over his muscular, bare chest. A very sexy, sculpted body Kodi was determined to keep to himself for as long as he lived. Even though it hurt he had to smile at the thought of his image. Not that he was ever going to make a move but even the hot, snarky still green for the job game warden wouldn't look at him twice now if he happened back this way before next season with his bruised, bloodied face outlined by the scars.

Downing several aspirin Kodi did finally allow himself a glance at his reflection in the kitchen window. His left eye was turning a Northern lights like hue of brilliant green and yellow, the right was already a ripe plumb purple. Cord had managed to miss the bridge of his nose with the length of wood or it would have been broken. Not that any of it mattered, Kodi could only hope the swelling would be minimal enough to allow him to see.

Drying off the young homesteader re dressed slowly and carefully, breathing shallowly as each time he drew in air his left side felt like it was filled with angry bees swarming up and down inside of his body. Which meant that he likely had broken or at least cracked ribs. Not an ideal situation to be starting a winter in the bush, especially a winter beginning like this one with an already dangerously low food supply.

Not to mention having a now missing brother.

Once bundled up properly against the cold night Kodi strapped a headlamp around the heavy knit cap he had pulled low over his ears and moved out into the darkness after carefully banking the fire.

The cold had caused the fresh snow to become slightly crystalized, it crunched under his feet beneath the soft tread of the mukluks. Being out in this weather, especially in the condition he was in was the last thing in the world he wanted. He would much rather have tended his wounds and let Cord sleep off his anger in the wash house but that was not the way Kodi operated. He knew he would only rest with his brother back in the cabin.

As he walked he tried to think of what to say to Cord, knowing that the words would not matter as much as the tone. His goal for now was just to get Cord back into the cabin, he was still furious with him and the ache in his side with each step reminded him that Cord's reaction likely meant he *had* hidden drugs and or booze on the property but after the fight there was no sense in trying to get that information out of him again today. Kodi would settle for getting Cord into bed quietly for the night so that he could start to heal.

Relieved to see light spilling from the tiny window in the sturdy log cabin wash house up ahead he pushed the heavy door open without knocking.

"Cordova?"

He was not surprised when there was no answer. Cord could be horrified or still furious about what had just happened. "This is serious man," Kodiak called out as he stepped farther into the wash house, his head throbbing. "But nothing we can't work out." He scanned the room, the door to the actual bathroom stood open but he could not see his brother inside.

Feeling dizzy suddenly Kodi reached out to steady himself against a chair pushed up under the table. This was not good, a blinding slash of pain cut through his head, his eyes involuntarily squeezed shut.

"Cord, I need some help man," he managed as another knife of pain cut through his head, the bolt of discomfort searing through him so hard that he had to reach out and grab the edge of the nearby table to steady himself. Something was very wrong, and this was not the place or time to be having this kind of pain. As someone who had experienced pain in the acid attack, Kodiak knew that this kind of feeling required medical attention.

Fast.

"Cordova!" he shouted sharply as the pain in his head

subsided. Swiping his hand over his forehead Kodi was relieved to see that it was not covered in blood.

Turning Kodi closed the door to the small cabin then checked the bathroom. No sign of his brother there either.

Glancing around the room Kodi felt his stomach knot again as he realized that while Cord might not be there at the moment, but he clearly had been there. Cabinets were open, clothing was scattered around; a roll of maps had been unfurled across the table.

Looking at the carnage Kodi groaned. Everything he saw pointed to the fact that Cord had filled a pack and was attempting the unthinkable.

To hike out.

Even in mid-summer under and under the very best of circumstances Kodiak would not have tried to cross the vast terrain which lay between the homestead and the nearest other humanity.

Cord had even less experience in the wild than Kodi. It was a suicide attempt to leave the camp even this early in the winter as there was snow (which would help Kodi track his brother), but rivers were not frozen fully, moose were still foraging with food getting scarce; wolf packs were on the prowl and not all the bear would yet be settled in. With the fish runs would be all but gone soon and the few berries left covered in snow. Every creature in the wild, animal or human, were now prey.

Not to mention that a giant cross marked bear had moved into the territory.

A large pack had been taken from off the wall, a quick inventory of what was missing showed that Cord at least knew what he might need in the wild. A sleeping bag, dried foods including salmon and berries were missing;

oats, a small cooking pan and a roll of land maps proved his brother was serious about leaving the homestead on foot. Kodi groaned inwardly again, the nearest village was a several days hike in the summer even with a fully supplied pack. Under the circumstances and with the short load of supplies missing the trip Cord had set out on was nothing short of a fool's errand.

Moving around the wash house, putting clothing back in place and reviewing the now alarmingly even more depleted supplies Kodiak realized that in addition to finding his brother he was going to have to go to the cave and break into those supplies much sooner than he expected.

Which made him think of fish, which made him think of the bear in the river and the hot-if-annoying game warden, Hunter. Even in the middle of this current crisis he could not help but feel a tingling tightening in his crotch at the thought of sexy guy.

What *did* cool his desire was remembering that Cord did not have the extra mukluks. The perfect winter homestead footgear were still in the possession of the hot young game warden.

Kodi hoped Hunter had been responsible enough to have mailed the boots back already. The boots carried powerful memories for Kodiak and he did not want to lose them.

The temperature had dropped again, even with his lifetime of experience in the bush Kodiak shuddered in the cold. He knew it was not a good idea to start after Cord, who could be just over the rise or miles away. He also knew that even as exhausted as that he was a long way from sleep. Unhooking his own back pack from the wash room wall Kodiak began filling it with essentials, not knowing how long the journey in front of him might be. He would use the emergency radio to call for help then have some food and rest before striking out for the cave to bring supplies in, much earlier than he had planned to be going back there.

Back in the cabin Kodiak rummaged into the dark opening of the small bar, hoping his fingers would bump against the SPOT radio. Once he had fired that off he would get the cabin squared away and wait for the arrival of the plane or helicopter arrived he would help with the hunt for his run-away brother before going to the cave for supplies.

His fingers scrabbled from corner to corner in the small space, finding nothing. Tilting his head down Kodiak shone the light beam around in the space, but the emergency call beacon was not there.

Hoping the beacon had just been pushed out when Cord was raiding the bar, Kodiak carefully scanned the cabin floor, leaving nothing un checked in the small space and the bedrooms until he had to admit to himself that Cord had either taken the device with him or somehow lost the important piece of equipment.

His brother was homestead savvy enough to know not to call for help when he really just wanted a ride out of the bush.

Frustrated at the waste of time spent looking for the SPOT, Kodiak knew he had to head out on his own to look for Cord. If his brother did deploy the signal it would only be a matter of time before Kodiak heard the rescue flight in the still, cold air. It was certain that if he heard airship movement that Cord was being picked up and he would eventually send a message on the radio communication line that he was safe.

With a deep sigh Kodiak began to gather what he would need for a few days in the arctic bush.

Once he had all the supplies needed from the wash house Kodi carefully maneuvered the door latch back into place. He was grateful his great grandfather had copied the latching device he had built into the cabin door for the wash house, which was much smaller back in the day before Kodiak had expanded and piped in the running water. Limping along Kodiak moved back to the cabin, where he completed the task of packing, rolling an arctic rated sleeping back tightly he lashed it and a waterproof underlay onto the bottom of the backpack frame then dressed. He chose his layers carefully, knowing he would be heated as he hiked and would need to shed layers as the day moved on.

His side ached like a sledge hammer was being driven into it with each movement. Checking his bruised face in the window again Kodiak cleaned off his nostrils then swabbed antiseptic gel lightly over the smaller scratches and cuts.

Choosing items from his large kit of First Aid supplies Kodiak tucked them into pockets of his pack then with a series of groans removed his shirt. His side was a rainbow of muted colors, deep purple and yellow streaking up and down his body. Breathing slowly and deeply he carefully wound a wide elastic bandage around his torso, leaving it loose enough for him to be able to move without constriction.

Kodiak did hope Cordova had taken the electronic beacon and had the sense to use it soon. Closing up the cabin Kodiak hitched the pack up onto his back, the last thing he grabbed on his way out was his small hunting rifle. The bolt action .22 caliber would not stop big game but the 30-ought six would be a heavier load in the snow.

The sun had risen but little light filtered through the heavy layer of grey sky that far north. As he moved along the snow-covered trail leading toward the river Kodi could still easily make out Cord's tracks in the snow in the murky light. His brother was going to become harder to track as the trail got older so Kodi was glad to have forego sleeping to try and catch up to him. He'd go as far as he could then make camp, musing that if he did catch up to his brother and could not talk him into coming back to the homestead he would at least get him to the village and figure a way to get Cord back to Anchorage.

If it came to it, he would take Cord back himself and if need be stay with him in the city for the winter. The media frenzy would die out for a while and he would have to live with the occasional flare up of pictures and inquires. He would still be trapped but at least Cord would not be bull headedly storming through the wilderness alone. Life in Anchorage would be hard on Kodiak, perhaps even harder on him than on Cord. The few friends, true friends Kodiak could trust, were scattered around the state and he was now suspect of anyone new who wanted to buddy up, he would suspect motives for the rest of his life after Finn. Sam Chigliac was his closest ally, but Sam spent most of the winter running his dog team up and down his long trapline and Kodiak had no intention of burdening Sam with his brother problem. He could always count on Sam to close up the homestead cabin for the season if needed.

The thought of leaving the homestead soured Kodiak's stomach as he plodded through the snow, his side aching with each step. He'd much rather be here in the peace and quiet of the wilderness than be held hostage by reporters in the house in the city for the rest of the winter.

Tired, head aching Kodi gave himself a shake. He wanted to be sick and cry at the same time but negative thinking like that was not going to accomplish anything. He was upright and moving, that was what mattered. He didn't know what he was moving toward other than trying to find signs of his brother's footsteps in the snow.

Re focusing on finding Cordova he slogged on through the knee-deep snow, each time he lifted his feet was an exercise in agony.

As the sun rose higher, flooding the bright white un touched snow, he finally caught sight of a lone pair of tracks moving toward the river. The holes in the snow were not caved in at the sides, which meant they were not that old, causing Kodiak's un settled stomach to lurch in a moment of expectation. Cord could not be that far ahead of him, and if he had stopped and made camp there was a good chance that Kodi would be caught up with him very soon.

Picking up his pace Kodi moved mechanically, stopping only to fish some aspirin out of his pack and dry swallow them. The throbbing in his head continued but he was feeling so hopeful he chose not to stop. His side felt like razors were being run up and down from his armpit to his hip.

Late-morning, according to the shadows being cast across the blindingly white snow, he came across a rough camp at the base of a tall spruce, boughs now sprung free of the heavy snow which weighed down the dark green limbs. Cord had carefully shaken snow from a few of the lower branches then scooted down under the others still being held tightly down by the snow. Following his childhood bush training Cord had found a safe shelter and would have constructed the fire second.

When Cord had left was the question, hours ago? Minutes ago?   The snow had easily come off the lower branches. Kodiak could not help being pleased that Cord had kept the snow in place in the crude shelter, his body heat would have held well in the emergency setting. In addition to that Cord had successfully made a fire pit in the snow. Boughs from a nearby spruce had been thickly lined in the bowl he had dug out of the snow. Kodi noted several long patches of bark had been peeled from the trunk, exposing the pitch. Which would have made a fast, hotfire starter with a flint.

A makeshift spit with a thick cross branch held the remains of one of Kodiak's summer caught salmon, reaching below the scraps of fish Kodi felt the coals, they were still warm. If the coals still had this much warmth Cord was not that far ahead of Kodi.

The former model was anxious to have this ordeal over and get back to the cabin where he could clean up and figure out how they were going to get through the rest of the winter. He wanted to soak in the stone tub, have a decent meal with what was left of the food then sleep for about two days. He was still furious that Cord had lashed out but knew that once the drugs were out of his system that his younger brother was a good kid at heart and that he would be reasonable once they were back at camp.

Or if it came to it back in the city.

Rising Kodi saw that the set of tracks continued northwest. Cord would be getting back to the river soon and Kodi hoped he would not try to cross the icy current alone. It would be dangerous enough if there were two of them but alone would be suicide if you fell into the rushing water alone.

Kodiak knew where the wide, shallow spot in the river near the old trapper's cabin was, Cord did not. Even though the mukluks he wore were sealed to the point of being water proof, crossing the river alone was not a thing to be done. The cabin was located on the edge of the river just ahead, Cord would not have known that either or he wouldn't have camped under the tree so close to shelter. The cabin would be open of course, it was rule in the bush to leave cabins unlocked in case of emergency.

Or emergencies involving numbskull brothers running trying to run back to civilization after going Cain and Able on each other.

All of this was doing a slow crawl through Kodi's mind when he heard only the tiniest crunch of snow behind him. Anyone not well versed in the way of the wilderness would never have noticed the sound, even standing stock still as Kodiak was.

Slowly turning his head, careful not to make any sudden moves, Kodiak's stomach twisted back into a knot when he saw a wolverine bigger than the average pit bull peering at him from a stand of trees, long yellowed canine teeth bared, course black and brown hair bristling from the shoulders of the muscular animal. Dark fur hid the massive muscles of its back and forelegs.

As lone hunter's wolverine were vicious foragers, eating bone as easily as the skin and fur of prey. The fierce predators feared nothing and attacked everything. They also did not hibernate, Kodiak had seen many kill sites scavenged by wolverines at all stages of the winter.

Moose, bear, caribou carcasses stripped to crushed bones. Once the fierce predators had flayed an animal to skeletal remains bones had been cracked open for the marrow to be gnawed out. Wolverines didn't leave enough behind for the crows, ravens and ground animals to scavenge and if one of those intruders tried to sweep in while a wolverine was feeding, they met a similar grisly fate.

Territorial, curious animals Wolverines were known to bury caches of food in their range area. It was too early in the season for this sleek brown and black fur coated animal to be starving, the feral creature had likely followed the smell of the cooked fish or even Kodiak's scent. However wolverine were curious and this one had likely never encountered a human, while hanging back and being cautious Kodiak knew the heavily breathing animal knew no fear.

Kodiak also knew better than to make a sudden move, the wolverine could move through the snow nearly as fast as they could on dry land.

Steadying his breath own Kodi slowly stood, moving a fraction at a time as the wolverine's black, glassy eyes bore into him. With each tortured move he was aware of the animal, his body beginning to ache as the homesteader waited for the animal to flinch.

But the wolverine did not move so Kodiak drew in some long, quiet deep breaths before beginning the agonizing work of easing the rifle from his shoulder. Thankfully the sling moved smoothly and silently down over his outer jacket inch by excruciating inch and the canvas strap did not catch against the buckles of the pack. If he were to get a shot in it would likely not take the small animal down, the best he would be able to do would be to get a slug into the wide chest of the wolverine and hope to hit a lung as the bullet of the .22 would likely not penetrate the rock like skull of the deadly little animal.

Just as the strap of the rifle reached the crook of his arm the wolverine moved, suddenly trotting half the distance separating the two, causing Kodi to freeze again.

He had to make a move, any closer and the animal would be on him.

The wolverine had stopped so Kodi let the rifle fall into his grip, his freezing fingers moving like lightning over the bolt he at the same time lowered the barrel and aimed as best he could while applying pressure to the trigger. The small popping sound of the bullet detonation startled both the man and animal, the acrid smell of discharged gunpowder burned Kodi's nose as a small plume of smoke curled from the end of the rifle barrel. A split second later the wolverine was hit, the small caliber bullet striking the animal square in the chest, pulling it's hind legs up off the ground the wolverine twisted it's head in pain while giving a horrible squeal pulled up from its bowels.

The only thing worse than a wolverine on the attack is a wounded wolverine on the attack. As Kodi had known the rifle did not have the power to kill the animal and he had only caught a corner of the muscular little beast's right lung, but the fury and anger now flooding through the animal made it oblivious to the white-hot pain searing through its body.

Front paws falling back down into the snow the wolverine charged as Kodi fired off another round, this one went high, missing the animal completely, he did not have time to slam another round into the chamber.

Turning Kodi let the rifle fall into the snow, using all

of the energy he had Kodiak gave a powerful shrug of his shoulders, managing to slip the pack down over his shoulders while pushing it toward the wolverine, which was at that moment was literally snapping powerful jaws against Kodi's left heel.

The heavy pack hit the mark as it knocked against the wounded animal. The pack momentarily distracted the wolverine as it stomped a powerfully muscled leg into the straps and rolled forward onto its snout as Kodi managed to get a slight lead, turning and tearing through a grove of young birch trees and not looking back as the animal became more entangled, and enraged, in the backpack, stopping finally to take it's anger out on the flying material, food, extra ammo and dry socks. The angry wolverine tore at the backpack the same way he would have torn into the human; bits of aluminum framing flew through the air, the snow was quickly flattened into a wide circle as the wolverine shredded the supplies in a rage.

Running through the deep, powdery snow as fast as he could, legs plunging into the deep, soft snow, side feeling like it had been doused in kerosene and set on fire, Kodi turned his head for a moment to make certain the animal was still in place attacking the pack and not on his heels again.

He did not see that he was running full bore into the river until he was in the tumbling icy water up to his knees.

Eleven

The moment his feet hit the freezing, frothy water, before the wet even had time to soak through to his skin, Kodiak knew he was in serious trouble.

The momentum of running launched Kodiak into the strong current, as his feet slipped over the smooth stones on the bottom of the river for just a moment Kodi thought, hoped, he was going to hold his balance and perhaps only soak the outer skin of the mukluks.

But then, like a nightmare set in slow motion, Kodiak fell forward. His entire body was suddenly engulfed in water so cold it felt as if he had been wrapped in a white-hot robe. Struggling to push himself up against the current, fingers grappling the loose stones on the bed of the river Kodiak was too startled to think or breathe.

His already cold hands scrabbled over the smooth rocks trying to find one fixed in the bed of the river for leverage but the slick, immobile stones only caused him to push himself farther out into the churning water. His one clear thought at that moment was how happy he was to have struggled out of the pack as its weight would pushed him face down into the river and would not have allowed him to have moved at all.

Trying to catch his balance again Kodiak did manage to rise up out of the water, screaming despite the futility of the situation the young man tried to take a deep breath and calm down but the freezing water had knocked the wind out of him and his body was already getting numb.

Steadying his feet Kodiak managed to spread them apart on the slick rocks in the riverbed. The water rushing around him was about waist deep, he looked back at the cut through the snow bank he had made stumbling into the river. The wolverine was likely still not far away but if he got back to the river bank that was just a chance he was going to have to take.

Death had Kodiak DePaul penned in.

Lifting his arms, soaked clothing weighing him down, Kodi tried to balance himself. He was managing that task better than even he could have imagined when a large tree branch came barreling through the water toward him, punching him square in the middle of the chest.

Reeling backward as his feet slipped on the rocks under his feet Kodiak screamed, a tiny voice in the back of his head telling him that the sound was the last he would ever make as he fell backward into the current, arms still flailing above the water.

The long, supple clump of willow which had recently been broken off due to the undercutting on a bank of the river snagged a partially sunken tangle of deadfall mostly underwater just as it hit Kodiak. Holding tightly to the slender branches he managed to push his head up from under the water, where he tried to keep his eyes open against the freezing waves. That little voice in his head this time assuring him if his head went back underwater that it would be for the last time.

Holding his head up out of the churning water Kodiak struggled to keep his breathing steady, and to see if he could clamber up onto the brushy debris which held him in place.

Moving could easily dislodge the raft of driftwood he clung to, but he had no option. The seconds were ticking by and it would not be long before shock set in. He had ten, fifteen minutes tops, less than that if he remained submerged and the heat was leeched out of his body. His fingers were white and seemed to have been carved out of marble as he tried to move them. Moaning through his now chattering teeth Kodi slowly, painfully, managed to get his fingers to flex slightly, peeling away from the slick willow branches as the roiling water tore at his legs.

The water was not deep but the current was swift and the water freezing. Kodiak had escaped an acid attack by a mad man, out maneuvered both an angry bear and an angry wolverine and spent a lifetime in the wilderness but it looked like this time the wilderness was going to win the Man versus Wild contest.

But Kodiak was not a quitter, now nearly five minutes into this ordeal he drew in a long deep breath and *willed* his cramped, curled fingers from the branches just as he was hit by something again.

It was of course impossible, but he saw a rope trailing in the water next to him. A rough length of sisal with a fist size knot had suddenly hit his hands. Without question or thought he managed to uncurl his nearly immobile fingers again from the bare tree branches and hooked them around the end of the rope, letting them slide to the knot where he held on with all the strength he could muster. The muscles he had built while chopping his winter wood supply were paying off despite the conditions.

"PULL!" was shouted from the shore, "PULL!"

Floundering for a moment, his head ducking briefly

back under the water, Kodi felt the rope go taunt, then used the force to slowly brink himself back upright against the strength of the rivers current.

"PULL!" was shouted again from the shore.

Finding his balance again the current Kodi managed to get to his feet, then wrapped the rope around his wrist and held tightly, energy nearly depleted as he drew in another long ragged breath, the cold burning in his lungs.

 he drama in the river was set against a brilliant blue background, the sun blazing the in the midday sky by then with each wave in the river topped by a dazzling diamond of white reflection. The rest of the landscape was freshly coated with a blanket of snow, an idyllic winter scene save for the struggle playing out in the river and the imminent death at hand.

"PULL!" was yelled again.

Like I need to be told.... somewhere in the farthest back, most primal spot of his head Kodi said this to himself while mustering every ounce of energy he could to follow the command. His body was racing on adrenaline, not having had time to recover from the wolverine encounter before charging into the river and starting another death defiance.

Inch by agonizing inch Kodi slid his feet slowly, carefully over the smooth, slick stones of the riverbed. His hands, while numb and aching from the cold, managed to keep grip on the rough rope. Drawing another deep breath he slid forward again, his footing faltering slightly as the rope gave a slight jerk when pulling him forward but Kodi managed to keep his balance and pulled himself forward far enough so he was by then back water only thigh deep. The current was still very strong and the cold unbearable but Kodi began to feel the best kind of relief of all; hope.

Pressing on, the assistance from whomever was pulling the rope helping move Kodi forward, the homesteader soon found true footing on the much smaller gravel near the edge of the river. His grip still steady on the rope Kodi managed to find strength he could not imagine he possessed and suddenly found himself on the edge of the river then stepping up onto the bank into the deep snow and solid land.

Falling face down into the soft, fluffy snowbank, panting, Kodiak's fingers still clutching the rope. He wanted to get up but could not. The events of the last 24 hours were the stuff of nightmares, eyes will closed he wished he were just in the middle of a horrible dream.

Moments later he was suddenly rolled over onto his side, then his back and looking up into the red, sweat dripping face of Hunter Davis.

"Let's get you into the cabin," the panting Hunter managed to chop out, "help me if you can."

Kodiak, still unable to move, would have helped if he could but he had reached the end, his energy was expended. He had no idea what kind of delusion he was having that made him imagine the phony game warden had appeared to save him but did not care. He was out of the water and that was all that mattered. Jimi Hendrix or Captain Kangaroo could have been standing over him and he would have been just as happy.

"Fuck," the very real Hunter muttered, realizing Kodiak was going to be no help getting back to the cabin.

This situation, the prey Hunter had come for landing on the bank of the river next to the cabin he had taken over, while convenient, was far from ideal. Even desperate as he was Hunter would not stoop to photographing Kodiak in this state.

Having lost the fire-starting material on arrival Hunter had spent the night shivering in his sleeping bag after searching the cabin and finding no matches, flint or starter kit tucked away. Despite having no way to start a fire he had lain a base of tinder, kindling and three small, paper dry rounds of wood in the fireplace then left the cabin to try and find two smooth rocks to chip together to see if he could force a spark to get the assemblage to catch into flame.

The moment he stepped outside he heard the commotion in the woods of the wolverine destroying the backpack, followed by seeing the figure of a man bolting from the woods into the river. It didn't take a lot to figure this was a bad situation.

Rushing back into the small cabin Hunter tore through the debris, precious seconds ticking away until he found the length of rope under the small built-in bunk and raced to the river, where thankfully the rope hit Kodiak's fingers on the first throw.

Steadying himself by a thick birch tree Hunter used the leverage of the tree trunk to anchor the rope and help Kodiak up onto the shore and into the powdery depth of snow he currently was resting in.

There was no time to try and lash a litter together, it was not that far from the cabin so Hunter reached down and slipped his hands under Kodiak's arm pits and began to drag Kodiak to the relative safety and warmth of the cabin. Despite no fire being inside was certainly better than outside at this point.

Sweat and the wet from Kodi's clothing soaking through the front of his own clothing, Hunter muttered curses as he drug the dead weight of the former model through the snow. He had not closed and latched the thick cabin door when running out with the rope so was thankful to just bounce it open with his backside as he bumped Kodiak inside and drug him over to the bunk. Reaching over Kodiak he pushed the sleeping bag aside and nestled him down onto the thin feather mattress on the bunk.

The only light came through a small, dusty window above the door, it helped that midday sun was streaming through the window, placed where it was to not only afford light but to keep bears from breaking through a window set lower in the walls of the thick logs.

Pushing the sleeping bag aside to keep it from getting wet he arranged Kodiak on the bunk then went back and closed the door to retain as much interior heat as possible. The small cabin already smelled musty, and now the smell of *wet* permeated the space.

Hunter had drawn a sharp breath when he finally got a look at Kodiak's bruised face. The fall in the river had not caused the blackened eye and goose egg size knot rising from his forehead. The young homesteaders gorgeous face was a mess but there was little Hunter could do about that at the moment. Fire was the priority, but getting Kodi into the sleeping bag was now higher on the to do list.

Kodiak's lips were blue, his teeth chattering uncontrollably as Hunter began stripping the soaking wet outer coat off his body. In a moment of lucidity Kodiak's eyes blinked, raising an arm slightly he pointed toward the fire place.

"Sorry, no matches man," Hunter said while pulling Kodiak up to peel the jacket off his back. He wished this cabin had a rock hot water basin like the one at Kodiak's homestead. The hot water would do wonders to raise his temperature. But if wishes were horses, beggars would ride.

"Mmmmuck….," Kodiak said through his telegraph chattering teeth.

"Shhhhh, man. Just lemme do this," Hunter said, his own teeth clamped together as sweat trickled down over his back from the exertion.

Kodi, while still making the odd "Mmmmmm" sound, kicked first his left leg up, followed by the right.

"Calm down dude! I'm trying to help you and this is difficult enough as it is!"

Ignoring Hunter, the soaking wet former model again kicked both legs while humming that weird "Mmmmmmm."

Working as quickly as he could Hunter moved to the end of the small bunk to begin working on the soft (now water logged) mukluks laced up over Kodiak's muscular calves. As his fingers worked at the knotted laces Kodi tried to kick his legs again, moaning that drawn out "Mmmm" sound as Hunter swatted his legs back down against the table.

"Stop it man! Damn! Tryna help here!"

With that Hunter began to roll the high-topped Mukluk down over Kodiak's leg as the model gave another violent kick and lifted his head slightly to growl out, "*TOP!*" through his clattering teeth.

Hunter had never been much interested in puzzles or anagrams or the kind of clever word story in which a hundred ducks flying in formation over a train and who would reach Baltimore first, but the force with which this freezing guy said the word TOP made him stop for a moment and realize that while his chattering, struggling and kicking were annoying that Kodiak was trying to communicate with him.

In some primal way but communicating, nonetheless.

TOP meant something. Slowing himself even though Kodiak shivered below him, Hunter scanned the roofline of the cabin interior in case he had missed a shelf holding some kind of fire starter. His head was still pointed up when Kodiak's left leg *whumphed* down against the bed frame again.

Time was passing quickly, and Kodiak's shivering was growing more violent, his lips were nearly indigo. Grabbing the top of the wet mukluk Hunter again began peeling it back down over Kodiak's leg.

If I don't get him out of these clothes and into the sleeping bag he's going to die, were the exact words freighting through Hunter's head as his fingers curled around the upper part of theboot.

Just as the thought finished his fingers felt something at the top (TOP!) of the mukluk boot. A wide seam had been folded over and sewn at the top of the footwear under the slick fur ringing the top of the boot. Sliding his fingers along the top of the boot he felt several lumps, then came across a tiny, carefully hidden zipper had been sewn in. Sliding the zipper open along the bottom of the wide seam small things began falling around his fingers.

Stopping the course of the zipper Hunter quickly sifted through the items, finding a tightly rolled length of high test fishline, two razor sharp (and carefully sheathed) fishhooks and the grand prize of the secreted survival cache; a flint stick.

"Holy FUCK, man!" Hunter cried, dropping Kodiak's leg and bolting to the already laid fireplace.

Hands shaking he struck the flint against the metal fire

grate. The first two fumbling times produced only tiny yellow jagged streaks of light. By the third strike Hunter had steadied his hand and managed a long bolt of energy which caught the dry tinder. Cupping his hand down around the tiny flame Hunter blew gently on the fire, which leapt up through the kindling, the flame catching as it touched the wood. The crackle of the burning wood was like the best music Hunter had ever heard.

"I could fucking kiss you man!" Hunter yelped as the flames wrapped around the wood as the fire was fully formed, stopping in front of the blast of heat for a moment before he jumped back up and went back to the shivering Kodiak.

Fingers now limbering up he quickly sat Kodi up and wrapped an arm around the homesteader, grabbing a handful of wet shirt to steady him Hunter clumsily stripped the shirt and up over Kodiak's torso, biting his lower lip as his hands skimmed against the handsome young man's body for the first time as he peeled the thermal underwear union suit top over the homesteader's muscular arms and chest.

Fuck, oh fucking damn...he thought, his cock beginning to swell as he lay Kodiak back down and swept his fingers over the homesteader's waist and unfastened his belt.

Wet jeans are difficult enough to get out of. Getting a pair of them off an inert form was even more challenging. Gulping Hunter struggled to peel the soaked denim down over Kodiaks legs. The white waffle weave thermal long underwear Kodiak was wearing peeled down over his legs along with the jeans, making that maneuver a twofer. Hunter did not bother averting his eyes from Kodiak's naked, muscular (and shivering) frame. He took a second to appreciate the thickness of his thick dick nested in a thick tangle of blond pubic hair as it flopped around his body as Hunter managed to roll him into the arctic rated sleeping bag. The temptation to grab his camera was nearly overwhelming but this was life or death.

But he would not above mentally making a sketch in his head to include in the book.

Thankfully even in his inert state the young homesteader had saved the day with his built-in survival kit. Kodiak had quickly passed back out, his body continuing to herky-jerky twitch in the down filled bag.

Once Kodiak's soaked clothing had been removed Hunter carefully un wound the equally wet length of elastic bandage Kodiak had managed to coil around himself, the young homesteader wincing through grit teeth as Hunter removed the bandage as carefully as he could.

Hunter gasped at the multicolored bruise streaked up over Kodiak's body, marveling that he could move at all, let alone walk. And those bruises, while fresh, certainly had not been made running and falling into the river.

Trying to ignore his new sleeping bag mate's nakedness Hunter hung the bandage to dry then tossed a few more substantial logs onto the fire.

Arranging Kodiak down into the sleeping bag Hunter then carefully pulled out one nicely formed leg at a time to massage the perfectly shaped feet one after another, his hands working up over Kodiak's bulging calf muscles while keeping his mind on the work of circulation and going no farther north on his new cabin mates' body. He longed to stroke his fingers up and down over the muscular leg, the tightness in his crotch becoming almost unbearable as he carefully kept his fingers from wandering up into the warmth of Kodiak's.

When he finished working the sexy homesteader's lower legs and feet Hunter tucked them back into the sleeping bag then went back to the fireplace. Stoking the flames with several more large cuts of wood he then returned to the bunk and quickly stripped out of his own clothing then wedged his body into the sleeping bag next to Kodi. Survival one-oh-one; skin-to-skin body heat was the best way to warm up someone who was freezing.

The cabin was quickly heating up also; already over heated from the exertion of dragging Kodi into the cabin, then struggling to strip him down and into the bag and building the fire had Hunter slick with sweat and sticky inside the down filled sleeping bag. Not to mention the fact that he was now naked with a man he had been dreaming about for a long time.

Wrapping his own arms around Kodiak's muscular arms Hunter managed to work the zipper of the sleeping bag only part of the way up, thankfully he was so uncomfortable that even when his hands accidentally brushed over Kodiak's genetalia his own piece remained flaccid.

Despite his over-all discomfort (the agony and ecstasy of the situation!), Hunter pressed himself up against Kodiak as hard as he could, his arms pulling the homesteaders muscular frame up against his.

This next part was the most difficult. Hunter burrowed down into the sleeping bag to wrap his hands around Kodiaks feet, pulling the icy pair up against his own calves. He then carefully worked Kodiaks hands down into his own groin, it was the best way to get his icy fingers to warm up given the circumstance. And was one of the most amazingly agonizing things Hunter had ever done. Holding a naked Kodiak, while naked himself, while not touching him in an intimate way.

Agony and glory rolled into one.

Sweat, slick skin against skin, his crotch seamed tightly against the former model's thigh. Hunter grimly held his arms tightly around Kodiak while trying to keep his thoughts on international politics, professional ice hockey (which worked until his thoughts derailed to skaters in the locker room), kittens in the rain and on to doing algebra equations in his mind in an effort to keep from focusing on the fact that his piece was being driven deeply against this man of his dreams.

The men lay that way for another half an hour, Kodiak trembling against Hunter, until the fire had to be tended. The small room was very warm by then; the place was old but had been well insulated with thick hands full of moss chinked in between the logs and the interior walls lined with flattened cardboard boxes. Black and white 8X10 glossy studio shots of movie stars of the 1950's and sixties were carefully tacked on the walls around the room. The trapper who had done that portion of the work certainly had a sense of whimsey to have packed the head shots this far back into the bush.

Slowly peeling himself out of the body heat warm but now body and sweat wet sleeping bag Hunter got up, shuddering as his own bare feet hit the wooden planks on the floor and poked the fire while adding a few more large rounds of wood. He would have to go outside and get more eventually but for then the wood box was full.

The sleeping bag, though, needed to be dried. Kodiak was still trembling, more now that Hunter had left the bunk. Pulling some dry clothing and socks from his own pack Hunter quickly dressed, re stoked the fire then brought a silver space blanket from him his pack. Another struggle ensued as he managed to ease the now much calmer Kodiak out of the sleeping bag and roll him into the thin blanket. Hunter then turned the wet sleeping bag inside out and tented it over two wooden chairs near the fire place. He then set about mixing several packets of dry soup mix with water into a canteen cup and put it on the metal hanger over the fire, all the while checking on Kodiak.

He kept his longing looks to himself but did allow himself to use a towel he had brought to carefully dry the model's soft, silky blond hair. Hunter wanted to rake his fingers over Kodiak's head, to toy with the curls but chastised himself at the thought of touching Kodiak in an inappropriate way. He needed to revive Kodiak but keep his paws to himself, although he longed to stroke his fingers down over the grooves formed by the acid attack, the lanes curved down the left side of his face now mostly covered by the thickness of beard Kodiak had let grow but clearly kept neatly cut back.

The scars up close made Hunter's stomach clench. He could not imagine the person who would do something like that.

He felt even worse when he remembered what he was there to do. Was taking pictures to sell any different than attacking someone in a physical way? Let alone setting them up to be broadcast on an international live video feed without their knowledge. Shaking his head Hunter realized that morality would have to be put on the back burner to get through this.

Stirring the now hot soup Hunter removed the metal container from over the fire and poured it into a mug.

Re fluffing the sleeping bag to distribute the feathers for faster drying he slipped on a pair of thick work boots a size too large but dry to shuffle outside to the woodpile stacked next to the cabin and brought several arm loads in and placed them carefully into the wood bin, thankful the movie star loving trapper had left the place stocked enough to get by wood wise for a few days.

Once the wood box was filled and he had quickly eaten something Hunter picked up the mukluks Kodiak had loaned him and smoothed his fingers around the top edge, smiling to himself when he felt that the same series of survival tool lumps had been sewn into the top seam of the expertly handmade boots Kodiak had loaned him. He had spent the night before freezing when a flint had been as close as the boots on the floor.

It was hours since the river rescue, the sun had set, and the cabin interior was lit only by the yellow glow of the fire but the cabin was nicely warm, too warm in fact, but Kodiak was still shuddering violently from time to time even after Hunter had managed to get Kodiak to sit up, feeding him sips of the warmed soup until the mug was empty.

"So cold, so cold," Kodiak muttered, "Gotta get Cord," his voice a near whisper, his eye's remained shut the entire time until he slumped over against Hunter. Brushing a hand over Kodiak's head Hunter soothed him then lay Kodiak back down onto the bunk as he fluffed the mostly dry sleeping back up Hunter struggled Kodiak back into it then tended the fire and stripped his clothing off and again to snuggle back down into the bag next to the model, his body yearning for the man he was saving.

The man he was touching but could not touch.

Twelve

The men slept as if they had been drugged. Kodiak was exhausted from the fight, his wounds, cleaning up the mess made by the brawl then tracking his brother and being chased by the wolverine and hypothermia from racing into the river.

Hunter was worn out from lack of sleep the night before, followed by struggle to warm Kodiak up.

And to keep his hand and erection to himself.

The fire had died out as the two slept, but the old cabin, run down as it was, still retained heat well.

Sometime early the next morning Hunter woke, his hard shaft pressing deeply into Kodiak's muscular upper thigh. The model's hands had fallen away from Hunter's crotch and did not stir as Hunter carefully felt the fingers and hands, then feet to make certain they were warm. He was very relived to feel Kodiak's circulation had returned and that his rough hands and sexily large feet were back to a normal temperature before pulling himself out of the sleeping bag, dressing and slipping out of the cabin. He hated the wade through fresh knee-high snow to the sagging log outhouse to empty his bladder. It was still dark but a full moon hung low in the sky giving a brilliant white light which cast long dark shadows of the bare tree branches across the snow and gave Hunter more light than if he was using a flash light to lead him to the privy. Although the sky was clear the temperature had risen, Hunter could see in the distance the brilliantly shining stars were slowly again being covered by a layer of grey and he knew by morning more fresh snow would be covering the woods.

Hunter stamped his feet against the cold as he relieved himself. As he finished the temptation to have a quick go at himself with the thoughts of Kodiak fresh in his mind were tempting but he reprimanded himself. The fire needed to be tended so he quickly re buttoned his jeans and followed his own footprints back through the snow to the cabin.

Back inside Hunter re stoked the fire and finally picked up the rest of the wet clothing strewn about the cabin floor, wringing out what he could he hung the pieces to dry on pegs thoughtfully made by the trapper who had built the cabin. Turning each pair of the soft, carefully made mukluk books inside out he propped all four of them around the fireplace to dry, again marveling at the emergency supplies sewn around the top of the boots.

Looking at Kodiak, Hunter smiled. His quarry was *right there,* and he could not resist.

Crossing the cabin he pulled a small camera out his bag, adjusted the settings and began to snap pictures of Kodiak. The inexpensive camera was nothing compared to the rig he had he brought on the boat the bear had sunk, but in the case the subject mattered more than the device-that old saw about a picture being worth a thousand words was true, and in this case the quality did not even matter as the shots could be sold for almost any sum Hunter would ask. The value of something rare always drove up the worth.

Even if the price would cost him the chance of ever having even a friendship with the handsome model.

The flickering yellow flames of the fire gave just enough light for the shots, Kodiak's sexy, tousled hair curled perfectly around the side of his face, the light was just bright enough to show the furrows of his scars as he slept. The model's face was finally relaxed and calm since he was again warmed through again. The sleeping bag had fallen far enough down Kodiak's shoulder to expose his muscular chest, without realizing it Hunter began to become aroused again as he took the photographs.

The Murdering Model!
Runaway from the Runway!
Wildman of the Tundra!

Tabloid titles flew through his head with each click of the shutter. Hunter reminded himself that if he were not taking the pictures someone else would. Cold comfort for the pain he knew he would be causing Kodiak.

He truly wanted to think that he would just keep these shots for himself but deep inside he knew this was a mercenary mission and that any photograph was going to be available for sale to the highest bidder. Finn would certainly cause a stink that Hunter had sold photo's but the only degree Finn held was in causing stinks. Finn's goal was to embarrass Kodiak and drive him back into the public, not tabloid pictures.

Empires were built on candid photographs in this day and age.

As soon as he got the camera installed in Kodiak's cabin Hunter knew the value of the shots would plummet once the world had full, if illegal (not to mention immoral), access to the scarred model.

Hunter carefully slipped the camera back into his pack on the table, sliding it down to the bottom and shoving socks, gloves, underwear and maps on top of it. With everything back in place he removed his clothing and carefully maneuvered back down in against the warmth of Kodiak's body, his partial erection subsiding as he sternly reminded himself why he was there in the first place.

Greed.

But when you had nothing, was it really greed or survival? It was much easier to live the lie of the latter.

The crackle of the fire soothing him Hunter was just about to drift off to sleep when Kodiak turned roughly against him in the tight confine of the sleeping bag, their naked bodies now face to face, Kodiak's fully hard erection pressing hotly against the flat muscles of Hunter's stomach.

Before he had a chance to react or untangle himself from the gnarl of limbs, body held tightly together inside the sleeping bag, Kodiak moved a hand up to the back of Hunter/s neck.

Splaying his strong fingers over the back of Hunters head the young homesteader gently but firmly pulled their faces together until their lips met in a deep kiss, Kodiak's soft tongue gently but firmly probing between Hunter's lips until he had forced them apart, causing Hunter's heart to and cock to begin racing like a jack hammer.

Startled, but not enough to dismiss the kiss, Hunter met Kodiak's lips in return, greedily, sliding his hands around Kodiak's now warm body, cupping his palms down around the hard cheeks of the homesteader's magnificent ass.

Oh fuck...Hunter sighed as Kodiak eased his tongue out from between their lips then back in between them again, their pre-come sticky cocks smoothing slickly together. Smoothing a hand down between their bodies Kodiak circled the throbbing members, holding them tightly against each other as he began slowly pumping his hips up, moving their dicks as one with Hunter throwing his head back to give a long, low moan.

All that time he had spent longing for and now photographing Kodiak, dreaming and fantasizing about a moment like they were having and now here he was, naked and in his arms.

Hunter slid his fingertips slowly down over Kodiak's smooth back, tracing lightly over his hot, damp skin until his palms were cupped under the homesteaders hard ass cheeks. Pulling Kodiak tightly in against his body while parting his lips and smoothing the tip of his tongue along the models neck. Shuddering Kodiak pulled his own head back and slammed his lips hard back against Hunter's.

If this was Kodiak's way of showing appreciation for the saving of his life Hunter planned to write one hell of a thank you note!

The young men were soon wet again, this time slick with sweat as they continued to passionately kiss, their bodies grinding together with hands roving lightly over each other's skin once Kodiak had released their cocks. Pushing, pulling, prodding; their tongues roved from mouth to neck; passion building with moans and grunts as they ground together, thrashing out of the tight confine of the sleeping bag to roll around on small bunk.

Face to face, bodies pressed tightly together, Hunter moaned as he slid his lips along the column of Kodiak's neck, not breaking the suction of his mouths on reaching the smooth expanse of Kodiak's chest. The model sighed deeply, arching up when Hunter began circling his tongue around this thickening left nipple.

"Oh!…been so long…" Kodiak moaned, eyes closed as he grabbed Hunter's head , slowly dragging it across his chest to his right nipple. As Hunter worked his mouth back and forth over Kodiak's smooth skin the young homesteader eased his hand back down between Hunter's muscular thighs. Grabbing his hard shaft and pushing it down urgently, his thumb sweeping back and forth over the wide head of Hunter's cock, a thick pool of pre come pumping out and oozing down over the throbbing shaft.

"No rubbers man, sorry." Hunter moaned back as Kodiak pressed his the head of his piece back between his thickly muscled thighs, trying to reach his tight hole. Cursing himself that he hadn't thought in a positive enough way that something like this *might* have happened to have brought that kind of protection. "Just relax and you may like this as much."

Rolling off Kodiak, Hunter traced a hand down over the homesteader's muscle ripped body and tightened his fingers around his slick, throbbing cock.

In certain circles a photograph of *that* would have set him for life, but Hunter was too caught up in the moment to even consider stopping the action to dig out his camera.

Gripping Kodiak's hard shaft Hunter began stroking Kodiak off as they continued to kiss, smoothing the thick clear line of pre come oozing from the model's piece over the wide head of the homesteader's dick with his thumb. Hunter had perfected his technique over the years which had never been met with disapproval.

"Oh yeah," Kodiak groaned as Hunter worked him, fist pounding in a blur up and down the length of Kodiak's throbbing cock. It felt like a red-hot poker in the grip of Hunter's fingers.

Fire crackling in the back ground, the only other noise in the small cabin came from Kodiak's increasingly choppy breathing and Hunter's continuing long deep sighs.

"Oh…," moaned Kodiak his body again writhing but not in the way he was shuddering hours earlier. These moves were sensual, his hips rising to meet Hunters grip. "Oh yeah!"

"Like that?" Hunter whispered, bringing his lips up to Kodiak's earlobe to gently take the small, rounded flap of skin lightly in his teeth. "I've wanted to do this for so fucking long." His own thick shaft throbbing as it strung a line of clear, sticky pre-come down onto the sweat damp sleeping bag.

Moaning, his body raising up off the small bunk made of carefully stripped medium size spruce logs which were now squeaking a symphony against the thrashing of the men, Kodiak gave a loud yowl as his piece began to throb in the hot, slick grip of Hunter's fist, thick spatters of come slashing up over the tiny black happy trail of hair which ran down the length of his torso to end in the now slightly matted tangle of glossy blonde pubic hair his cock pushed out from.

Both of their bodies where tightened, muscles tense as their climaxes built at the same time.

"Yes, Hell YES!" the young homesteader cried while reaching out with his own fist, grabbing Hunter's fingers and holding them tight as his load continued to pump out hot slashes, his sticky come trailing down over Hunters hand as the scent of his load filled the small cabin space.

"Oh, man, oh…" Kodiak trailed off, eyes still tightly shut as Hunter slid a hand down into his own crotch while still finishing Kodiak off, the model's load trailing sexily over his own fingers. Tightening his fist around his own piece Hunter grit his own teeth and finished himself off with an eye rolling orgasm of his own, his hot come slashing out over Kodiak's thigh in a hot, thick line.

By the time Hunter finished with his own orgasm Kodiak was gently snoring again, snaking an arm out of the again sweat damp sleeping bag to snag a thick wool sock from the floor and managed a fast-sloppy wipe down before snuggling back down into the bag. He drifted into a deep sleep of his own wrapped against the man he had just been intimate with, thinking of the irony that he had not only just saved Kodiak's life but that he had come to the bush to exploit him in the worst possible way and thankful that he had restrained himself, that Kodiak had been the one to initiate the intimacy they had just shared.

By the time the pair woke with a start again hours later the fire had burned down to a glowing bed of embers and several new feet of snow had fallen around the remote cabin.

Grudgingly Hunter pulled himself away from the warmth of Kodiak's body. With a shiver he padded naked and barefoot across the cold wooden planks of the floor. Stoking the coals he then added several thick cuts of wood to the rapidly re igniting fire, smiling to himself as flames curled up over the logs. Turning back toward the single bunk his eyes met Kodiak's, the smile fading from his lips immediately.

The hot homesteader had shoved a hand down into his crotch, bringing his now come sticky fingers back up and was staring at them, slowly pulling the digits apart and glaring through the web like strings of his release at Hunter.

"What the…" he growled, "what is *this,* why are *you* NAKED and where is my brother?"

"Sorry, I didn't do a very good clean up job," a startled Hunter replied in a low voice. They had just been as close as humans can be. He wasn't expecting Kodiak would be in a good mood or even grateful but for fucks sake, he did expect the coupling would have left his new cabin mate relaxed at least.

"Why am *I* naked? Did you take advantage of me?" Kodiak demanded prudishly, pushing the flap of the sleeping bag aside to pull his legs out, bunching a handful of the sleeping bag modestly down into his crotch. Kodiak had never expected to see the interloper to his homestead life again, let alone to find himself naked in front of him in a remote cabin.

"NO, I didn't fuck you! *YOU* grabbed me and then some stuff happened," Hunter sputtered while grabbing at his now dry clothes and beginning to scramble into them. "You ran into the river and I literally fished you out. We were naked for warmth and body heat. Some bushman *you* are. I've saved your ass literally twice now!"

Carefully keeping himself covered Kodiak winced as he began to move his aching and stiff body up out of the sleeping bag, snagging the edge of the bright silver space blanket he lifted it from the side of the bed where it had been tossed and wrapped it around himself as he got up, feet stumbling as he moved to the wall where the drying clothing hung on pegs and began rummaging for his.

"Where's my brother?" Kodiak demanded while feeling the mostly wet clothing and trying to ignore the sticky situation in his crotch for a moment.

"I have no idea where your brother might be. Anchorage? Seattle? Tahiti?" Hunter, who had been pulling into his own clothing as the accusations flew, reached behind Kodiak and grabbed the sleeping bag, fluffing it and again carefully turning it inside out to dry.

"How long have I been here anyway."

Hunter shrugged, "Day and a half, about. Took a while to get your core temperature back up, man. What's the rush? Got a reservation somewhere for dinner?"

Kodiak, memory finally again fully engaged, was able to recall why he was in the cabin with the intruder in the first place, said nothing to Hunters snark. He was grudgingly impressed by the skill Hunter had shown in both keeping him alive after the accident and the care he was using in keeping the sleeping bag dry. Little things like that were the difference between life and death here in the bush.

"Well thank you for pulling me out of the water," Kodiak said, grumbling the words out as if they cost a hundred bucks each. "It was either the river or finish a dance with a wounded wolverine." Kodiak hated that he again felt a knot of attraction toward Hunter and hated even more that they had just clearly been intimate and he only remembered the encounter as a dimly lit dream. A very nice dream but one he had never intended to bring to reality.

Even more he hated that he wanted to grab the sexy intruder and kiss him right that moment.

"Actually, you kind of saved both of us," Hunter pointed to the still opened top of the mukluk Kodiak had been wearing. "Lost my fire-starting stuff in the river and you managed to let me know where the fire starter was. So on the lifesaving count I guess we are one up."

Fully dressed by then Hunter crossed the room and pulled a pair of jeans, flannel shirt and thermal undershirt out of his pack, along with a thick pair of wool socks and handed them over to Kodiak.

"It looks," Hunter said as he stepped up next to Kodiak with the elastic bandage, "like you may have tangled with something, or someone one, else along the way. You had this on so I probably should help you back into it. And we are now Even Steven on the dry clothes front too."

"Except that you still have my mukluks," Kodiak reminded him before going silent and allowing Hunter to begin wrapping the now dry bandage slowly and carefully around his body as he stared straight ahead. The homesteader offered no information about why he was wearing the bandage. Kodiak grit his teeth as Hunter cinched him up, trying to show that he was in as little pain as possible even though each move of the bandage felt like he was again being beaten by a length of stove wood.

Both men internally sighed as the warm flesh of Hunter's fingers grazed over Kodiak's body in the process of wrapping him back up.

The model, sweat damp hair sexily grazing his shoulders, grunted a thank you as he stood, quickly moving to the rough chair next to the table he sat down and began to dress. The thin space blanket was still wrapped around his shoulders and now floated around him like the cape of a superhero. Without wanting it to Kodiak's body had begun to react to the slight touch of Hunters fingers and he did not want the reaction to show so was happy to have the billowy material floating around his frame. It took every ounce of will power each of the young men possessed to keep from grabbing each other again. Kodiak did not make a move as he was determined not to let this phony, liar and cheat take him again and Hunter knew Kodiak would snarl as loudly as the rouge bear they had seen if he tried to make a move after the lecture he had just been given about taking advantage. Even if Hunter knew he had certainly *not* put the move on Kodiak. He had just been in the right place at the right time.

Kodiak grudgingly admitted to himself that Hunter did have some survival skill. He had wrapped the bandage with the care of an ER nurse and knew enough to begin drying out the sleeping bag as soon as Kodiak had gotten out of it. He hadn't figured out that there was a flint stick sewn into the top of the mukluks and hadn't produced a bush plane to help search for Cord, but in Kodiak's book his basic skills were on point, for a lying schemer.

"Then my mom saved us," Kodiak said while struggling into the clothing. "She always sewed the survival gear into our Mukluks. I have to find my brother." The homesteader gave a brief explanation that Cord was trying to hike out of the bush with only a few supplies and a bad attitude. He left out the details of the fight between the two young men because Hunter just did not need to know. Thankfully his various wounds including the probably cracked ribs and black eyes blended right into the story of the wolverine. He decided to let Hunter think nature had a hand in tearing him up instead of his own brother.

"I hate to be the one to point this out," Hunter began slowly, "but wouldn't *this* have been a good time for you to have fired off that SPOT signal for help?"

Kodiak gave the intruder a glare that could have cut diamonds.

"Cord took it with him and I do hope he uses it. Meantime I'm going to need to borrow some of your supplies."

"You are kinda outa luck there man, I'm only up here for a short time so I didn't bring much," Hunter shrugged while tossing another log onto the fireplace.

"But take what you want." Hunter said with a nod toward the small pack he had left on the table, it took only moments for Kodiak to plow through the assortment of dehydrated food. With a snort of disgust he stroked his fingers through his thick hair and shook his head.

"That's about enough for two meals each," Kodiak muttered, "When is your pick up?"

"Waddya mean, pick up." Hunter challenged, cagily wanting to keep as much of his own information to himself as possible.

"I mean when is the plane or boat or dog sled or snow machine or UFO coming in to haul your sorry butt out of these woods. No one comes in with that little food without having arranged to get the hell out of here someway. I don't even see any snow shoes so I know you weren't expecting to walk out of here. Since you saved me I'm not even going to grill you about what the hell you are doing here anyway."

"Not that it involves you," Hunter said with defiance and guilt, "and why I am here is none of your business."

He was only there *because* of the sexy homesteader. "But I'm checking snow levels and I'm going to monitor winter fish run."

His words had lost conviction by the time he finished, still holding onto the now flimsy mask that he was a game warden.

"The snow is deep and fish don't run in the winter." Kodiak sighed, it was pretty simple. He was not really listening to Hunter anyway, his mind was racing like he was running a marathon. Cord was out there, miles from nowhere, no shelter and very little in the way of supplies with an angry bear stalking the territory and now a wounded wolverine could be on the prowl as well. Not to mention wolf packs, moose foraging for tender willow branches, huge animals who could crush a human as quickly and easily as a person smashing an aluminum can.

While Cord had made it through one night as evidenced by the camp, but how many more would he get through? Kodiak's own meager inventory of supplies had been destroyed and this dope, Hunter, might as well have brought a handful of magic beans to the party for all the good the meager supplies he had brought would do. In his mind Kodiak saw an over view map of where they were, the river and how far it was back to the cabin and on to the nearest village.

Every point of reference was wilderness spread hopelessly far apart now covered in fresh snow. If Cord had gotten cold or hungry enough he might have gone back to the homestead but there was no way of knowing unless the homesteader went back there on his own. Which would be useless. The last tracks of Cord's were heading away from the camp, he was not going back there.

Of course Cord could also have fallen into the river by then, not to mention that he likely had some injuries from their fight.

Kodiak put his head down into his hands in momentary despair.

"Hey, it's going to be alright." Hunter said softly as Kodiak lifted his head then raked his fingers sexily back through his hair.

Ignoring the platitude Kodiak drew in a deep breath and slid to the edge of the bed and began to struggle into his still damp mukluks.

"Hey, c'mon man." Hunter said, "it's nearly dark and look," he said while opening the front door to the cabin to reveal the thick new blanket of snow that had fallen in the hours since he had been up to use the outhouse, "it's still snowing."

The news caused Kodiak to pause, he hated that Hunter was right as much as he hated being trapped in the cabin with the sexy intruder to his world.

"C'mon. I'll make us something to eat, we'll get some more rest and head out first light."

"You can make food and in the morning *I* will head out."

Keeping his mouth shut Hunter set about mixing several packets of dehydrated stew with water he had gotten from the river into a small cast iron kettle, which he hung over the now roaring fire as Kodiak slowly backed his feet out of the wet mukluk boot and set about arranging it in front of the fire to dry. Pulling a length of the leather lacing out he deftly twisted the soft strap until it broke. Sitting back down onto the edge of the bunk he again drug his fingers through his thick, unruly hair and used the piece of leather to tie his hair back then stared into the flames in the fireplace with another deep sigh.

Sometime later, when the simple supper had been finished in silence and the pair sat quietly in front of the fire, Kodiak finally spoke again.

"Ok, here's the plan." He wasn't looking for or asking for input, Hunter could tell. "This is a bad situation; my brother's life is at stake and you are putting your own stupid self in danger by just being here. For which I am stupidly grateful because if you hadn't been here to pull me out of the river *I* wouldn't be here, so I am not asking questions because I don't think you would tell me the truth and because if you did tell me the truth about why you are here I would like that even less."

Hunter said nothing.

"Whatever you are up to I can't imagine and don't care. I don't expect you were planning to be here for longer than three weeks or so based on what I see you have brought. Your pick up is certainly going to be here faster than anyone checking on me, but I don't have time to waste with Cord out there."

Again, being sensible, Hunter was keeping his mouth shut.

"I've changed my mind. Tomorrow you *are* coming with me. We are going to go over to the cave where I keep my deep winter supplies. As you can see I am pretty banged up and I don't feel confident I can make it on my own. I don't like saying it, but I need you. I don't want you, but I need you."

There was a pause before Kodiak continued.

"Then we will go back to check the homestead to see if Cord came to his senses and gone back there. I don't think he has but with all of this new snow there is no way to follow a trail."

Standing Kodiak poked at the fire and added another log. He had stripped back down to his long john top, the warm waffle weave material tightly formed to his chest, allowing a small tuft of slick dark blond hair to spill out from the button fastening, the teasing view of his chest driving Hunter crazy. This was the shot he wanted, it would bring him a small fortune. The homesteader in this cabin exuding sexuality as he stood in front of the flickering flames of the fireplace. Hunter's crotch was filled, head nodding absently as Kodiak continued. While Hunter itched to ease over to the table and try to get his fingers wrapped around the camera he knew he had no choice but to sit this shot out. Selfishly he wanted the picture of the former model for himself.

"If he hasn't gone back to the cabin then I have to go on in the direction of the nearest village, I have to go, I have to." Hunter knew Kodiak was saying this to himself, not to Hunter. Given the condition the former model was in Hunter doubted Kodiak could make it to the outhouse, let alone to a village.

"I'll mark a map back at the homestead for the route out I am going to try since I won't be able to track Cord now because of the new snow. When your pick up arrives you will then take that route and hopefully not find our bodies." Kodiak ran his fingers through his hair again, causing Hunter's crotch to leap as his sexiness. "I have a roll of bright orange plastic survey ribbon back as the cabin that I will use to mark where I am each night. It will easily show up against the snow from overhead."

"Um, yeah, that's, whatever works for you." Hunter mumbled as Kodiak limped his way painfully across the cabin to the fireplace to pour himself another cup of coffee from the pot Hunter had hung over the fire after he had cleaned up from dinner.

Kodiak was in no position to be tracking any one, but Hunter knew it would be futile to try and talk him out of trying to go farther while looking for his brother.

However, he thought devilishly to himself, *there might be a photo op while they were slogging through the snow. Hell, I might even get him to legit pose out on the tundra for a picture!*

Rising, a slight smile forming on his lips, Hunter went to the table and rummaged in one of the small packs. Bringing out a small silver flask he took a fast hit, then offered it over to Kodiak.

"That's illegal up here," The homesteader said flatly, "remember?"

"Don't be sanctimonious. I've seen your bar, remember?" Hunter shrugged on his way back to the only chair in the cabin. Settling down into it he took another small pull on the flask then offered it over to Kodiak.

"Make it a sip in celebration to your being alive. It's still snowing, we can't do anything until morning so c'mon and have a little snort or two with me."

This time Kodiak, with some hesitation, reached out and accepted the flask, taking a heady swallow.

"Shoulda pushed some of that down you yesterday, woulda given you a real kickstart."

Hunter smiled. Kodiak took another gulp and shuddered as the fiery liquor burned down his throat as he handed the flask back to Hunter then moved back to the small frame bed.

"What the fuck is it like to be so fucking hot." Hunter said, realizing he had allowed his body to voice what he meant to keep in his head.

"Huh" was Kodiak's startled reply.

"You. You are just hot in every way." Hunter gushed on, cock beginning to thicken. He hadn't meant to take this plunge but since he was here there was no holding back.

"Wha, I mean, we are in a crisis here and you want to talk about what I look like? And stop with the eff bombs man, they are rude!"

"It's hard not to wonder what it's like to be wanted by *everyone.* I mean, yeah, I know we are in trouble. Well your brother is in trouble. You have a plan." Hunter took another drink and handed the flask back over to Kodiak. "But meantime," he went on, an arm waving expansively around the air in the cabin, "we have a roof, fire, food and some time to reflect." The liquor had taken over, somewhere in the primordial back of his brain a whole crew of neurons were going into over drive hoping to shut him up but the train seemed to have left the station and was in runaway mode.

"I mean come on! You are a model for freak's sake! Why the hell are you out here in the middle of nowhere when you should be in New York walking a runway or getting waaaay over paid to sit and look pretty! Man! Why the would you give that up!"

Hunter reached for the flask, but Kodiak held it away from him.

"You've had enough."

"C'mon man, just give me an answer. Why does a guy who has it all give it all up and come up here?"

"Not that it is *any* of your business, but as you have figured out I am damaged goods." Kodiak said quietly before suddenly reaching out and snagging the flask from

Hunter's hand.

"Hey! C'mon, give it!" Hunter protested, swiping a hand through the air as he tried to grab the cheap metal container from Kodiak's grip.

In one smooth move Kodiak turned the small flask upside down, emptying it onto the floor then tossing the empty container back into Hunter's lap.

"How do you know I don't have a bottle in there?" Hunter said with a nod toward the pack on the table.

"Because even you don't seem to be that stupid."

Making a "pistol" of his thumb and forefinger Hunter pointed it Kodiak.

"Then you, my friend, are wrong because I am that dumb."

Jumping up and jamming a hand quickly back into the bag on the table Hunter pulled out a small bottle of amber colored whiskey more than half empty. Twisting the cap off he took another fast swallow, his face puckering cartoonishly as the liquor burned down his throat.

"C'mon, I'll let you have swig if you promise not to pour it out again."

"What's your game, man. Why are *you* here, with no supplies in this cabin after showing up on the river. Not to mention all but raping me."

"Dude, *you* initiated that fun with me, man, and both times I showed up I saved your ass. Literally. In some cultures that means a debt to be paid." Hunter said with a grin and a long stretch. The liquor had relaxed him enough to offer a grin at Kodiak, who looked sexy even with a scowl on his face. "Besides, we made out and I jacked you off. That's not a lot more than a gay handshake."

Kodiak gave Hunter a scathing look as he crossed the

small room in just a few steps, grabbing the pack still on the floor and slamming it onto the table. Lifting the bag Kodiak emptied it, scattering Hunters goods across the rough-hewn planks. Socks, underwear, and the camera tracked out over the table top.

"Is that all of the liquor?"

"Yes, offer still holds through," Hunter stepped toward Kodiak, taking another sip he pushed the bottle out toward Kodiak.

Grabbing the bottle Kodiak capped it then slammed the bottle into the pocket of his own jacket. He rummaged through the assorted clothing on the table top then without looking at Hunter picked up the camera.

Clicking through the digital pictures Kodiak moved the random shots Hunter had taken over the last few weeks, which included the shots he had just taken of Kodiak.

"Hey, that's mine!" Hunter snapped as he unsteadily got up and lunged for the camera. Kodiak, head still down and looking into the viewfinder.

"Gimme!" falling forward Hunter tried to grab the camera out of Kodiak's hands again as the former model kept his eyes glued to the device, rage crossing his features as he slowly clicked through the shots Hunter had taken of him in the sleeping bag.

Moving like lightening Kodiak lifted the camera, holding it away from Hunter he side-stepped him and moved to the door.

Flinging the door open Kodiak cocked his arm back and pistoned the camera into the air. The small device arched high through the cold night, the homesteader kept the door open until he heard the satisfying splash of the camera landing in the murmuring rapids of the river.

Thirteen

Slamming the cabin door shut, well, slamming the cabin door closed again as best he was able in a hand-crafted log shed built with no plumb or level, his side still feeling like a bowie knife had been plunged into it, Kodiak turned and went back to the table. Sifting through every item he turned the pack inside out, inspecting the seams until he was satisfied no other camera had been secreted in Hunter's belongings.

"You can't just take my shit!" Hunter finally protested, weakly, knowing Kodiak was in the right. And that at least one piece of his *shit* had already been taken and tossed into the river.

"You are lucky I didn't throw your ass out there, too." Kodiak said as he crossed the room and stoked the fire again.

"I'm sorry. Like I said, you are so damn hot, and I've seen you in magazines and on television all these years I just thought I'd have a souvenir of my moment with *the Kodiak DePaul...*"

"Bullshit. You can't even just say *I'm sorry, I messed up!* You were going to sell those pictures to the highest bidder."

"No, I," Hunter started, quickly cut off by Kodiak.

"I knew you were a phony from the second you rounded the bend in the river piloting that skiff."

"And again, had I not come around when I had that bear would have eaten your ass." Hunter tried to argue, not bothering to try and defend his lie of being a game warden.

Despite the flaring anger from both young men the unspoken underlying sexual energy crackled between the two as they stared at each other before Kodiak finally spoke again.

"The confirmation that you were phony the minute I took your hand to take the quill out of your stupid thumb." Kodiak went on, ignoring the interruptions by Hunter. "Your skin is as soft as rabbit fur. If you'd worked a summer in the bush your hands would be like river rock. Damn cheechako."

"Hey! I'm a lot of shit but I ain't no fuckin' cheechako!" Hunter countered, furious to be referred to as a tenderfoot in the bush. "I was born and raised here just like you, buddy boy!"

"Sure, Anchorage? Eagle River? Or were you raised in the "wilds" of the state capitol down on the panhandle?" Kodiak challenged, "Might as well be from Seattle."

"Palmer, dipshit." Hunter muttered, wondering how the fuck he could be so turned on by this asshole at that moment. "I'm from Palmer."

"Palmer might as well be Anchorage and Anchorage is pretty much the same as Portland these days." Kodiak said with a laughed that sounded more like a snarl. "Doesn't matter where you are from anyway, what *matters* is whether or not you have any more camera's and if you have set one up in here.? Is that why you had sex with me? Gonna build a Kardashian empire by selling it for a million bucks? Got a buyer lined up already I bet." Kodiak snorted, angry with himself for being as turned on by Hunter as he was angry with him, fully dressed in the small cabin with the fireplace roaring was causing sweat to track down the faces of both men.

"Cheap slime is all you are and ever will be!" Kodiak snapped. "Besides, I'm old news buddy. The joke would have been on you."

"Fuck you," Hunter fumed back as he began to suddenly undo the buttons of his shirt. Peeling it off he balled the material up and heaved it across the table, the flannel bouncing off Kodiak's chest and falling to the cabin floor.

Sitting down Hunter stripped back out of the soft leather mukluks then stood and shucked the flannel lined jeans he was wearing down over his muscular legs then began popping the buttons of the skin-tight waffle weave union suit underwear next to his skin.

"Hey! What are you doing man?" Kodiak protested.

Peeling the top portion of the form fitting long underwear back over his shoulders Hunter shoved the material down over his body, skimming the long johns over his hips then exposing his groin as he pushed the leg portions down over his calves as his socks balled into the bottom of the underwear and he shook his now bare feet free of the tangled material.

"There!" Hunter said, spinning his naked frame in front of Kodiak. "Does this prove that I don't have any hidden cameras on me? Huh?"

Kodiak felt his dick start to thicken as this enemy, this man he was in the middle of an argument with and was now wearing only a sexy strap of leather around his neck which dangled sexily down over the center of his heaving chest, suddenly had him more excited and turned on than he could remember being in a very long time.

"Put your damn clothes back on," Kodiak muttered, hating the way he felt his body betraying him.

"What, you are suddenly King of this cabin and in charge of what everyone does? You are a guest here in *my* space." With that Hunter grabbed a small flashlight that Kodiak had dislodged from the backpack on the table and began shining it into the corners of the cabin, the light refracting off the cracked, grey logs.

"I wish I *had* installed a camera and was going to try and sell a sex tape for a million bucks. You fucking flatter yourself with that, by the way." Hunter shouted all the while guiltily knowing that was *exactly* his money-grubbing little plan.

"Stop," Kodiak said, bending down and snagging Hunters shirt and tossing it back at the naked young man. The homesteader was suddenly tired of this argument and just wanted to sit down to hide the fact that he was now fully, ragingly erect and wanted nothing more than to sit down to hide the embarrassing situation. "And I told you, knock off the eff bombs." Kodiak finished half-heartedly.

Coming around the table, flashlight beam crisscrossing back and forth into the dark upper corners of the cabin.

"Happy? See any lens reflections up there?"

Hunter was standing right next to Kodiak, holding the light up afforded Kodiak a view of the sexy dark tuft of hair under his arm. Kodiak suppressed a moan, he didn't know how his throwing out the camera and making an accusation had so quickly led to his forgetting about the camera and concentrating on the now naked man next to him.

Both men were nearly panting by then, both from the heat and, yet to be known to both of them at the same time, the sexual tension which filled the room.

Hunter swung the flashlight down into Kodiak's crotch.

"What's that?"

Kodiak took a fast, short breath, the circle of bright light was fully exposing the fact that he was sporting a full, throbbing erection.

"Looks like you are ready for round two…" stepping forward Hunter brushed the wide head of his thickening shaft feather like across the side of Kodiak's exposed neck, which caused theyoung homesteader to shudder involuntarily.

"Cat got your tongue?" Hunter whispered as he snapped off the flashlight and dropped a hand down into Kodiak's crotch. "I think," he said as his fingers caressed Kodiak through the thick material of his pants, "it would be better to say that *I* have your dick."

Suppressing a moan Kodi stood, pulling away from the naked man next to him. This was the second time his body had betrayed him next to Hunter and Kodiak did not like the feeling. Especially the feeling that if they ended up next to each other like this again that he might give in to the temptation.

"Stop it." was all Kodiak managed to hoarsely croak, he wanted Hunter, wanted him as badly as the giant bear had wanted salmon; as much as Hillary wanted that seat in the oval office. It had been a long time, too long, since Kodiak had allowed himself to act on raw feelings and look where that had gotten him, a ruined face and self-imposed exile.

The two men looked at each other intensely, the light

from the flames giving the room and Hunter's skin a golden glow. Even from where he stood Kodi could smell the lingering scent of soap on Hunter's body, his fingers nearly vibrated remembering the touch of Hunter's mouth,of his smooth, taunt skin and the ripples of muscle riding just under the tan flesh. Kodiak's dick throbbed as his tongue could almost taste the salty skin of Hunter's shaft.

Easy, it would be so easy to reach out for Hunter, to accept his embrace. Despite Kodi's anger at what Hunter had tried to pull by stealing his image, Kodiak was still a man who knew what he wanted, and what he wanted was presenting itself right in front of him ripe and ready for the taking.

But want was not need, and right then Kodiak knew that this situation called for him to keep all his focus and energy on finding his brother. He would have to deal with Hunter's deceit later.

"C'mon man," Hunter urged in a low, sexy growl sounding exactly the way the snake must have sounded to Adam.

"Put your clothes back on." Kodiak said again sternly with grit teeth as he turned to face the fire while willing his dick into submission. "We have a lot to do and need to get some rest."

Hunter crossed the room, picking up discarded clothing with each step, slowly re dressing then sitting down on the edge of the bunk.

Despite his honesty (and theatrics) in showing Kodiak he was not holding a camera on his person Hunter was glad to have carefully tucked the small video camera he had packed in under a floorboard of the cabin soon after he had arrived at the old cabin. He knew no one was around for miles but after Sam Chigliac and the beautiful lead dog of his team, Yukon, had materialized out of nowhere on Kodiak's homestead his gut had told him that anything was possible even here in the far north and that some secrets should be kept secret.

"Have you really wintered over up here, alone?" Hunter finally asked while buttoning the thick red flannel shirt up over his chest.

"Of course," Kodiak snorted in reply. "You think I did all of that now destroyed prep work for fun?"

"What do you mean, destroyed."

"Cord and I had a fight. He messed some stuff up before storming off. We'll get by." Kodiak said by way of an abbreviated explanation.

"I kind of figured you guys weren't reading poetry by the firelight when I saw your face." Hunter said, settling back down next to the hearth. "Isn't the isolation unbearable?"

Kodiak shrugged while sitting back down into the chair.

"Cities are full of crap like you."

Hunter had nothing to argue back with there.

"Christmas, New Year's Eve, Valentine's Day-do you celebrate anything?"

"Look, you have no idea what it is to be able to live with yourself," Kodiak snapped. "I *like* myself and that is all I need to get by. Being alone up here alone is paradise for me." There was a long pause before Kodiak slowly moved his head and locked eyes with Hunter, a smile crossing his lips. The same sexy smile Hunter had seen look back him in numerous magazine ads.

"You can't take that from me. No one can."

"I wasn't trying," Hunter started.

"Sure you weren't," Kodiak countered flatly. Standing the young homesteader moved toward one of the small grime covered windows. "I live, the rest of you survive. You may think you are doing better than I am but this, here, this, forest, snow, cabin, is living for me."

Hunter, the heat of the liquor still working on him, felt weak and started to tell Kodiak why he was taking the photos, what the security of the money being offered meant to him but knew the abused homesteader could not understand. If he were in Kodiak's position he would not be able to understand either.

"We are going to have to work together to at least try and save Cord. I don't want to, but you are here so we are stuck. Up here I don't have to protect my image from people like you," Kodiak quietly finished.

Turning his profile breathtaking to Hunter, Kodiak looked up above the door, his eyes drawn out of the small window set into the logs. Hunter's stomach clenched at Kodiak's beauty when he smiled.

"Look!" Kodiak, exclaimed, his voice suddenly trembling with excitement.

Rising Hunter looked out of the window, Kodiak brushing by him. The homesteader grabbed his outer coat and began sliding his arms into it then re crossed the room, throwing the cabin door open again, standing in the open doorway.

"Hey!" It took forever for me to get this place warm and now you are trying to heat up the great outdoors!" Hunter bellowed

"Just look." Kodiak said without looking back into the cabin.

"I don't know what you are doing," Hunter said, teeth clenched as he buttoned his shirt all the way up and grabbing his own coat and zipping it up while pulling his gloves on over his fingers, "but I'm freezing again."

Stepping out of the cabin door he closed it and looked up, gasping in awe.

The sky was ablaze with color, emerald green, azure blue shot with ribbons of pale yellow moving in slow, lazy streaks like a symphony across the vast sky.

"This, this is why I'm here." Kodiak whispered as the Aurora Borealis played lazily above them, the vibrant colors stretching as far as their eyes could see, dotted behind with glistening white stars. That far north in the crystal-clear skies the colors were deep and crisp as they moved in long, easy waves under the stars, the galaxy looking like a black velvet backdrop.

The two young men stood silently side by side, huffing plumes of the cold air out as they breathed, transfixed by the curving colors moving around night sky.

"It's like a Georgia O'Keefe painting." Hunter whispered, his right arm raising he traced a finger to outline a ribbon of green rimmed with electric yellow. "I've seen a lot of night sky shows but never anything like this."

"O'Keefe used almost these exact colors. She painted music just like Picasso painted light in the air. It's ethereal." Kodiak whispered in return, as if raised voices might break the spell.

Shoulder to shoulder the pair stood quietly for some time watching the colors move languidly across the sky, the cold night air seeming to crackle around them. They likely would have stayed there longer had Hunter not suddenly shuddered violently.

Kodiak had made the move to pull Hunter in against

him involuntarily. He was cold as well but he was not ready to go back into the cabin.

"Aquarius is there, Pegasus over there," Kodiak said in a low voice as he pointed out the clearly outlined constellations visible at that time of year. "Cancer and Orion are over there," the homesteader used his finger as a pointer to trace the stars with his finger.

Reaching up with his own hand Hunter pointed at the Big Dipper which was standing out brighter than the stars around it, with the North Star looking as big as the moon.

Boldly moving a hand over to Kodiak, Hunter reached over and traced a finger over the area of Kodiak's jacket where the constellation was tattooed on his chest then turned his face toward the handsome homesteader.

"I like where it is there better," he whispered.

Kodiak turned just as Hunter was speaking to say something more about the amazing light show of the Northern Lights being displayed above them, their lips meeting accidentally, but the resulting kiss was far more than just an un planned moment.

As their mouths met under the gently moving lights of soft yellow, green, blue and blush of pink in the sky the men turned, bodies pressing together, thickening erections pushing at the heavy winter gear as their gloved hands began to rove up and down over each other's backs. The tentative meeting of lips became a passionate kiss, after the impromptu strip tease by Hunter a short time earlier even Kodiak's Fort Knox like defenses were down. The romance of making out under the multi colored natural lights moving slowly across the sky would have tempted the most rigid mother Superior to break her vow of chastity.

Kodiak did not *want* to be involved in the kiss, but it

was as natural and easy as the involuntary sex had been earlier.   Something he could not control and in the deepest part of his mind did not want to control.

Hunter's lips were soft, he still tasted of the liquor, but Kodiak didn't mind. He allowed his body to melt in against the phony game warden, his hands roving slowly up and down over the young man's muscular back as they ground against each other with the brilliant, soft Northern lights wavering back and forth above them.

The moment was the first in a long time that made Kodiak feel whole. He was in that brief time with his lips firmly pressed against Hunter's complete again. There was no before or after the incident. No missing Charles or Jimmy, just the delicious feel of being lost in the feeling of the moment.

The kiss ended slowly, naturally. Hunter was smiling from ear to ear, trying to get Kodiak to look him in the eye but the young homesteader only coughed and shuffled his feet, turning away and averting his eyes back to the sky before he finally spoke again.

"Show's over, back inside," Kodi mumbled, feeling guilty over the un intended kiss although he enjoyed every second of it. "Last thing we need is *you* getting sick."

Deciding to accept a half-loaf accidental kiss rather than no kisses at all from the homesteader, Hunter silently followed Kodiak back into the cabin where the pair settled in front of the fireplace.

"If I promise to behave could I have another shot of that booze?" Hunter pled.

Against his better judgement Kodiak reluctantly brought the bottle out and handed it over to Hunter with a stern look. He was still reeling from the kiss, while he did not want to give Hunter the bottle Kodiak knew giving him the liquor was a good distraction from what had just happened under the stars.

After a drink Hunter handed the bottle back to Kodiak, who took a turn, the bottle silently passing back and forth between the men a few times before Hunter spoke again.

"So, the kiss, what was that all about?" Hunter finally asked.

"Shouldn't have happened. You were cold, and I was caught up in the moment." Kodiak mumbled through grit teeth. He wanted to be kissing again, to press against Hunter, taste his mouth and feel his lips again but he knew he had to keep those feelings tamped down. Once he found Cord and got him back to the cabin he would leave Hunter on his own. The dope had managed to get himself up here into the wilderness which meant he could certainly get himself out of the wild.

Despite the temptation of a hot intruder Kodiak DePaul was out of the love business.

"Or, and just hear me out here, you are so attracted to me you couldn't help but kiss me."

"Isn't there a dumb old song that says something like *a kiss is just a kiss.*" Kodiak said flatly.

"Don't you ever feel like that tree frog, the one who freezes solid for the winter? No social life, seeing people? Is that what you want to be like for the rest of your life?"

The Wood frog which lived that far north did not freeze solid. It's metabolism did slow to that of near death, for months at a time the far north amphibian would hibernate in the frozen world. The small frog could cycle in and out of a state of near animation over and over through deep freezing temperatures. In the spring, break up as it is known in Alaska, the frog would burrow back out of the mud to eat and mate.

Kodiak knew how closely his life had come to resemble the frog but was not about to admit that to Hunter. It was not a life to suit everyone but it suited him.

"Seen enough people to last me," Kodiak retuned in a low voice.

"What about, you know," Hunter jerked his head toward the bed where the sleeping bag lay like an open yawn. "Don't you miss that."

Kodiak absently ran a thumb along one of the crooked edges of one of the raised scars on his cheek.

"What is it with your concern about my life and wellbeing? You just can't let that go. It is no business or concern of yours." There was a pause before Kodiak continued. "I've learned you can get used to almost anything," he said softly, his fingers absently tracing along one of the scars on his face.

"But you had everything and gave it up, man! This huge career as a model with looks that are like a,ah,a, I, I don't know, a superpower!" Hunter stuttered, "your pictures were everywhere! That would have led to movies and television. Not to mention that you could write your own ticket in the states! And here, up here you could have run for fucking Governor! You were more well-known than Sarah fuckin' Palin!"

"*Language!*" Kodiak snarled. A few minutes later when he had calmed down, he continued. "Everything has a price," Kodiak said softly, eyes fixed into the fire, "a price more than I was willing to pay."

"Yeah, tough work." Hunter said with a grimace,

"Put on these nice clothes while someone takes pictures. Hard life."

For the first time since they had been together Kodiak laughed, a deep, rich chortle which filled the small room and made Hunter smile, a smile which travelled all of the way down into his stomach and continued tingling down into his crotch. He was getting used to the sullen, angry sexy as hell Kodiak so this fun, exciting laugh took him totally off guard.

"Everyone thinks that," Kodiak said, remembering the anger and degradation of some of his experiences as a model. "I guess it does work for some people. But those are the ones who never realize that they have sold their soul." Kodiak said, reflecting to himself how on one of his first shoots after the reality show the photographer had just assumed the young model would easily and quickly strip out of his underwear. The man had shrugged and assured Kodiak that there were many, many more who would do that and much more to get to where he was. Then there had been the photographer who had simply taken what he wanted despite Kodiak's protests.

"Are you really even from Alaska? Kodiak asked after another long period of silence had hung between the pair. Kodiak needed a distraction to keep his hands to himself and his mind from churning with worry over Cord or turning back to the dark moments with the abusive photographer.

"Do you think a tenderfoot could have gotten back up here, that a pilot would bring someone who didn't know the bush back to this cabin? I'm here to set some snow depth meter's and monitor fish runs. I'll come back up in February and again in April to check the meters." Hunter smoothly lied.

"Why don't you have any equipment? Measure sticks, stuff like that?"

"Going green man, just going to cut some willow branches and notch them. I'll measure 'emin the spring." Hunter at least had experience snow depth measuring with his grandfather.

"You are as much a game warden as I am a Las Vegas show dancer."

"Bet you've got some smooth moves then." Hunter deflected, a wry smile crossing is face.

"Don't start that again," Kodiak warned, but for the first time since the faux game warden had floated into his life there was a hint, just a hint, of warmth in his voice.

"Seriously, you can't spend the rest of your life as a bush rat. Yeah, it's pretty and all but what about living. Travel, movies, restaurants you don't have to fly three hundred miles to get to then drive another forty-five minutes to once you leave the landing strip."

Kodiak shrugged. "I did that. New York, Milan, Paris. I'll take this," the handsome young homesteader waved his arm around the cabin, "over any of that for the rest of my life and be happy."

"What if you met someone, someone you couldn't live without?"

After a long silence Kodiak spoke.

"I did. And I lost him."

"Not everything lasts, what if there was another guy." Hunter prodded, not caring if Kodiak exploded over his nosiness.

"Not for me."

"Tell me about him."

Much to his surprise, with the fire crackling and the

sky alive with vivid green, yellow, blue and pink lights whipsawing over the roof of the remote cabin Kodiak did tell Hunter about Jimmy.

And Charles, and his life outside of the forty-ninth state.

It was like a dark doorway blocked shut had been opened, the pain, happiness, trauma came out in a tsunami of words, Kodiak could not have stopped telling the story if he had wanted to.

The question had come as easily as when Jimmy had asked him to tell him about his mother. The liquor had calmed him enough to talk in a way he had not in years, Kodiak didn't want to feel safe and comfortable with Hunter, but he did. Perhaps the words were to take his mind off his missing brother, perhaps because, while he knew in his heart of hearts that Hunter was a phony that he also was enjoying (a tiny bit) of the time he was spending with the cute (if fake) game warden. While not drunk the few stiff drinks Kodiak had taken had unlocked the memories locked in his heart. Although he wanted to stop, he could not, the torrent of words going on until he had told Hunter more about his life than even most of his family knew.

Including the photographer's attack.

Despite the fighting they had done, the mistrust, there was a certain kind of prison bonding going on with the total stranger who had, quite by accident, recently saved Kodiaks life twice.

"Didn't you tell anyone?" Hunter asked in disbelief when Kodiak told him about the attack by the photographer.

Kodiak shrugged.

"Who? Was I going to go to the cops and tell them

that I'm a model who stripped down to my underwear and then he screwed me? Was I going to tell my agent, who would have applauded and gone out to price a new condo over all the work he would think the guy was going to get me? There was no one to tell. And no reason to tell. But I knew I had to get the hell out of there. I would have but then, well everything else happened, and just like back in the day all roads led to Rome, all of that leads us right here to tonight." Kodiak finished, suddenly even more exhausted than he had ever been.

The only part of his story he left out was the part about throwing the knife, taking the life of the man who had maimed him to avenge the death of his innocent friend.

"I'm sorry, man," a still tipsy Hunter said, reaching out to Kodiak when he finally brought the long story to a close.

While Kodiak was far from trusting Hunter. and would have burned the cabin to the ground in anger had he known the sexy young man he was feeling charitably comfortable toward had a camera hidden under a floorboard which he still hoped to hide and activate in his cabin, he was given the circumstances, having a pleasant enough evening. After Hunter had truly saved his life this time Kodiak felt he could extend as olive branch of courtesy to Hunter.

And the chit chat at least kept Kodiak from lunging forward to press his lips against Hunter's as he wrapped his muscular arms around him and from needless worry about Cord.

"Thanks, but I don't need your sympathy, it happened and it's over." He said quietly, ignoring Hunter's reach.

"Besides, even if I had stayed in the game I would only have been a novelty for a while. I'd have been the guy with the face scars but eventually another younger guy with a different story would have come along and the vultures would have gone after him. There may be a few who make a career of modeling but most end up on the discount rack before long and even with the advantage's I might have had I would have ended up marked down as damaged goods and eventually would have come here anyway."

The fire had burned to nearly nothing but a bed of low embers. Unless they broke up the table, chairs or bed frame there would soon be nothing left in the cabin to burn.

"It'll be daylight soon," Kodiak said, "I hate wasting time, but it is going to be a tough go out there in the un broken snow so we are going to need as much energy as we can get. Besides, we can't go thrashing around in the bush in the dark. Let's catch some sleep."

"This is not the invitation you think it is. We need to rest and conserve heat. That's it." With that Kodiak rose and poked at the fireplace, banking the fire with some rounds of wood then going to the single frame bunk and slid into the down filled sleeping bag then held up the edge of the bag to indicate that Hunter should slide in next to him.

The men slowly settled into a deep breathing pattern, Kodiak's right arm slowly settling over Hunters rising and falling chest in the most natural, if involuntary, way. Hunter was even being mindful of the bandage still wrapped around Kodiak's body.

The emotion of the day, concern over Cord; the confession of his deep, secret along with his now mixed feelings over the man he was holding finally caught up with the usually strong Kodiak.

Without realizing it tears had begun sliding down the former model's cheeks, the slow moving dampness building to a steady stream, his body shaking until he was wracked with sobs.

Hunter held Kodiak tighter than he had ever held anyone in his life, knowing the scars the former model bore on his face were no-where nearly as severe as the scars on his heart.

It was at that moment that Hunter knew he would not be carrying out his plan of setting up the camera in the cabin for a live video feed of Kodiak's life.

The stack of bills offered by Finn could have filled the cabin and over flowed into Kodiak's washhouse and it still would not have been enough to make him invade Kodiak that way now.

As the young men relaxed, Kodiak's tears slowly easing to nothing, their bodies naturally took over, lips meeting in another soft, passionate kiss; hands roving slowly up and down over each-others smooth, bare skin as a longer, more intense session of love making took place before they were again physically exhausted and drifted back into a deep, satisfied if sweat slick sleep.

Fourteen

"Fuck! I was gonna say it is cold as the north pole in here but that's a little too close to home. Literally." Hunter said through chattering teeth, breath chopping out in front of his face in small silvery puffs. "So wadda we do now?"

Kodiak had pulled free of the groove their bodies had been snuggled into a short time earlier and was now breaking apart the chair, feeding the pieces into an again growing fire in the stone hearth. An almost too bright strip of sunlight came through the main window of the cabin, motes of dust and debris swirling in the clear brilliance.

Kodiak would have stayed in the sleeping bag had his raging erection not been furrowed deep against his accidental host. As he lay there snugged up against Hunter he had begun thinking how nice it would be to wake up pressed against the attractive pretend game warden on a regular basis. A lazy, dark little fantasy he knew would fade away just like his thickened shaft once he was up and moving about the important work of the day, finding Cordova.

Facing the frigid cabin was a better alternative to those thoughts so Kodiak had launched himself out of the warm burrow they had created in the narrow bunk. His heart was still broken;

Hunter, while cute, had none of Charles sass and wit and certainly none of Jimmy's charm. He was just a run-of-the-mill guy who was clearly up to no good in Kodiak's world, but still the homesteader could not shake the attraction he had begun feeling toward the young man.

Between needing to get outside to pee, his hard on and his head throbbing from the booze he was not used to and his aching, battered body Kodiak had enough on his plate to keep his thoughts away from his now very mixed feelings about Hunter Davis, fake game warden. Hunter had turned and held him as Kodiak sobbed himself to sleep, limbs tangled in a knot. by then Kodiak was fully aware of what had happened between the two of them and now hoped that Hunter would at least be gentleman enough to not mention that little episode or his break down now that they were awake and his head was fully clear again. Kodiak was ready to get back to the mission of finding Cordova.

If it was not too late for that.

"Not many options, but we start with you cleaning up your language and both of us being thankful to be alive, that is what counts," Kodiak said as briskly as possible. "We won't last here until your pick-up so we will follow through with what I said last night. Go to the cave, get home supplies then back to my cabin. We'll at least have food and a firewood supply there. We'll write up clear directions to the homestead and you will bring them back and post them here. We'll likely hear a plane from there. If we get bad weather your pick-up is gonna be delayed." Kodiak poked at the fire then stood.

The young homesteader hated that he had just voiced defeat for the season by including himself in the pick-up plan but knew he had no other option but to head back to the city for the winter and start living on the homestead again in the spring.

But if he were returning to the city he planned to be going back with his brother in tow. Cord could be anywhere by now, could have gone in any direction even though he knew the basic movements of the sun and stars to know which general direction to be heading. The wilderness was still just that, the wilderness.

Vast and unforgiving.

And this portion of the wilderness was a maze of trees, rivers, mountains, ice and snow and more snow.

"You go get some snow to melt so we can make some water to eat some of that freeze-dried crap you brought before we go. I'm going to get us some branches and boughs to make snowshoes. It's going to be a long tramp in the snow but the cold will help form a crust at least."

His mind buzzing with plans kept Kodiak from focusing on Cord and what he might be going through.

Kodiak gave himself a mental shake, not moving and getting lost in the emotion of what might be happening with his brother was not going to help in any way.

"Home made snow shoes? How Martha Stewart is that…." Hunter began, shutting up as soon as Kodiak cut him a vicious look.

"Wouldn't it be better if I stayed here and kept a fire going. In case your brother...," Hunter switched tactics then trailed off as Kodiak continued the stare then without further comment went on.

"You wanna eat anything other than spruce needle soup for the next few weeks you'll get your ass outa that bag and get ready to hit the trail and pack your share of food back to the cabin." Kodiak thundered.

"You'd have been great on a cattle drive circa eighteen eighty-eight," Hunter grumbled with a smile while sliding from the sleeping bag. Stretching long and tall, his erection tenting out the front of his pants, a waste of man-power ignored by both men in the frigid air.

In just under two hours the young men had finished the meager meal and Kodiak had lashed together two pair of sturdy enough emergency snow shoes by scraping four long sections of spruce down to bare poles, cross hatching more sturdy branches through the openings then tying all the pieces together with bits of string, twine and rope salvaged from the cabin interior. The shoes were heavy and clumsy but kept them on top of the heavy snow, which could have plunged hip deep with each step without Kodiak's primitive craftsmanship.

When gathering the branches Kodiak had carefully slogged through the deep snow along the edge of the river to the spot where the wolverine had attacked him. There was nothing left to salvage of his pack but he had located the frozen rife and brought it back to the cabin so he could retrieve it later to clean and oil.

While cutting the spruce branches Kodiak also cut a wrist thick cottonwood pole nearly as tall as himself. Sharpening the end of the soft wood he hefted it a few times until he was satisfied to have found a balance in the stick. He had not taken a lot of time to put a fine point on the primitive weapon but it was better than having nothing in his hands, the point was just sharp enough to be a danger to anyone or thing who crossed Kodiak. He could poke with the sharpened end and club with the blunt end if needed.

The thin layer of frozen crust on the snow did help

J A M E S   B R O C K

their movement as they started off into the forest, their progress painfully slow. The young men were quickly winded and covered in a light sheen of sweat despite the fact their breath was still billowing out into the frigid air of the day like old fashioned steam engines. The numerous times they had to stop and re fashion the snow shoes did not help the travel time of the day. Kodiak's side was aching like a bad tooth after only a few steps but thinking of Cord he simply blocked the pain as best he could and kept moving on.

As Kodiak held on, trudging through the snow as if he were walking across bare summer moss it was uninjured Hunter who finally spoke up after chuffing along for hours.

"How. Much. Farther," Hunter panted just as the men noticed a sudden drop in the temperature. The constant movement and their labored breathing had kept conversation to a minimum, the sun was quickly getting ready disappear.

Lifting the make shift spear doubling as a walking stick Kodiak pointed at the dark dot of the cavern, they were three quarters of the way across the vast field at the glacial front.

"Keep moving," Kodiak panted while lowering the staff. Each step of the day had been agonizing, his side feeling as if it were made of crushed glass. Luckily his battered face had gone numb early on the hike and he could not feel the cuts and bruises. Only the thought of finding Cord had kept Kodiak moving forward all day. There had been no sign or track that Cord had passed anywhere near the route he and Hunter were travelling.

"It's like in that scene from the *Wizard of Oz*," Hunter managed with a gulp of frigid air, "When the characters wake up in the poppy field in the snow and see Oz across the way."

"Yeah," Kodiak returned flatly, "that is exactly what this is like."

Through his exhaustion Hunter managed a small grin, his body reacting through his exhaustion with a slight thickening in his crotch at the memory of their bodies entwined only a few hours earlier. This Kodiak, this model, this homesteader had taken Hunter's heart long before he had taken the rest of him wholly and completely now that they had shared intimacy.

Another few more kisses from Kodiak and Hunter could have hiked on across the state, the Bearing Sea and on into Siberia.

Through the veneer of exhausted euphoria Hunter knew this was hardly the time to drop to a knee and proclaim his feelings.

After the brief exchange the pair trudged silently on through the snow for another half an hour before finally reaching the wide gravel pathway leading up to the mouth of the cavern just as the sun hit the horizon. Sweat covered, panting and exhausted they stood next to each other silently.

"Another nice place ya got here." Hunter laughed through his weariness, happy to know they were only a short distance from sitting down. He was lightheaded from lack of food and the hours of exertion marching through the snow.

Wind had kept the opening of the cave clear of snow, a scree of smooth stones making a kind of bare path to the dark opening around the huge boulders.

Exhausted the men stopped, finally out of the snow they noisily began kicking at the sticks tied to their feet, leaning against one another they alternately pulled at the makeshift snow shoes until they had kicked the branches from their feet. Kodiak could hardly speak, let alone breathe. Side aching, head ready to split open like a ripe melon he could hardly stand but his determination to find Cord kept him going despite the pain.

Panting Kodiak had just told Hunter they needed to re gather the sticks and to pull up some of the dried grasses sprouting around the rocks to use as fire starter when they heard the first noise in the cavern. A faint rustle but just enough of to give the pair notice that they might not be alone in this vast wilderness.

"Did you hear," Hunter began, before could finish the next word in a bewildered voice both he and Kodiak caught of whiff of what smelled like death heated and re fried wafting out of the cavern mouth. Kodiak's stomach turned to liquid, this was a scent he knew, a scent even more dangerous after a long hike on an empty stomach through the snow with nothing but a stick to defend himself and Hunter.

It was the distinct scent of the renegade bear Kodiak had last seen charging across the tundra in front of the glacier.

Kodiak had never relied on luck or his looks. He depended on as few people as possible and had built a good, solid life for himself. He didn't want for much, certainly did not ask for much, depending on his own hard work, planning and determination to get through the hard life he had chosen for himself.

At that moment he did, however, ask the universe, fate or any old deity listening, to please, please, please give him a break. His brother was wandering the wilderness, his winter food supply had been destroyed;

he had been molested (well, kind if, and that certainly wasn't the worst item on his list), and it felt like molester had been chattering like a chipmunk all the live long day as they had trudged through the wilderness to get what he hoped with all his heart was going to be a safe place.

On top of those issues he wished that Hunter were not so damned attractive. That was one little issue Kodiak really did not want to deal with but here it was.

And now there would not be a chance of friendship or anything else ever working out between them as they were likely to die if something other than a fox, wolf or black bear which had strayed too far north wandered out of the cave.

"Freeze!" Kodiak managed to hiss as they saw movement in the blackness.

"What," Hunter said through chattering teeth, "do you think it is," he managed as a black snout the size of a mailbox poked out of the cave, fist size nostrils snuffling the air.

As if expecting the men the great beast of a bear brought its massive body fully out of the mouth of the cavern, it seemed to take forever for the huge animal to rise onto its hind legs, the prominent white cross Kodiak had seen earlier in the summer and fall was now on full display nearly close enough for him to touch as the massive animal stood. Between the rancid smell and the marking it was certain this was the same marauder from the river attack.

"Do not move," Kodiak hissed as quietly as possible, lips twitching only slightly. The words were hardly out of his mouth when two things happened; the huge animal began swaying its Volkswagen size head from side to side and Hunter turned back toward the unsafety of the vast snow covered tundra the men had just trudged across.

For Kodiak the next few seconds moved as if they were being played out underwater, every movement slow and defined. With a snarl which echoed around them the bear stepped forward, following the movement of Hunter.

"Unless," Hunter began, freezing in place again, said in a whisper of his own, his mouth going cotton dry, "you learned to create and hurl lightning bolts in the last few minutes we are so dead."

Reflex alone caused Kodiak to lift the makeshift walking stick. It was only when the giant monster of a bear moved again that Kodiak realized how much of its summer winter weight gain had already been burned off in short time since he had last seen the animal. Fur hung around the frame as if the bear were a cub playing dress up in the skin of one of its parents.

Throwing that great solid block of a head back the bear tried to give another mighty roar, tossing that snout into the air, the long razor-sharp claws of the animal's forepaws slashing wildly in the air.

The men expected another horrifying snarl from the bear but instead of a powerful roar a deep, course cough racked the air, a gasping, gurgling sound coming from deep in the animal's chest. As the bear lowered its head the cough was followed by a series of sneezes, the blasts hurling long, white ropes of phlegm to the ground as the bear stopped and wobbled back and forth for a moment. While this was certainly the same animal that had capsized the boat Hunter had foolishly brought zooming down the river weeks earlier this was also a very sick animal.

It might be weak the bear was still a nuclear event

waiting to happen that close to the pair. Hunter had at least stopped moving. The novelty, even while running for his life, of seeing a

giant wild animal break into a sneezing fit had stunned him into stopping.

Medusa like the bear held their attention, between noticing the draped and matted skin and fur hanging off the animal and now the guttural coughing and sneezing Kodiak knew they were not only dealing with a powerful animal but a *sick* powerful animal ready to destroy anything annoying it.

An agonizingly long split second later the huge animal did manage another mighty roar while again lurching forward, this time not quite making it around one of the huge boulders between the mouth of the cavern and where Kodiak stood rooted, makeshift spear still firmly gripped in his fist.

Deftly as any skilled athlete Kodiak sensed what was happening next. Glancing off the stone pitched the bear forward, the illness causing the animal to be off balance. Kodiak in that instant re tightened the grip his fingers had on the piece of wood in his hand.

Falling forward, huge muscular paws outstretched, the bear's body slammed down on the roughly sharpened staff. Despite the pain and exhaustion wracking his body Kodiak held the sharpened stake firmly in place while managing to leap out of the way as the huge animal fell forward, the ragged point of the cottonwood pole driving deep into the stinking pelt of the bear.

The weight of its body drove the bear forward, a snarl of rage coming from between the finger thick razor sharp teeth as the pole plunged into its chest, passing between a set of ribs and driving directly into the chambers of the machine-like pounding heart of the huge beast.

The men remained statue like, as if the bear had truly turned them to stone as the great animal gave a few involuntary lurches, unable to push back up off the stick which had impaled it's heart. The huge body flopped a few times then with a long, low release of air the animal settled back down onto the frozen ground. Carrying the slightly sharpened stick had been the turn of dumb luck Kodiak had been waiting for. Perhaps not the same as a National Guard helicopter suddenly appearing over the horizon to take them to a hot dinner followed by an even hotter bath but it was the kind of small miracle he would take right then.

"Holy crap," Hunter hissed as he looked down at the huge right paw twitching near his foot.

"Careful," Kodiak cautioned, adrenaline pounding. "I'm certain its dead but the nerves could still be twitching and those claws could shred you."

"A trophy for sure," Hunter was at least thankful no one had driven this huge beauty to its death by running it toward some rich dolt with a gun with a snow machine.

"There was one chance in infinity of this kind of thing happening. Something was watching over us or we've just had the dumbest luck of anyone in North America." Pausing the young homesteader stood, panting heart racing as the giant animal's muscles again twitched and contracted, the huge claws skittering across the rocks uncomfortably close to their feet. "It was beautiful but sick, wouldn't have made it through the rest of the winter," Kodiak continued as the twitching bear's giant form contracted a few more times before finally going still.

"We need to get inside and get a fire going and see if

there is anything left in there." He finished with a grimace. The sun had gone down as they carefully threaded around the boulders until reaching the dark mouth of the cavern, Kodiaks heart nearly leaping out of his chest when he saw a bed of red, glowing embers in the firepit. The bear certainly would not have been the one to have started the fire.

"CORD! CORDOVA!" he screamed, the stench of the now dead animal filled the small space, catching in his lungs but that did not stop Kodiak from rushing into the dark. He made his way to the inset in the rock where he had laid in a supply of firewood still yelling for his brother.

Even in the dark his fingers traveled correctly; first to a handful of shredded wood followed by strips of kindling.

The most experienced woodsperson could not have choreographed the re starting of a fire with such precision. As the kindling caught fire Kodiak grabbed larger pieces of wood, feeding them onto the leaping flames as he continued to call out for his brother.

"Oh does that feel good!" Hunter moaned as the first tendrils of heat began to radiate from the leaping flames of the open fire. Stripping the frozen gloves curled around his fingers from his hands Hunter gave a deep sigh, tossing the frozen material aside while extending his open palms toward the open flames.

Once the fire had caught Kodiak turned to scan the cavern. It had been trashed worse than his cabin, gear strewn in mangled pieces across the gravel floor. Kodiak's stomach lurched when he saw bits of orange plastic on the hard, cold dirt floor. He didn't need to pick the pieces up to realize they were parts of the SPOT signal device. Taking a step forward his foot crunched on more plastic, bending down he then did pick the debris up and verified that the "indestructible" call box had been crushed beyond recognition between the massive teeth of the bear, clearly before an SOS signal for help was sent or there would be a search team at the cave by then.

The reality that they were totally on their own hit him like a sledgehammer, in his condition he didn't know how much longer he could go on without medical help and they still did not know if his brother was in the cavern or what condition he would be in when and if they did find him.

There was no reason to concern Hunter with any of that information just then.

"CORD!" he managed to bellow once more, dropping the broken signal device piece back onto the cave floor. The bear certainly hadn't started the fire, it had to have been lit by his brother.

Fumbling up onto a high ledge inset in the rock Kodiak muttered, "Yesssss!" to himself as his fingers wrapped around an Led flashlight stored there. Without doing a full inventory he let his fingers wander over the small First Aid pouch, his nearly numb fingers finally landing on a zip lock baggie of power bars stored next to the light.

Smiling to himself Kodiak congratulated himself on thinking ahead (planning his own luck!) while turning on the light and snapping the seal on the plastic pouch all at the same time. Tearing open one of the bars and taking a greedy bite he turned and tossed one of the bars to Hunter as he stepped away from the main room of the cavern.

Sweeping the light across the floor of the niche where

he had stacked salmon like cordwood the previous summer and fall he quickly found his brother. Cord's body lay in a broken, twisted knot at Kodiak's feet, head hidden in the tangle of his limbs.

"No, no, no no…" Kodiak groaned, his tone brought Hunter to his side.

"Is he dead?"

"I hope not," shining the flashlight over his brother's body Kodiak truly did not know where to start.

"Cord," he began, "I don't know if you can hear me, but we have to move you buddy."

Handing the light to Hunter, Kodiak began slowly pulling at his brother's limbs, moving each arm and leg as if it were shattered, and they may very well have been for all Kodiak knew. At that point Kodiak would have been grateful if Cord had been fully unconscious. His brother's crippling fear of bears had brought him to this, being opened like a tin can by one of the biggest, meanest animals this part of the north had ever seen. If Cord was going to get through this Kodiak needed to be calm and take things step by careful measured step.

Cordova's right leg had a huge gash in it, the pants he wore were tattered around the gaping wound. A piece of material, soaked with his blood, had been wrapped crudely around the upper part of his leg. Kodiak began doing a mental timeline as he slowly, gently, manipulated Cord's body.

The wound was long, but it had not bled him out, so it might not have been that old. The fire in the cave still had embers (and how the bear managed not to scatter the fire pit would be one of the unsolved mysteries of time), so the bear attacking Cord could not have happened that long ago. Between ten and twelve hours perhaps. Bears were known to guard food and continue playing and toying with wounded food sources for hours and it appeared that Cord had done exactly the right thing and gotten down into a corner as deeply as he could to try and wait the bear attack out. Fear and panic had likely saved his brother.

After straightening Cords head, his lips sealed, and eyes closed, Kodiak slid his fingers around Cord's left wrist and eased two fingers along the side, searching for a pulse, his stomach clenching until he finally found one. It was weak and thready, but there.

Cord moaned slightly as the men moved him carefully as they could back into the larger area of the cave, where they settled Cord onto the small sleeping shelf he had obviously been using before the bear found him as the sleeping bag he had carried from the homestead was unrolled and open on top of the bagged moss mattress.

Searching through the scattered supplies Kodiak found several more unbroken lanterns, lighting them all to access the damages.

The disarray was not as bad as he had first thought in the dark. Supplies were scattered but not too many items appeared to be broken. It was likely Cord had cooked something and the bear, probably hibernating in one of the other nearby caves or ice caverns, was drawn in by the smell.

Crossing the cave Kodiak put another piece of wood on the fire then lowered the canvas tarp back across the opening to the cave, the small area was already beginning to feel warmer.

Rummaging around he found the stout pieces of wood he used as a spit roast for either side of the fire and got them back into place then re attached the thin metal rod which went between the pieces of wood to hang pots on.

Taking a metal bucket off a hook he had set into the stone wall he handed it to Hunter, who had been standing quietly still warming his hands once Cord had been re settled.

"Here, we need water and for now snow is going to have to do. Fill this with as much as you can."

"But my hands were just getting warm," Hunter whined.

Cocking his arm back Kodiak slammed the light metal container into his chest, eyes blazing. "In case you haven't figured this out, asshole, we are in a life and death situation here. Life or death. Yours, mine and his," the homesteader growled in a low, ominous tone.

With no further comment Hunter picked up the bucket he had allowed to bounce off his chest and disappeared behind the stiff sheet of canvas.

With Hunter settled into a routine of melting snow for water and transferring it into a larger container, Kodiak found the wire rack and arranged it over the fire as a make shift grill. He would have preferred preparing steak for them but knew the fish would be faster to cook.

Throwing one of the frozen salmon onto the grill over the fire Kodiak turned his attention back to Cord.

His breathing was as shallow and weak as his pulse, but the wound on his leg was no longer bleeding. Grabbing the small First Aid kit he kept in the cave Kodiak fished out the packets of sterile cleaning pads. Carefully unwrapping the gash he began swiping the edges, cleaning it the best he could. He was pleased to see that he had been right in the triage, while the wound was long and ugly it was not deep. Infection from the bears dirty claw was a big concern, the homesteader fervently hoped they could get Cord back to the cabin where he could clean the wound properly.

Leaving the rest of Cord's clothing in place Kodiak carefully worked him fully into the sleeping bag and zipped it up. Chipping some ice from the back of the cavern Kodiak eased a few slivers at a time between his brother's now badly chapped lips.

The smell of roasting salmon was filling the air, Kodiak flipped the portion of fish then carefully broke off the cooked edges. Dropping the meat into a smaller pail he added some water and settled the kettle down into the coals to make a broth for Cord. If they were stuck here while he healed they might be in for a long few days and all them needed as much strength as they could get.

Catching his breath Kodiak finally winced at a pull in his side. With the rush of adrenaline he had found in finding Cord he had forgotten his own wounds. Gritting his teeth he drew in a deep breath then tried to relax. He didn't have time to be concerned about his own recovery at the moment.

When the salmon was nearly done, the smell driving both Kodiak and Hunter quietly crazy, both began to realize how hungry they were. The energy bars they had wolfed down hardly made a dent toward filling them up after the slog to the cave.

Going back into the icy niche at the back of the cave Kodiak brought out a large handful of frozen wild asparagus and a small container of frozen raspberries he had cached back there. He rolled the vegetable onto the grill to char then sprinkled a packet of sugar from the "pantry" over the berries. A short time later the men tore into what would have been a very expensive meal at any restaurant in the world.

"Thank you," Hunter said with a stone face as Kodiak passed a metal plate of food over to him.

"You are welcome." Kodiak said bluntly back.

"This is all bad enough, why do you have to be a dick?" Hunter said with a passive smile.

"Said the man with the secret cameras who came here to steal my image." Kodiak countered while shoveling a piece of the delicious fish into his mouth. "You'd steal and sell my soul if you thought you could get away with it." The warmth the two had shared the night before had again been shattered.

"You'd have drown and he'd have been eaten by the bear if it had not been for me," Hunter shot back a bit too smugly for someone who was every bit guilty of the crime he had been accused of.

Kodiak set his own metal plate aside and brought the broth up out of the coals, carefully pouring some into the cup from an Army canteen he had left in the cave.

"Possibly," Kodiak shrugged while tilting the watery fish broth and deftly skimming up a spoonful and bringing it to Cord's lips. After a few bites of food Kodiak had set his own food aside and begun to feed his injured brother. "But at least I would have at least died with dignity while trying to save my brother. Open." Although his eyes were closed Cord managed to part his lips slightly, the weak soup trickling in with Kodiak carefully holding the spoon in place to make certain each drop went into his mouth.

Hunter watched that in fascination. He couldn't imagine anyone in his family showing such compassion, even in a situation like this. He could not have loved Kodiak any more than at that moment, when he was showing such care to his errant brother who had gotten him into awful   place. But telling him, especially now, would not be the right time, Hunter knew.

Never might be the only right time for him to say something like that to the man whose kisses and embrace he would savor for the rest of his life, even if the intimacy had been accidental.

Both times.

And now they were on their own, the nearest help might as well be on Mars. No one knew where they were and only Kodiak had any idea how to get back to the remains of either cabin. A lot of long shots were in play for their survival, their youth tended to block out a lot of the bad they were facing. A situation like this called for step by step thinking anyway.

Hunter finished the delicious food as Kodiak continued to feed the broth to Cord, carefully scraping the sides of his mouth with the spoon. Cord was not exactly eagerly eating the improvised broth but some did appear to be getting inside his mouth and hopefully oozing down into his stomach.

The homesteader had to have been as famished as Hunter but still fed him first and was now feeding his brother even before he finished eating his own food. Hunter wished again that he had been able to meet Kodiak under a different circumstance, one in which they might have had a chance.

Declarations of love had more than likely been made under more awkward circumstances, but it was highly un likely that they involved a former runaway model, a dead giant bear and a five-star salmon dinner prepared over an open campfire.

Even if he were able to put his pride aside Hunter knew he would never be able to convince Kodiak that he wasn't just out to make a buck off the stolen photographs he had taken.

Despite the liquor infused confessions of the night before, followed by the intimacy, Kodiak had cut Hunter off.

Rising Hunter crossed the cave and brought another piece of wood to the fire as Kodiak put the pail with the broth aside. Cord had drifted off to sleep so Kodiak picked up the plate of food he had prepared for himself and began to eat finally, his mind spinning with thoughts of what needed to be done and soon, to try and get them out of this mess.

The food certainly helped, and there was enough for all of them for a while, and wood was going to be a problem. Tufts of tundra grasses could be wound together to make a longer lasting fuel but one of them would have to cross the marsh to get real wood soon. They could stay in the cave a few more days, long enough to get some strength in Cord then Kodiak would fashion a sled out of the ski's he had stored in the back to haul Cord back to the cabin. It was going to be a challenge to get back to the cabin and dispatch Hunter, the shit, back to the trapper's cabin to leave a message for the pick-up pilot but Kodiak felt confident they could make it if their luck, if you could call Cord not being dead and a hot meal luck, held out.

At that moment fate laughed, sending a pair of cantaloupe size rocks crashing down from the ceiling, one of them crushing Kodiak's right shoulder, knocking him to the floor of the cave and totally unconscious.

Fifteen

Hunter, squatting near the fire, was thinking how much he wanted a Coke. An ice cold, sparkling beverage which would sizzle and fizz as he popped the can tab open. That first sip would be slightly burning but crisp and sweet as that first swallow went down his throat.

In his fantasy the soda would be delivered by a squadron of Marines in a Huey helicopter. They would be hot, muscle ripped Marines carrying the soda. And they would be pretty naked save for their helmets, safety first! If he wasn't going to be able to have Kodiak again he might as well have a decent fantasy.

These were the happy thoughts going through Hunter's head when all hell broke loose in the cave.

One second he was briefly lost in his fantasy of cold soda and hot un uniformed military men, the next second the air was filled with plumes of dust and the noise of crashing rock falling from the ceiling of the cavern.

Soda forgotten Hunter managed to push back on his heels and tuck himself into a ball, not knowing if the cavern were crashing in or if a grenade had gone off.

In the eternity it seemed Hunter lay there, rolled into himself as tightly as he could manage, he considered his life, in the end knowing that he was young and wanted more. More of everything: food, hot water. He wanted to feel the sun, be warm, and have sex again. With

Kodiak. He wanted more of that, even more than he wanted the soda. He still wanted the Marines and helicopter more than anything else but if he were killed in the next few seconds it all wants and needs were going to be moot.

He was at least glad that the last sex he *had* indulged in had at least been with someone he really had wanted to be with, even if Kodiak might not have been fully aware that they had engaged in a great time.

More than anything he wished he had never run into Finn, had never been tempted by the bound bricks of money offered to spy on Kodiak, to indulge a wealthy eccentric at the cost of someone he was fast falling in love with.

Seconds turned into minutes and on into what seemed hours before Hunter finally crossed his arms over his head and carefully sat up.

"Kodiak, y'ok man?"

It was hard to see in the gloom of the cave with a sheet of dust hanging in the air, the flames of the fire casting shadows on the rock walls was hardly the electric light he was used to.

"KODIAK! ANSWER, MAN!" Hunter shouted, desperate for a reply.

When Kodiak gave no response Hunter stood, stomach knotting as his eyes again adjusted and he realized the jumbled pile of stone and gravel now piled on the cavern floor opposite him was not just rock. A low groan came from the mound of stone, Hunter managed to suppress a gasp as he realized Kodiak's body was part of the debris.

Scrambling across the un even dirt floor Hunter began tossing rocks aside as Kodiak sat up with a moan just as another small stream of fist size rock and gravel crumbled from the ceiling.

"We've gotta get out here. Change in temperature from the fire and our body heat is causing fissures to open. This whole thing could collapse." Kodiak said in a whispered voice. He knew any further disruption in the natural order of the cavern could cause more damage. Noise, movement, more heat. They had to get out and fast.

"Are you alright?"

"No," Kodiak, said with a grimace as he rubbed his shoulder, "but we don't have a choice. We have to get back to the homestead. The wood supply was going to run out fast soon enough in here anyway."

"How are we gonna carry your brother?"

Kodiak tried to stand but was hit by a wave of pain and nausea so lowered himself back to the floor of the cave.

"You can't even walk!" Hunter challenged, "how are we going to transport *you* and your brother? He's not even awake."

"Put another piece of wood on the fire and stay calm," Kodiak began as an ominous rumble from deep inside the rock above them caused another plume of gravel and dust to sift down over the exhausted young men. Even Cord groaned from the other side of the cave.

"We are fucked," Hunter began, his words cut off by Kodiak.

"Stop it. Being negative is not going to help. Now put another piece of wood on the fire then go into that niche behind you. There should be a pair of skis and a pair of round, bear paw snow shoes in there." Kodiak gulped, "Hand me the water, and I have told you before to watch that language."

"What is it with you and that word?"

"Doesn't matter," Kodiak said flatly, "I'm in charge and it is a word I don't like. It shows lack of willingness to think and find something more appropriate to use."

"In case you haven't noticed," Hunter said while reaching across the fire and plucking the tin container of recently melted snow over to Kodiak. "we aren't exactly in an English class here."

The homesteader downed most of the tepid water, handing the metal cup back to Hunter.

"Civilization is still necessary anywhere," Kodiak said primly before going then went ahead with instruction on their survival. Hunter smiled as Kodiak echoed nearly the same words he had used when quoting regulations on the path to the cabin on their first meeting.

"Pull down some of those shelf planks I stuck up and use them to make the best sled you can to transport Cord. Since the snow stopped and temperature fell it may have crusted over enough to pull him." Even in the dim light of the flickering fire Hunter could see Kodiak was beginning to sweat, long beads were tracking down over his suddenly pale skin.

"You don't look good," Hunter started, only to be cut off again.

"In the top of the Mukluks we are all three wearing there is fishline where the fire starter and fishhooks were. Use it. I'm dizzy..." Kodiak managed before wobbling and crumpling over onto his side again.

"Fuck," Hunter muttered, forgetting the most recent reprimand about use of the word already before stepping over the rubble and pulling Kodiak into a prone position. There was nothing he could do but follow the directions given him, first stepping back outside and filling the container with snow again and wedging it into the ring of rocks around next to the fire.

"Language…." Kodiak muttered almost dreamily as his eyes fluttered then shut tightly.

Hunter smiled, shaking his head before carefully centering one of the remaining pieces of firewood into the flames Hunter then set about finding the skis, snowshoes and shelving. Opening the sleeping bag Cord was tightly tucked into Hunter carefully pulled out each leg, the young man moaning, body flinching with each movement. Once his feet were assessable Hunter quickly found the fish line which had been sewn into the top of the soft Mukluks, pulling yards of the heavy gauge line out and mentally thanking the fingers which had thoughtfully stitched it in place just for an emergency like this. He followed the same procedure with the mukluks worn by Kodiak, then the pair he wore then quickly added more snow to the tin to melt before wiping Kodiak's face and tucking Cord back into the sleeping bag before going back to work.

This was serious, their lives were at stake. Hunters fingers began to shake as he poked at the fire then went back tying the length of fishline together then threading the strong material around the boards and through the bindings of the skis.

Even with the two brothers so close to him Hunter had never felt so alone.

"So, um," he began muttering as he worked. Hunter knew talking to yourself was not a sign of good mental health but the only sounds were the labored breathing of the young men and the crackle of the fire. The lack of noise was deafening, but the uneven pops from the fire and the by then constant rattle of gravel trickling through the rock were driving him crazy, so he began to talk. He knew his words were falling on deaf ears but any sound was better than waiting silently for the implosion of rock which could end this journey for all of them.

"I don't know if you can hear me, but I am sorry. I was desperate," his fingers moved steadily as he spoke, his words falling into a steady rhythm which slowed his heart beat. "I had this huge crush on you to start with, hell, who didn't in this state. Even the straight guys I know who called you a fag were proud that you went outside and were making a name for yourself. For us." Hunter carefully tied a tight little knot and moved on to the next.

"Then when you were charged with killing that guy they thought you were a bad ass. That news just made me want to kiss you even more. You are a *very* good kisser, by the way, even if you didn't really mean to kiss me." Hunters voice was wistful. "I wish we could have kissed under different circumstances."

"We all knew your story, your success brought us all a little closer to glory." Pausing Hunter looked up from the work in his hands and stared into the dark.

For a moment Hunter was not in a cave hundreds of miles from anywhere in the wilderness as a tightness formed in his crotch thinking of the touch and taste of Kodiak. Giving himself a little shake he took a deep breath and forced himself back to the task at hand.

Grabbing the tin pot from the ashes and cinders of the fire Hunter took a long drink then left his work to go re fill the container with fresh snow then set back to his tasks.

"I needed money. Who doesn't?" For what your *pal*

Finn offered to have me put a camera in your cabin I could have lived well for a long time."

He continued his work in silence for a few more moments before speaking.

"If we get through this he'll never see me again, I swear."

Moving to the down mummy bag where Cord was now sleeping soundly, Hunter unzipped it and reached inside, his fingers fumbling around until he found the young man's belt.

Unfastening the buckle Hunter slid it from Cord's waist and then re zipped him into the bag. Moving to Kodiak he bent to unbuckle the belt around his waist. "That's over now. I wouldn't do that now even if he doubled the fortune he is willing to pay to spy on you. You are kind of a hard ass, but I like the challenge of that." Exhaustion and genuine emotion overwhelmed Hunter, "Don't know what I was thinking of in the first place but I could never do that to you. Especially not after all we have been through. I may not be able to have you the way I want you but he sure as fu.." Hunter smiled to himself as he caught the word before it made its way out of his mouth, "*fudge* won't get any piece of you." A double tear made its way down over Hunter's cheek as he cinched the belt around Cord's leg's, careful not to touch the still open wound running down his thigh.

Turning back to Kodiak, Hunter was startled to see a faint smile on Kodiak's sexy lips. Slowly pulling a hand out of his pocket Kodiak reached out to Hunter.

"Quite a story," he whispered.

Hunter shrugged, "Didn't know if you were out of it or not. Had to say it for myself."

"Guess it doesn't much matter now," Kodiak said, "I

don't feel so hot. Get Cord out of here."

"Shut up!" Hunter growled. "We've been through too much for you to start that kind of crap."

"I think my shoulder is crushed. Probably have bleeding in my head. Get the kid back to the cabin and salvage what you can to get you through until your pick up arrives."

There was a long pause as the men looked at each other, then Kodiak managed to raise his hand slowly, hooking his rough fingers around the back of Hunter's neck, pulling him close. Their cracked lips met lightly, mouths parting as Hunter leaned into the kiss, both trembling as their mouths ground together.

A faint smile crossed over Kodiak's lips as they pulled apart, the scowl he had worn from the moment Hunter had first met him gone for the first time.

"Wh, what was that for," Hunter stammered.

"For finally being honest. And I wanted one last kiss. You may be a liar, but you are cute, I'll give you that. Now work on getting Cord out of here. I'm scarred, messed up on both the inside and outside. He deserves his shot, get him out of here." Kodiak said, his eyes closing again slowly.

"Knock off the last kiss shit. We are all getting outa here." Hunter smiled back down at Kodiak while gently tracing the side of his right thumb down the longest of the scar lines on his cheek.

"It wasn't personal, it was survival. For you survival is living off the land. For me it is getting by the best way I can," Hunter said. "I'm sorry you were the one I was going to exploit. Is this forgiveness?"

"No, that has to be earned, so stop it. I started figuring you out when you messed with a porcupine, then didn't know what a loon was and then you dropped your pants to prove you didn't have a hidden camera. Even the dumbest game warden wouldn't have done that. He'd have just hidden the camera." Kodiak said with a smile, his voice weakening in a way that scared Hunter.

"Look, I might very well die here so I guess I can be a little forgiving about your plan. But don't capitalize on my death. Don't sell these moments or details. And do not ever talk about my relationship with Jimmy or Charles. You would only hurt their families."

They hadn't come through all of this, to have Kodiak forgiving Hunter and kissing him just to have him lose the homesteader.

"Uh Uh buddy, this ain't over yet." Hunter whispered as he started to scoop Kodiak into his arms. "I'm not the dumbest of anything by a long shot because I do have a camera hidden back there but I wouldn't use it now for all the money in the world."

Kodiak's fingers gripped Hunters upper arm as the young man leaned over him.

"There is only part of the story I didn't tell you. I did it, Hunter, I killed him, The guy who scarred me. I couldn't get Finn, he had too much money and protection, but I got the piece of scum he hired. I got off, but I killed him. Not because of what he did to me, but because he killed Charles. I need someone to know that if I do die."

"NO death bed confessions!" Hunter roared. "You are not going to die now so shut with that talk!"

"Someday I want you to tell, I want the world to know. Just wait a respectful time because the press is going to come down on my family. Eventually the story will cool off again but let them get through with a burial for me," Kodiak said, wincing in pain. If ribs were not broken after the fight with Cord they certainly were from the rocks that had just fallen on him.

"You have been dead set on pinning a reason for me living here alone since the moment we met, so there it is. I can live with the scarring. I can live with people taking pictures and writing stories. But I have to live with myself. I took a life. Even for a good reason, to me at least, and that is wrong. This place is both my heaven and hell."

"Stop it! Stop talking and save your energy." Hunter protested, only to be cut off by Kodiak again.

"This is not a good situation man, and it IS likely I will die, and I had to say it. I didn't know him, he didn't know me. An eye for an eye. Call this a confession, whatever you want. I'm not looking for absolution, I did it and would do it again. You can tell that to whomever you want, sell the story to the highest bidder just save Cord first. Now. And get rid of that camera you hid. It's not likely that Sam is going to poke around in that cabin but there is no need to take a chance of him finding it by accident. He tends to be as protective of me as that bear was with food. Even if I'm not around he would come after you."

Kodiak's eyes fluttered shut again as Hunter, feeling more alone than he had ever felt and on the verge of tears, again prepared to lift him but stopped mid move as he heard the most amazing sound he had ever heard.

In the distance a dog barked. Not a wolf howl, a dog bark. A husky, one happy, working dog yelp followed by another and another until it was clear an entire team was heading directly toward the cave front.

Sixteen

Sam Chigliac and his team of beautiful, powerful huskies, Yukon in the lead, arrived at the remote cavern like Santa Claus and Spiderman rolled into one and more welcome than both fictional characters put together.

The dogs were beside themselves with anxiety at being near the smell emanating from the huge bear carcass but followed Sam's soothing commands as he calmed them.

After assessing the situation Sam brought out pieces of fresh mucktuck for the men, the thick cuts of pickled bowhead whale fat would give them energy to get them back to Kodiak's cabin, Sam smiling as Hunter grudgingly chewed the thick blubber at Sam's insistence.

Sam then quickly and skillfully organized the rest of the rescue operation much to the relief of the exhausted Hunter. Turning the sled and dogs around Sam pulled the thick seal skin parka with an ermine ruff over his head and snugged it down over the still unconscious Cordova before easing him into the carry basket of the dog sled. After retying some of the fishline and straps on the skis of the makeshift sled now holding Kodiak the very quiet artist told Hunter that while he would have to walk, the dogs would be going slow due to the load of carrying both brothers so Hunter should be able keep up the pace.

"How did you know where we were anyway?" Hunter asked, squatting to tighten the small round snow shoes now strapped to his feet.

"Stopped to check in on Kodiak and found the cabin trashed. Then checked the trapper's cabin and found it worse. Figured he was headed here for supplies." Sam shrugged, making the plan sound easy and thought out instead of a fly-by-night-seat-of-the-pants rescue mission turned disaster.

Filling a pack with still frozen salmon and packages of the wrapped moose meat Kodiak had stored in the cave Sam strapped the heavy load onto his back then positioned himself behind the runners of the sled holding Cord.

Calling out *HO!* the musher pushed off with his right foot and releasing the sled brake as the excited working dog's lunged forward, eagerly dashing back down along the trail they had just broken into the dark night lit only by a slice of moon.

There was no rest through the long night, Hunter was exhausted after the first hour but was not going to ask to stop. Despite the horror in the cave Kodiak DePaul had kissed him and told him he was cute. While Hunter's body was running on empty his heart was pounding like a humming bird on crack remembering the taste of Kodiak, his smell, words carrying him on. If they made it through his (and he now believed they would) he thought there might even be a chance. A chance at what between them he wasn't certain, but he wanted to be available for whatever that might be.

Hours later after what had been the longest night of recorded history they neared Kodiak's homestead camp. When it was finally in sight   Hunter felt that the collection of log cabins was almost a mirage, an illusion in the forest.

But thankfully it was not.

The reality of being there did not set in until Hunter and Sam had Kodiak and Cord in their bed's and a fire roaring in the hearth. Sam let Hunter pass out on the sofa then went out and un harnessed and fed the dogs, bedding them down before going back in and catching a sound nap of his own.

When Hunter finally woke from his hibernation like sleep hours later he found Kodiak stumbling around the cabin, putting things to right. He had a fire going in the small wood stove in the kitchen, the most amazing smells were coming from the oven and top of the range again.

The homesteaders left arm was hung in a makeshift sling made of olive-green material hanging from around his neck. Even hampered with his injuries Kodiak was making magic happen on the little wood stove.

"You are going to overdo yourself," Hunter cautioned as he moved into the kitchen, amazed Kodiak was able to move at all.

"I'll be ok," Kodiak said with a wince while clutching at his side with his free hand. "You and Sam did the work of getting us here, so I need to take care of you."

"Sam got you and Cord here. And you killed the bear!" Hunter said as he grabbed Kodiak, leading him to the sofa. Sliding an arm around Kodiak's waist Hunter led him across the cabin, easing him onto the sofa.

"You can hardly move!," Hunter said before Kodiak could protest, "How's Cord?" he continued while moving back to the kitchen and taking over the duty of serving up the hotcakes and coffee Kodiak had somehow managed to put together in his battered condition.

Kodiak shrugged as Hunter, carrying a plate filled with food, sat down next to him and began cutting the soft flapjacks swimming in homemade blueberry syrup into wedges then pushing the fork toward Kodiak.

With a bashful grin Kodiak opened his mouth and accepted the food, slowly chewing as Hunter cut another wedge out of the pancake. Hunter was all but drooling over the smell of the food but happily put his own wants aside to continue feeding Kodiak first, just as the model had fed his brother first in the cave.

"Sam washed and fed him before he left and cleaned up the wound, it's not that deep and Sam wrapped and dressed it really well. As long as Cord stays still it will be ok until rescue gets here." Kodiak said while swallowing, Hunter leaning in and pushing the next bite forward. "Sam said Cord complained about not having his phone and music, so I think he'll live. He told Sam he was in the cave when the bear came in, it knocked him around but did not use those horrible claws to slash him to ribbons for some reason, just that one cut on his leg. He fell and hit his head on the rocks and that's where we found him after he went into shock. All of that must have been happening as we were crossing the field going toward the cave. Being unconscious saved the kids' life. If he had stayed awake and fought back it would have been the end for him. We are all lucky, damn lucky." Kodiak said before leaning in for another bite of pancake. "Sam brought supplies up he salvaged from the wash house, so it looks like we have enough food to get us through until the help Sam sends arrives. And I was ahead of getting my wood supply in so we are set with that as well."

The men sat in silence, Kodiak chewing as they slowly, shyly smiled at each other.

"So, I lived," he finally said, "But I am a man of my word. When you get back to civilization sell my confession to the highest bidder. I expect there will be trouble and I'll likely have to go back to New York for that, so I'll just ask that in addition to telling about my confession that you consider adding our little story of survival. Sam will photograph the remains of the bear and I'll ask him to document the trapper's cabin and cavern as proof. It would take the edge off my story." Kodiak said quietly, his face as sexy as ever and solemn as a judge.

"Fu….," Hunter began, then cut himself off with a grin at Kodiak. "I mean to heck with that."

There was a long silence as the men looked at each other, grins slowly breaking into wide smiles.

"I was thinking," Kodiak said slowly, "rather than me sleeping in with Cord it would be easier on both of us if you and I bunk in the other bedroom until Sam gets a plane here to pick him up. I can't kick too much. I can hardly move." he lifted his wounded arm slightly.

The men continued to look at each other, the tiniest of smiles curling at the edges of Kodiak's lips.

"What exactly are you proposing?"

"It doesn't seem like you have anywhere special to be," Kodiak went on after taking a deep breath and giving a lopsided shrug, "the only immediate errand you have to run is to get over to that old cabin and smash a camera up. Even when I am patched up I'm going to need some help putting this place and the wash house back together. Not to mention that even after he gets out of the hospital and is sewn up Cord is going to need more care than I can give him alone."

Kodiak took a deep breath, "So I thought you might hang out for a while. I could use some help getting the place back together since I don't want to be back out in the world."

Kodiak's smile had fully formed across his face by then.

"I don't know if you have anything else going on except your career with the fish and game department of course."

"I'm thinking about taking early retirement," Hunter smiled sheepishly at the verbal jab. "I don't have any money for my share of supplies, why the change of heart. You think you kinda

like me after all?"

"NO!" Kodiak said, wide smile still in place.

"Liar." Hunter grinned back, darting his tongue forward and swiping a tiny dot of blueberry syrup off the edge of Kodiak's upper lip.

"Hey! That's disgusting!" Kodiak roared back, smile still stretched over his face, causing Hunter's heart to race the way it had when he had seen Kodiak on television and on the cover of magazines.

"You need a bath like that all over," he said in with a low growl, "but I am going to take you to the wash house for a real bath first. Now c'mon, tell me. Why the sudden change of heart about me."

"Well, we almost died out there. You aren't much to look at," Kodiak snarked with a beaming grin," but since you and Sam, really did kinda save me again I guess I do have to give that forgiveness thing some thought. Three times saved is some kind of record."

"*I* can do better than *you*, pretty guy." Hunter huffed

with mock indignation.

"No one else is going to put up with a weaselly mutt like you," Kodiak smiled back, then continued with a serious look on his face.

"I know you hate being in the bush but I think the help you could give Cord and I could more than take care of your share of the supplies."

"Well I do hate being stuck out here in the sticks." Hunter said while pushing the fork forward, with another piece of flapjack toward Kodiak's soft, supple lips, "but I think I can force myself to hang out with you for a while, but there will be a price."

"I'm not rich, and there won't be any trapping this season so think about this price tag before you attach it," Kodiak cautioned.

Settling back on the sofa Hunter finally took a bite of the pancakes on the plate he still held. "Let's see, room and board, use of the wash house tub, continued use of these mukluks and another one of those kisses under a Northern Light show thrown in sometime very soon."

For the first time since the pair had trembled on top of each other with the giant bear nosing around them on the river bank the men smiled at each other at the same time.

"What about the story, the fast, easy money you could make?"

"I think if we tried making love when you are fully conscious that might make up for some of that loss…" Hunter said, wanting to make a grab for Kodiak's fun parts but not wanting to hurt him with a sudden movement.

"That's both complimentary and weird." the battered homesteader replied, heat growing in his crotch.

The cabin was again silent save for the crackle of the

fire in the hearth as Hunter eased the breakfast plate onto a low table at the end of the sofa and turned to lean in to Kodiak, wrapping his arms around him, Hunter silently smiling as he melted in against Kodiak neck, snugging in against him.

"We lost a lot of the winter supplies both here and at the cave, but I bet we can get at least one more supply flight in. Might have to live on powdered eggs and milk for a while," Kodiak mused.

Then with voice lowered he went on, "Gotta warn you, I lost at love once, if there is a next time around I plan to mate for life like the loons."

Hunter traced a finger lightly along the longest scar running down the side of Kodiak's face. "I think those birds have the right idea," With a grin Hunter held up his still bandaged thumb which had been pierced by the porcupine quill. "It's gonna scar you know, because of your bush removal method but I can live with that. I also think a couple of scarred up guys like us stand a chance."

"Not a chance in hell, but I'm willing to give it a try if you are."

"About that camera," Hunter said slowly, every fiber of his body tensing as he felt Kodiak's muscles tighten against him. "I could clean up the old cabin and still set it up. Show up over there in a parka with the hood pulled up and light off a fire. When we get you guys back to Anchorage to see doctors I'll set the camera up on line and show Finn. It'll take a while before that dope figures out it isn't you. But by then he will have sent at least some of the money to my account. Which I will close as soon as his funds show up and move to another bank. It'd help get us through the winter."

Relaxing again Kodiak leaned back and smiled at the

intruder, the invader, the fake game warden he had just been through hell and back with Kodiak leaned into his recent enemy, gently pressing his syrup sticky sweet lips against Hunter's, feeling safe and content for the first time in what seemed like ever.

"I guess if you are willing to turn over a new leaf and use your super power of being sneaky for the forces of good and not evil I'm willing to go along with that plan. But it also shows how devious you can be so no other cameras for you until I say so. And that could be a long time."

Hunter made a very somber face and raised two fingers.

"I promise to take no unauthorized photos of Kodiak DePaul. Former pretend Alaska Game Warden's honor."

Kodiak smiled and sighed.

"You are one true piece of work. Now put those mukluks on and get me to the wash house for that bath!"

Hunter leaned in for another kiss while reaching down and grabbing the fur that ringed the top of the soft boots while thinking life bush might not be so bad after all.

57731291R00158

Made in the USA
Middletown, DE
01 August 2019